KILLER PRINCESSES

Jennifer R Hollis

PROLOGUE: A HOT NIGHT FOR COLD BLOOD

Friday 3rd August 2018 - Janice, Caitlin, Killer

"Thank God for that," muttered the tall red-haired woman to the shorter dark-haired one. She sighed as she slammed the staff exit door of the supermarket.

"Starting at midday, ending at nine-thirty on a Friday night; it's no life," Caitlin continued.

Though the sun was down, the evening was unusually warm and sticky, even for early August. It had been a long shift, plagued by many hot and bothered customers. Their endless complaints and demands had exhausted her.

"I'd do anything for a bit of breeze too," added Caitlin. She pushed her long red curls into a high ponytail and wiped the sweat from her freckled forehead. They plodded together alongside the store towards the dimly lit car park.

The shorter woman, Janice, hummed in agreement. She loosened the top buttons of her shirt and rubbed the back of her neck to relieve the tension of the day. Flies circled above their heads, buzzing with an energy that the women very much lacked.

"Jan," sighed Caitlin as she moved her hand towards her friend's arm. They paused.

"I'm sorry, Cait," whispered Janice. "I know I've not been myself lately. But what we've found out, it's awful, and you know that someone at work is behind it."

"Not here, Jan," hushed Caitlin. She raised her eyebrows and glanced through the glass panels into the supermarket.

"I know who you think it is," Caitlin continued. "But you've been going around in circles. Theory after theory, all as unlikely as the rest. It's time to go to the police and tell them what we know."

"And give them the chance to cover their tracks or run?" replied Janice, her voice louder.

Caitlin closed her eyes, took a deep breath, and urged herself to remain calm.

"We're having a drink tomorrow evening,

4

right?"

Janice nodded glumly.

"Then let's have a proper talk then, yeah? I'm tired, and we shouldn't be discussing this here of all places."

Caitlin walked ahead of Janice. As they reached the car park, she took her car keys from her pocket.

Janice followed her friend in silence and opened her car door to let the day's heat out. She sat down in the driver's seat and almost slammed her door closed without saying good-bye.

But then, a loud bang and a cry from Caitlin stopped Janice in her tracks. She heaved herself out of the car too quickly and hit her head on the hard door frame.

Caitlin stood a few parking bays down, alone, with her fists on the top of the car.

"What on earth is the matter?" asked Janice, as she clambered out of her car and rubbed her head.

"I've left my handbag in my locker. I was too keen to get out," groaned Caitlin, with her hands on her hips.

At that moment, Janice was reminded more of her teenage daughter than the 29-year-old colleague she knew so well.

"Oh, just smile then," grumbled Caitlin. "Don't offer to come back and get it with me." She banged her fists again, though not as hard, on the car roof.

"Do you need it tonight, Cait? You have your car and house keys, don't you?"

Caitlin glanced from her car to the supermarket. She was rarely without her handbag and phone. But the store had creaked in the heat all day, the car park lights were flickering, and there was an unfamiliar, dark-green car with tinted windows in the corner. Plus, she thought bitterly, Janice had put her on edge by talking about the secret they'd uncovered.

"You know what," sighed Caitlin, "I'll come to get it first thing, on the way to that job interview."

"Good luck," mumbled Janice. Caitlin returned a half-hearted smile, and they both slammed their car doors closed.

It was the last time the two women, colleagues and friends ever saw each other.

They drove out of the car park in opposite directions, yet both women were thinking about the same thing.

What started as idle gossip had turned into an investigative hobby for them. It was an almost welcome distraction from their mundane jobs.

They had played to their strengths. Caitlin, who was everyone's friend, collected information and gained people's trust. Janice separated rumour from facts and started spotting patterns. Before long, they had uncovered a dark and dangerous secret.

There was one final piece of the puzzle remaining: which colleague was behind it all? Who was pulling the strings and putting vulnerable staff members in danger? Janice vowed to heed Caitlin's advice and go straight to the police as soon as they were sure who the culprit was.

Halfway home, roadworks which had blighted Janice's journey home for weeks delayed her once again. She already felt guilty about how she had left things with Caitlin.

"Should have gone back in to get the bloody bag," she muttered to herself, as she tapped the steering wheel.

Janice turned the radio up, pulled her phone from her bag and typed a message.

Sorry, Cait – I know you won't get this till 2m morning....

Had Janice not been so focused on the message, she might have noticed the car with an obscured number plate, creeping up behind her. She continued to type and pressed the send button, as the makeshift traffic light in front of her flicked to green.

The car behind her was bottle-green in colour, very much like the one in the supermarket car park. It was slow and quiet, with tinted windows and dimmed headlights. It was the perfect vehicle for the intended crime.

Yet the driver was not so sleek. As they carefully followed Janice, they wiped the sweat from their forehead and top lip. Their heart pumped with adrenaline, and their body shook with nerves, but they still possessed a cruel, cold intent to murder. A gun, fully loaded and deadly at a short-range, lay on the passenger's seat.

Janice arrived home with a sense of relief. She looked forward to a day off to relax, catch-up with errands and have a few drinks with Caitlin in the evening. But as she got out of her car, her thoughts returned to the secret they'd discovered.

Her last thoughts were not of her husband and children asleep upstairs or of her best friends. Instead, she dwelt on the mystery colleague she planned to turn in to the police.

As Janice fumbled in her bag for her house keys, the bottle-green car crawled across the front of her drive, and the driver positioned themselves for the kill.

They opened the car window and aimed the gun, complete with a silencer, at Janice's back. As they squeezed the trigger, their hand shook by a fraction of an inch. The first bullet flew past Janice's head into a window, which fractured into thousands of shards.

Janice spun round. She gulped for air as her heart thumped against her chest. Her mind was blank, her arms and legs paralysed. When she recognised the driver, her eyes widened in shock.

"You?" she whispered in disbelief. It cost her every last bit of effort to force the word out of her mouth.

"Yes," confirmed the driver coldly.

That was the last word Janice heard before the second bullet pierced her chest and heart. She was dead before she hit the floor.

The bottle-green car sped down the street, out of sight and sound. Gone, by the time Janice's husband had jumped out of bed, run downstairs and found his wife lying at their front door in a pool of blood.

The killer felt calmer as they headed towards the next victim; their secrets were one step closer to remaining safe.

Yes, they had misfired the first shot into the window, alerting the husband and neighbours. But that would work to their advantage. The police would flock there, leaving the killer free to do as they liked on the other side of town.

Soon, there would be no-one apart from themselves and a trusted other who knew the secrets they kept. This time, there were no nerves, and the intent to murder was colder and crueller.

Caitlin was already home, roaming her flat in her loose-fitting pyjamas. She felt bereft and bored without her phone, so she finished her glass of red wine and got into bed with a sigh.

An early night was best, given the day ahead. She had a job interview for a hospitality manager role at a prestigious hotel in central London.

Afterwards, she had a lunch date with her new boyfriend, who worked as a stockbroker in town. She already adored him; she had never fallen for someone so hard or so fast before.

As her eyes slowly closed, a loud knock on her front door made her jump violently. She gathered herself; her boyfriend must have decided to surprise her with a late visit. Or, he'd texted her without reply, and had come to check on her. She pictured him behind her front door holding a bottle of wine, his handsome face smiling back at hers.

She checked herself in the mirror, ruffled her long red hair and smiled as she flung the door open. Her smile vanished, as she saw not her boyfriend, but a colleague who'd never visited her before.

"It's a bit late for a visit," commented Caitlin, with no attempt to cover her disappointment.

"Yes, it is," conceded the visitor, though they did not explain themselves. They looked pale and clammy; their hands stuffed into the pockets of an oversized, dark linen coat.

"Can I come in?"

"Why?" asked Caitlin suspiciously, as she held the door ajar to prevent her colleague from entering.

"I need to talk to you, Caitlin. I have some, um, suspicions about someone we work with closely. I know you and Janice do too, and I think I can trust you."

Caitlin rolled her eyes. It seemed Janice had spoken to someone else about this awful thing, which they'd agreed to keep secret. Caitlin relaxed her grip on the door and pulled it wide open, to let the visitor into the hallway.

As Caitlin closed her front-door and moved her hand towards the chain lock, she made a connection in her mind. A link so obvious, she couldn't believe she hadn't made it before. It all fitted, and she now knew who the colleague behind the dark secret was. Unfortunately, though, it was the one she'd just let into her flat.

Sure enough, as Caitlin turned around with fear in her eyes, she found herself staring down the barrel of a gun, with nowhere to run.

"Stay very still," ordered the killer.

Caitlin raised both of her hands in a sign of surrender.

"You don't have to do this, I won't say..." Caitlin pleaded, but the killer smiled and shook their head in response.

"Oh, I do have to," they replied. "You really should've minded your own business, instead of poking around in mine."

Caitlin turned to grab the door handle, to no avail. This time, the killer only needed one shot, straight to the back of the head. Their work was complete, their secrets were safe.

The killer stepped over the body, opened the door as far as it would allow and squeezed through the gap. They jogged to the car with their hood up and drove away at speed. Ten minutes later, they were off-grid and out of sight of cameras. They torched the car on the edge of a field and walked into the woods under cover of night.

A few days later, the supermarket, which looked so ordinary from the outside, buzzed with gossip and speculation. Why were two checkout supervisors murdered in cold blood on the same night? The police also seemed perplexed by the crimes, and both the staff and local shoppers worried about the lack of arrests.

Unbeknown to them all, the killer had wandered around the supermarket ever since, basking in the knowledge that their secrets remained safe.

Police Media Statement: Monday 6 August 2018, 12:00
DCI Vincent Okafor, Croydon police

On Friday 3 August 2018, at 22:06, Croydon police received a report of a woman (Janice Locke, 41) being shot outside her house in Melwood, in the south of the borough. Officers attended the scene to confirm the fatality and to collect evidence. An investigation was started immediately and is underway.

On Sunday 5 August, at 18:09, Croydon police received a missing person's report and attended a flat in Homestead at 19:05. The tenant (Caitlin Murphy, 29) was found dead at the scene; her death also caused by a single gunshot wound. It is estimated that her death occurred late on Friday night or very early Saturday morning.

Mrs Locke and Ms Murphy were friends and colleagues – both working as checkout supervisors at the same supermarket in Melwood. This, together with the similarities in their deaths, have led us to assume the two crimes are related.

While no possessions were taken from Mrs Locke, some personal items of Ms Murphy's, such as a purse and phone, were not present at her address.

We are working as quickly as possible to establish a full picture of the events leading up to these crimes, from the time the women left work at the supermarket on Friday evening.

We encourage anyone with any information relating to these women, the incidents, or the missing items, to come forward immediately using the following phone number: 0800 445 5426. Any information will be treated in the strictest confidence.

1: MEETING AT THE MANOR

Sunday 30th September 2018 - Gillian & Kevin

Gillian Prince rearranged the eight seats in the reading room for the fifth time that evening. It had been a busy weekend; living rooms were spick and span, fires stoked, and bathrooms cleaned from top to bottom.

Her mini-mansion - 'The Manor' - in its gated, suburban estate - 'Fair Lawns' - was ready for visitors. It hadn't looked so pristine since her and Kevin's 20th wedding anniversary party, two years ago.

Tonight's guests were her team of checkout supervisors from the Melwood supermarket. She'd arranged an important meeting to discuss their poor performance and behaviour in the aftermath of the untimely deaths of their two colleagues.

The polished floorboards creaked as Gillian paced up and down the hallway. She gazed proudly at the framed picture of herself and the Borough's Mayor, next to a portrait of her and Kevin.

Yet she also felt a nagging sensation, as though something wasn't quite right. She turned to the wall-length mirror and scratched her chin. Her fitted cream day-suit and neat, curly ash-blonde hair were, like the house, perfect.

Her eyes drifted to the console table next to the front door. She opened the right-hand drawer and found three badges. They all had 'Gillian, Customer Service Manager' printed on them.

She removed them and placed them in a straight line on top of the console, with a satisfied smile and sigh. Her shoulders finally relaxed.

The doorbell rang at 6.58 pm, and as she opened the door, Gillian received precisely the reaction she'd hoped for. The two women facing her hadn't been to The Manor before, and they were visibly impressed. Their eyes swept past Gillian, down the hallway, and rested on the badges lined up on the console.

"Debbie, Karen!" she greeted them in her high-pitched voice.

"Come in, come in," continued Gillian with a smile. She waved her hand to usher the two women, who were roughly the same age as her, inside.

Karen's straight blonde hair was down, rather than tied up in its usual tight ponytail. Debbie looked as dishevelled as ever. Gillian's eyes lingered disapprovingly over her messy dark hair and the food stain on her baggy jumper.

"Shoes over here on the rack, coats on the pegs over here, and then we're going to the third door on the left, the reading room."

The two women smiled back, entered The Manor and followed her instructions. Though, as Gillian turned to lead the way down the hall, she glimpsed Karen rolling her eyes at Debbie, who bit her lip. Gillian made a mental note of the gesture but pretended, for now, that she hadn't seen it.

"Wine, tea, juice?" offered Gillian in a musical tone, as the two women reached the reading room door. "Kevin will get you whatever you want," she paused, 'won't he…'

"Yes," replied her husband's strained voice from a room on the right-hand side of the hallway.

Gillian smiled and wrinkled her nose, as she ushered the two women into the room.

"Sit anywhere you like ladies," she instructed, "except there - that's mine." She pointed at the largest armchair.

Debbie and Karen sat down on a small two-seater chintz sofa closest to the door. They exchanged another swift, meaningful glance.

Ten minutes later, three more of Gillian's team sat in the reading room. A teenage girl and boy who'd arrived together, and a fragile-looking woman in her late 40s called Dawn.

They'd all accepted their drinks from Kevin with thanks, but the conversation had floundered. Only the ticking of the grandfather clock in the corner broke the silence. As three more minutes passed, the ticking seemed to get louder and louder.

Gillian shuffled the agenda papers for the seventh time. She smiled awkwardly at Debbie and Karen on her left, and the other three colleagues on her right. To Gillian's increasing annoyance, two chairs remained empty.

"Well, I suppose we have waited long enough," she announced. Her high voice cut through the silence and made the young boy and girl jump.

"I was rather hoping to have us all here tonight, given we'd finally found a Sunday evening we were all available."

Gillian paused and stared at Debbie and Karen. She knew they'd tried to avoid the meeting, ever since she first suggested it four weeks ago.

Their eyes darted downwards, but they did not respond. Gillian didn't push the matter further; after all, at least they had bothered to turn up.

"So, I take it…"

But before Gillian could continue, three loud bangs reverberated down the hallway, into the reading room.

"There is a bell," muttered Gillian, with a roll of her eyes.

"Kevin!" she shouted, then turned to the others in the room with a wide smile.

As Kevin moved towards the door, he felt his chest and neck redden. He paused to wipe the sweat from his hands and delay the moment he'd come face to face with the woman behind the door. He usually couldn't wait to see her, but tonight was different.

Three things happened in quick succession. Another bang echoed through the house, Gillian shouted 'Kevin!' again, and Kevin swung the door open too quickly. It crashed into the console, knocking the neat line of badges onto the floor.

As he glanced up, he saw someone unexpected standing there.

"Ah, Marie, is it?" he asked, wiping his top lip in relief. "Come on in."

The short, weighty woman looked up at him with a rogue smile. She narrowed her eyes behind patterned glasses and a thick, strawberry blonde fringe and stepped towards him.

"Oh, I wouldn't close that yet Kevin," whispered Marie, as he leaned behind her to close the door. "She's just coming."

Kevin tightened his grip on the door, as a familiar aroma wafted through the gap; a concoction of Marlboro Gold and Chanel No.5. His neck began to redden again.

He turned away, but within seconds the door swung open and crashed into the console again. A tall, thin figure stepped into the hallway and cast a shadow over the portrait of Kevin and Gillian on the wall.

She flicked the base of her cigarette with a long, red nail, then smirked as the burning ash dropped onto the welcome mat below. As she threw the end of the cigarette back out of the door, Kevin looked at her coyly, and Marie gazed up in awe. Renee Beck had made her entrance.

"We're down here!"

Gillian's shrill voice punctured the tension. Her head poked around the door of the reading room, as she waved her short arm up and down. Renee grabbed Marie's coat from her, and threw it, along with her own, at Kevin with a wink.

"Big smiles, Marie." Kevin heard Renee whisper, as her long, golden-brown hair swayed behind her. She sashayed down the corridor, her stiletto heels still on.

"Gillian!" exclaimed Renee, as she leaned down to embrace her much shorter boss.

"Lovely house," she continued in her low,

husky voice. "What an amazing use of space here, lovely colours on this portrait, don't you think, Marie?"

Gillian withdrew from the embrace, which she'd neither enjoyed nor expected. In the reading room, the young boy and girl eyed each other nervously. Debbie and Karen whispered to each other while Dawn stared into space. Gillian's jaw twitched; she needed to start the meeting as planned.

"I'm so sorry we're late," apologised Renee, as she spun round to address the room at large. "My cat, Princess, went missing. Always happens when I'm in a rush, luckily Marie found her in one of my kitchen cupboards!"

"Lucky indeed. But let's move onto business," interrupted Gillian, with a pointed glance at the grandfather clock.

"No, thank you, Kevin." Gillian waved away her husband, who'd appeared at the door to collect new drinks orders. He didn't need telling twice. He turned on his heel, marched back down the hallway and stomped up the staircase.

"Marie, why don't you sit down here?" suggested Gillian with a smile, as she pointed at a single dining room chair, between herself and Karen.

Karen looked as though someone had put something unpleasant under her nose.

"And that leaves you over there, Renee," continued Gillian.

She pointed to a hard-backed chair in the corner of the room. It was opposite Marie and almost hidden behind the young boy and girl on the squashy velvet sofa.

Debbie and Karen exchanged another smile and glance, as Renee and Marie grudgingly took their separate seats.

"Let's try this again," said Gillian to the now full room. "I take it you all know why we're here?"

"Anyone?" she continued after a few seconds of silence.

"Because you invited us," answered Karen, though she received a sharp jab in the ribs from Debbie.

"Yes, thank you, Karen," replied Gillian with another hint of impatience.

"I invited you all to discuss our performance in this ah, informal, setting. It has been a slightly challenging time, but…"

Seven heads turned in Renee's direction as she attempted, and failed, to pass off her snort of laughter as a sneeze.

"Oh, come on," laughed Renee. "It's a bit of an understatement to describe two murdered colleagues as a 'slightly challenging' time, isn't it? It's been hell!"

Marie raised her hand to her head as Gillian glared at Renee.

"That may be, Renee," replied Gillian icily, "but it certainly isn't funny either way. If you don't want to take this seriously, you can leave."

Renee frowned, folded her arms and sat back in her chair. She stuck her tongue out at Marie, who shook her head in return.

"I," continued Gillian, "I mean, we, used to run the most efficient customer service team in the region. And we can do it again if we can learn to get along. But before we get into that, I'd like to welcome Jade and Ethan to the team."

Gillian inclined her head towards the young girl and boy sat together on the velvet sofa. They both blushed under the gaze of the older women in the room.

"As everyone is well aware, since Janice and Caitlin, well, you know, we have struggled to cover all the hours. Renee going full-time has helped," admitted Gillian, with a slight twitch.

"But the addition of Jade and Ethan should solve this fully and help make our work environment less tense. I wish you both the best of luck."

The other women in the room nodded solemnly in agreement.

"Does anyone have the latest from the police on what happened? Have they caught anyone yet?" Karen asked the room at large. Gillian rolled her eyes; this wasn't on the meeting agenda.

"You know, I think we might have heard something if they had," replied Marie.

"Well, not necessarily," retorted Debbie, as

she leant across Karen to defend her. "There might be things the police don't share with the media."

"Or with suspects, like some of us?" interjected Renee from the corner; she leant as far forward as she could, to get close to the conflict. Her large, amber eyes reflected the light from the fire.

"This is what I mean," shouted Gillian suddenly. "We're not suspects, for goodness sake."

The room fell silent again. Renee slunk back into her chair and stared at her bright red nails.

"Renee," sighed Gillian.

"What?"

"Why, whenever I hear reports of rows and inappropriate behaviour, is it something to do with you?" asked Gillian bluntly, though she kept her tone light and smiled.

"I couldn't tell you, Gillian. I don't go looking for trouble, but trouble always finds me. Story of my life." Renee laughed and paused for a reaction, which she didn't get.

"I wasn't aware there had been complaints about me, Gillian, and unless you're willing to share them with me, I don't know how you expect me to defend myself."

Gillian's eyes narrowed, and her cordial smile faded. Renee held her glare from across the room.

With a cough to break the tension, Marie paved the way for her entrance into the discussion.

"It's like Karen was saying the other day, it's you two who need to keep your tempers down. But then, Karen is the only one here who does have formal complaints against her."

Gillian's gaze switched to Karen, who looked nervously at Debbie on her left. Debbie stared at Marie with a look of loathing.

Renee exhaled, stood up and tip-toed past the bookcase towards the door with a swish of her hair.

"Bathroom," she whispered, and she smiled and winked at Marie as she left the room.

Upstairs, Kevin heard the sound of Renee's high heels against the wooden floor.

He leant on the doorframe of one of the guest bedrooms and watched Renee float up the carpeted staircase. She was smiling to herself, revealing small dimples on both of her cheeks. She withdrew a pack of cigarettes and lighter from her trouser pocket.

"You do know it is forbidden to smoke in the house?" he asked with a smile.

She reached the top of the stairs and looked deep into his eyes, with one of her dark eyebrows raised. His voice was more confident now, and he felt a different kind of tension as she walked towards him.

"Oh, you know me, Kevin," grinned Renee, as she grabbed his waistband. "I don't like to play by the rules."

Excerpt: Interview with Gillian Prince. Tuesday 7 August 2018, 15:00

Officer: Can you describe your relationship with Mrs Janice Locke and Ms Caitlin Murphy?

Gillian: I am, or should I say, was, their boss. Both of them.

Officer: Did you have any kind of personal relationship with either woman?

Gillian: No.

Officer: No after-work drinks, social dinners, children playdates?

Gillian: No, I don't tend to socialise with colleagues. As the boss, my relationships should be professional. And I don't have children.

Officer: Did you like Janice and Caitlin, get on with them?

Gillian: *Pause* Yes, as much as you can like and get on with colleagues you know very little about. They worked hard; I never argued with them at work.

Officer: Do you have any idea why anyone would want to harm these women?

Gillian: No.

Officer: Did they ever mention any personal problems to you, ever ask you for money or appear troubled?

Gillian: They never mentioned personal troubles. Janice asked me for a pay rise a few years ago – though I don't think that would be relevant. It was long overdue.

Officer: I have to ask, Gillian. Where were you on Friday, 3 August, between 21.30 and midnight?

Gillian: At home. I always spend Friday nights in, with my husband, Kevin.

Post-interview officer's notes: Alibi confirmed. Neighbour recalls seeing Kevin drawing curtains on the front windows at The Manor at 21:00. Kevin confirms Gillian was at home for the entire evening with him, in their reading room, lounge and bedroom.

2: THIN ICE

Sunday 30th September 2018 -
Renee

Adrenaline coursed through Renee's veins as she perched on the end of the guest bed at The Manor. Next to her, her boss' husband pulled up his trousers.

She watched him and wondered, as she often did, how Kevin had ended up married to Gillian. He was tall, dark and handsome, and in good shape for a man in his early forties, whereas Gillian was short, stocky and rather stern in the face.

Renee looked away before he turned towards her. She reached over to the balcony door, pushed it open, and lit a cigarette.

"Shouldn't you go back now? You've been gone 15 minutes," Kevin suggested, as he pulled his shirt back over his head.

"Now now, Kevin, we both know it hasn't been that long."

Kevin rubbed his stubbly chin and blushed.

"Won't they be wondering where you are?"

"Oh, they'll be too busy arguing to notice I've gone. Marie said it would be better if I dipped out for a bit. I need to let Gill focus her anger on Debbie and Karen, or something like that. Anyway, I'd rather be up here with you."

Kevin raised his eyebrows and looked at Renee. He couldn't entirely hide the glimmer of hope in his dark brown eyes.

"Oh," said Renee in a dramatic tone, "come on now. Don't look at me like that."

"You're all I think about. I want you to feel the same; I want you to be honest with me," he muttered.

"Well, it's been a year, Kevin. You're my longest relationship ever, and I keep coming back for more, don't I? Yet, I notice you're still married."

"But what if I wasn't? Do you think..."

"Well, who knows," interrupted Renee with a wave of her hand. "You'd have to roll the dice and find out, wouldn't you? But until you do, this is an affair with no attachment, nothing else."

Renee stood up from the bed and moved away from a deflated-looking Kevin.

She admired herself in a full-length mirror, next to a large wardrobe. Her long hair, good looks and perfect-ten figure made her look considerably younger than her 35 years.

"You're the one who keeps talking about ending it anyway," remarked Renee. She met Kevin's sullen glance in the mirror.

He looked at his feet, ran his fingers through his short greying brown hair and sighed.

"I don't want to end it, and you know that. It's just that, when we met, you were at the other store and you didn't know Gill. It was easier. But now you're at Melwood and she's your boss," he sighed.

"Oh, but that makes it more fun!"

"I don't want you to get hurt."

"Hurt? What do you mean by that?"

Before Kevin could answer, Renee held her finger to her lips. She could hear footsteps; someone was marching purposefully up the stairs.

She remained rooted to the spot, but Kevin acted decisively. He scooped up Renee's clothes from the floor, passed them to her and steered her towards the balcony door.

As she stepped out, she flinched at the coldness of the floor against her bare feet. Her heartbeat quickened as she pulled up her trousers and watched Kevin disappear into the wardrobe.

She hoped that whoever was now at the top of the stairs, would pick another room to enter. Yet, almost inevitably, the person turned right, as Renee had done, and entered the guest room.

"Oh God," muttered Renee under her breath. "Please, not Gillian..."

Whoever it was, she was sure they would notice the unmade bed and the open balcony door. As quietly as possible, she tried to put on her blouse, despite the newly missing buttons. An agitated voice sounded from inside the room.

"I am at a work meeting, Mum, so unless it's super urgent will you stop calling and messaging me because I can't talk now."

Renee breathed a silent sigh of relief; the young female voice was not Gillian's. She edged towards the open balcony door, to hear more of Jade's conversation.

"I've already explained to you, I know what I'm doing," Jade hissed down the phone. "Well, how else am I going to get the money for you?"

After another brief pause, she continued. "I'm not ungrateful, stop saying that, I'm under enough pressure as it is. I've got two jobs now, but I'm still behind on my rent. Ethan won't leave me alone. And I do not need you judging me when you're the one who comes begging for money every time you want drugs!"

On the balcony, Renee's eyes widened with interest.

"Mum, please, I know you've stopped, and I know you worry about me. Look, I got a promotion at the supermarket. I'm a supervisor now. I'll do more overtime, clear the bills and stop the other job, OK, then I'll lay low for a bit."

Jade was talking through gritted teeth. Renee was not surprised to hear a raised voice the next time she spoke.

"I've got nothing more to say, now I've got to get back to this work meeting, it's important!"

Without warning, Jade hung up and stomped onto the balcony, causing Renee to jump and Jade to gasp in fright.

"Hi," said Renee sheepishly, and she re-arranged her grin into a more sombre expression.

"What are you doing here?" asked Jade. She looked Renee up and down, her eyebrows raised.

"I was smoking, of course," replied Renee, as she took her packet of cigarettes and a lighter from her pocket. "And taking a break from the row downstairs. Would you like one?"

They lit their cigarettes and turned to look out from the balcony on the front of Gillian's house. A similar mini-mansion stared back at them, two water fountains on the front lawn.

"A bit different to where we grew up," commented Renee, sensing Jade's thoughts.

"Just a bit different from the New Grange estate, yeah," replied Jade with a sigh. "You heard the phone call?"

"Um, yes. Sorry, Jade, I should have let you know I was here, I thought I'd let you get on with it and then not mention it."

Jade sighed again.

"You know, girls like us don't have two-point-four families or thousands of pounds. But we don't need them, either. I've done just fine without it all..."

Renee trailed off as Jade looked at her with the same curious expression. Her eyes fell onto the open button holes of Renee's blouse.

"So, what's the other job then? Bar work?" asked Renee. For once, she was eager to divert attention away from herself.

"No, well, sort of," replied Jade. "Not that it matters, I'm quitting it soon anyway. Where are your shoes?"

Renee laughed nervously. Jade was inconveniently observant.

"Just inside there. I took them off because they were hurting. And I like having cold feet. Um, so Ethan won't leave you alone?"

"No," sighed Jade, "he's a little obsessed. I like him as a friend, and he's supportive of me. But I reckon he wants more, you know, in return."

"He's not pressuring you, is he?"

"No, nothing like that. Ethan is a nice guy. He's kind and smart. But it's just, I'm not..." she paused.

"Not a nice girl? Not interested in dependable men?" Renee filled the gap and laughed. "Well, join the club, Jade. I've lost count of the number of hearts I've broken!"

Jade balanced her elbows on the edge of the balcony and stared at the house opposite, lost in thought.

"Let's go back in," urged Renee, and she reached out to touch Jade's shoulder. Her feet were almost numb, and she'd been away for too long now. She steered Jade back into the guest room.

The wardrobe door was open; Kevin must have escaped while they were on the balcony. Renee hoped that Jade hadn't noticed that too.

"Oh, and don't worry," said Renee as she put her shoes back on. "I won't tell Gillian about your other job. You should stick at it, though. Make as much money as you can and get out of here!"

Jade looked down at the floor and shrugged her shoulders.

"So lovely of you to re-join us," greeted Gillian, as Renee and Jade returned to the reading room.

"Oh the pleasure is all mine, Gillian," replied Renee with a big smile. Kevin turned a dark shade of red, stopped handing out biscuits and shuffled out of the room.

"We have," announced Gillian, "in your absence, found a way to move forward as a team. I'll type up the notes and send them to you all in due course. I think we have made at least some progress. Jade, I will see you tomorrow at work. Everyone else, later in the week."

No-one needed a further hint. All seven guests stood and made their way to the hallway to collect their coats and shoes. They bade farewell to Gillian and split into smaller groups as they rushed towards the street.

In front of Renee, Debbie opened her car door and looked up at Karen. "I should offer Dawn a lift, she's on the way," she said.

But as Debbie looked around and called Dawn's name, there was no sign of her. It seemed that the woman, who had sat alone and not said a word for the entire evening, had disappeared.

Renee skipped past Debbie towards her car, with Marie beside her struggling to keep up. They got in and waited for Debbie to drive away, then Renee started her engine.

"Well?" she asked curiously.

"Oh, the usual," replied Marie. "Karen and I have to have mediation sessions, and before you laugh, so do you and Debbie."

"Urgh, anything else?"

"Well, we all have to go on a team-building day. I can hardly wait for the trust exercises."

Renee laughed and shook her head as they drove towards the front gates of the Fair Lawns estate.

"Where did you go for all that time?" asked Marie.

"Oh, well, since I've gone full-time, I don't see Kevin as much. So, I thought we'd make up for lost time."

"You didn't! Not while we were all down-stairs?"

"I did! And I nearly got caught!"

Marie raised her hand to her mouth in disbelief as Renee laughed.

"You're treading on thin ice, Renee."

"Oh, yeah, yeah. Shall we go get some wine?"

As they approached the front gate, Renee spotted Jade and Ethan talking on the pavement. Renee lowered her window to listen in.

"Just let me walk you home, please Jade," pleaded Ethan, with his arms outstretched.

"I'm only going home for a bit, and then I'm going into town. And you're not coming with me," warned Jade.

The last thing Renee heard as she drove through the gate was Jade shouting, "Ethan, I said no!"

Excerpts: Interview with Renee Beck. Wednesday 8 August 2018, 11:00

Officer: When did you start working at your current supermarket branch?

Renee: Oh, it was January this year, I believe. It would have been sooner but the store I moved from needed me to cover the Christmas period, it's such a busy time in retail – and the customers are so stressed, you wouldn't believe...

Officer: Just January 2018 is sufficient, Renee. Why did you transfer stores?

Renee: What's that got to do with anything?

Officer: Please just answer the question, Renee.

Renee: I wanted to work in a bigger store. Brighter lights, busier, closer to my house, you know.

Officer: Any other reason?

Renee: *Pause* I suppose you could say there were some personality clashes between me and the management at the last store. We didn't get on. I wanted to go, and I suppose they wanted me gone because they agreed to the transfer.

Officer: Can you describe your relationship with Mrs Janice Locke and Ms Caitlin Murphy?

Renee: Well, I knew them. I worked shifts with both of them. Sometimes I spoke to Caitlin at work drinks. Janice had children so she never really joined in. I wouldn't say we were friends.

Officer: Did you not get on then?

Renee: *Pause* Well, not really, it was like they didn't want anyone else in their conversations. They were always talking together and went quiet when I approached them. I think they were a bit jealous of me when I joined. I am quite popular you see, and it can put people's backs up when they've been trying so hard for so long.

Officer: Did you ever have reason to wish harm upon them?

Renee: Sometimes Caitlin would knock the lunch cover rota right out of order, and Jan took really long breaks *laughs*. No, sorry, of course, I didn't.

Officer: Do you know of anyone else who might want to harm them?

Renee: Well, no. But, isn't it always the men?

Officer: Can you clarify that, please?

Renee: Oh, come on! It's usually the men in women's lives, right? Caitlin had a new boyfriend, Christian. The way she went on about him, it sounded too good to be true. He's a stockbroker or something in the city. That sounds about right. And Janice, well I heard a rumour that her husband wasn't happy with her late hours and there was trouble at home.

Officer: Renee, I have to ask. Where were you on Friday 3rd August, between 9.30 pm and midnight?

Renee: *Pause* At home. Of course, I'm usually out on Friday nights, but I wasn't feeling my best, so I had no plans and stayed indoors.

Officer: Was anyone with you, or did anyone visit who can vouch for your whereabouts?

Renee: Not unless you have a way to interview my cat.

Officer: You made no phone calls?

Renee: Maybe I got a few messages from Marie, but I took no calls, and I don't think I replied. No, as I said, I really felt quite unwell. I expect I was asleep by 10 pm now I come to think of it.

3: JADED

Sunday 30th September 2018 - Jade

J ade Dimont had always admired Renee Beck. She'd grown up on the same dead-end council estate as her, yet she had somehow escaped New Grange to a better life. But now, Jade felt a sense of rejection and disappointment as she watched Renee's car speed out of the Fair Lawns estate.

It's not like they were close friends, but they got on well at work, especially since Jade's promotion. On the balcony earlier, Renee had seemed interested in her. She'd pledged, without prompting, to keep her secret safe from Gillian. Yet moments later, Renee had seen her trying to shake Ethan off at the gate and had not offered her a lift home.

It had been her last hope, and now she was left with Ethan, who seemed intent on chaperoning her back to Melwood. She wondered what he would say if he knew where she was going later.

"I said no, Ethan," repeated Jade with less conviction than before. She rubbed her temples with her small hands.

"Well, even if I don't walk you home, we're both walking the same way towards the bus stop, right? So, shall we…?"

Jade couldn't argue with him. With a sigh, she wrapped her long black coat around her small, thin frame and walked onwards, with Ethan in tow. She glanced back at Fair Lawns' iron gates before they turned a corner. It was like looking at a dream life that she'd never have, no matter how she tried to cling to the details - the warmth from Gillian's bathroom floor on her feet. The smell of old books lining the walls of the reading room. The sound of Kevin rustling through the cupboards stocked full of food to find the biscuits. The sensations were already running through her fingertips, escaping her.

She was aware of Ethan talking, but it sounded more like distorted background noise. The thoughts swirling around her head were drowning out everything else. Her mother's voice, for instance, was crystal clear: 'Please Jade, stop, you don't know what you're getting yourself into…'

She tried to focus on Ethan. At some point, he'd expect her to take part in whatever discussion they were having. "And I know you say you can look after yourself," he said, "but we all thought that about Janice and Caitlin. And look what happened to them."

"Ethan," she replied with a hint of impatience, "neither of us knew Caitlin and Jan that well, especially outside of work. We don't know what happened to them."

"We know someone killed them!"

"Yes, but in their own homes. Do you think it was a supermarket serial killer who might be after me next?"

"I just don't think you should be walking around, alone," he muttered.

They fell into silence as they reached the bus stop. Jade could almost hear Ethan's brain whirring, thinking of something to say.

"I saw Renee tonight when I took that call," said Jade, eager to change the subject. Ethan looked back at her with interest.

"I walked into one of the spare bedrooms upstairs; it wasn't perfect like the rest of the house. The bed was messy, and the balcony door was open. I walked onto it, it was cold, and Renee was standing there without any shoes or a coat on. She'd been there for the whole call, maybe for even longer before."

"Weird. What's the deal with Renee, anyway?" asked Ethan. "I don't think she likes me."

"She just doesn't know you," replied Jade. "She's from New Grange, and we don't trust posh people, you know. She had a bit of a reputation on the estate when she was growing up. Everyone, especially the boys, loved her. You can see why. But she left when she was sixteen, started some beauty sales businesses and didn't come back. She lives in a nice house in South Croydon now."

"Why's she working at a supermarket then?" asked Ethan, and Jade shrugged. She hadn't considered that before.

They discussed their colleagues until the bus had taken them to Jade's stop on Melwood High Street. It was only two miles from Gillian's house, but the difference was stark. There were no front gates, fountains or mansions on the street Jade had recently moved to. But after her mother lost their house in New Grange, she didn't have another option.

Ethan followed her off the bus, and its doors closed behind them before she realised what he'd done. She gave him a stern look but didn't object as he walked her the extra five minutes up the hill. They approached a small, terraced house at the top of one of the narrow roads. Jade rented a room in it from the council; the two larger rooms were often occupied by care leavers who flitted in and out.

There was a large crack across the single-paned, downstairs front window, and some fresh graffiti sprayed along the front wall. Opposite, younger teenagers were shouting and laughing in the small park.

"Bye then, Ethan," said Jade.

"Goodnight, Jade."

Inside, she turned on the bedroom light - a dangling bulb without a lampshade - and looked around. Not a lot to show for nineteen years of life, she thought. Her eyes burned and she felt a tightness in her chest and throat. The bed and small desk had been there when she moved in. Clothes piled up on a simple storage unit left behind by one of her old housemates; she couldn't remember their name.

Two photos were blu-tacked to the wall above the desk. One was of Jade's mother over ten years ago, before she'd succumbed to a persistent drink and drug addiction. The second was of Jade, her father and her older half-brothers: Junior, Joey and Jonny. It was one of the rare days they'd included her because her stepmother was away. Her brothers all looked similar: tall, olive skin, dark hair, blue eyes, and an air of mischief.

Jade had some similar features if you looked very closely. But to most people, she stuck out like a sore thumb, with her mother's petite figure, pale skin and blonde hair. Her eyes roamed left across the desk towards a pile of bills that she couldn't afford to pay. Then, her phone buzzed impatiently against the edge of the desk.

"Hello," she answered, her voice already shaking.

"Hi," replied a male voice with an east-end

twang. "I've spoken to the Boss, and she wants you at the Castle tonight. We've got guaranteed trade. You can expect a good haul tonight, girl."

Often, she thought about starting a different conversation with the man. Was he the same as her, forced into work by a boss he didn't know, for money he desperately needed?

"Did you get that, Jade? You'll be there, right?"

"Yes, yes I will," she replied, as she considered her next step.

"But wait!" she added before he hung up.

"Make it quick girl. I've got other people to call."

"I'll be resigning soon, giving in my notice. A bit more overtime at my supermarket job and I won't need this anymore."

"Oh, that's funny, girl," he said, chuckling. "You don't resign from this kind of work. The Boss thinks you're good for business; we're not letting you go anytime soon. And just think how much trouble you'd be in with the law after all these months."

"I'll stop answering your calls, and I'll move," she replied, channelling an inner strength she hadn't felt in a while.

"How's your Mum, Jade?"

"What?"

"This is why you got into this, right? Pay off your Mum's debts, get her food, keep her alive. You run away, and I reckon the Boss will ask me to visit Mummy at her new hostel. Now I don't want to do that Jade, and I'm doing you a big favour here warning you. You understand?"

After a long pause, he continued.

"Yeah, I reckon you do."

He hung up before she could respond.

She sat on her bed and started to shake. She turned to look in the small mirror on the back of her door, and the tears finally came. With a surge of rage, she stood up, threw her phone down hard onto the bed and punched the wall with a loud cry.

Tears fell from her eyes as she pulled her curtains shut. She took off her jeans and jumper and replaced them with a short skirt, vest top and tights. They laddered as she wrenched them on. She grabbed some old heeled back boots from under the bed and picked up the same long black coat she'd worn to Gillian's.

She removed the credit cards and loose change from her pockets and threw them on the desk, replacing them with her house keys, an old kitchen knife and some small, rectangle-shaped cards. Wiping her tears, she locked her bedroom door and tiptoed down the stairs. She took a packet of cigarettes and a lighter from one of her housemates' jackets and stepped back out into the night.

It took Jade twenty-five minutes to walk from Melwood to the south end of Croydon town centre. She took a shortcut by a row of old garages where gangs of teenage boys often hung around. They broke into long-abandoned units and abused anyone who happened to walk past. Tonight, though, it was eerily quiet.

A couple of times, Jade stopped to look behind her. She couldn't quite shake the feeling that someone was watching her. Was the man on the phone following her, to make sure she reached her destination? Or was it someone else, like the person who killed Janice and Caitlin?

She picked up the pace, dipped into a side street, and jogged around some large steel rubbish bins. She paused at the end of the street, which led to a busier road, and looked back. A figure appeared behind the bins, but ducked out of sight as soon as they saw Jade looking at them.

"What do you want?" she called, sounding braver than she felt. Inside her pocket, her right hand curled around the handle of her knife.

The hooded figure stepped towards one of the dustbins. In front of them, waste bags cascaded onto the street with loud crashes, making Jade jump. She turned and rushed down the road towards a small crowd of people outside a busy pub. She didn't have far to go now.

She veered off the beaten track, onto an old market street. A few flickering street lamps illuminated dozens of boarded-up shops. Many of them had homeless people and sodden blankets outside. She stopped outside one of the buildings, which, at some point, had been called 'The

Castle.'

Jade took the pack of cigarettes from her pocket and as she did so, a small rectangular card fell out onto the ground. She lit a cigarette and took a few puffs as a boisterous group of men turned into the road from the opposite end of the street. She sighed, crept towards the boarded door, pushed heavily on it, and entered the building.

Excerpt: Interview with Jade Dimont. Tuesday 4 September 2018, 10:00

Officer: Thank you for talking to us, Jade. I appreciate some time has passed since the events of the 3rd August. I understand you worked with both Mrs Janice Locke and Ms Caitlin Murphy?

Jade: Yes, they were both supervisors at the supermarket where I work. On my department - checkouts.

Officer: Did you know them well?

Jade: Not outside of work, they seemed nice though.

Officer: How so?

Jade: Janice bought me lunch sometimes, didn't get cross with me when I made mistakes, gave me the overtime slots first.

Officer: Why did she do that?

Jade: *Pause* I think she knew I was struggling with money.

Officer: Apologies Jade, I didn't mean to upset you. Let me cut to the chase. Do you know any reason why anyone would want to harm Janice or Caitlin?

Jade: No.

Officer: Did you see or hear anything on the evening of Friday 3rd August that was out of the ordinary?

Jade: No, but I wasn't at the supermarket or their houses.

Officer: Where were you, if you don't mind me

asking?

Jade: That night, I can't remember. Let me… *Pause* I was at home. As I said, I don't have much money. I was at home in my room, I think.

Officer: Anyone else in the house who can verify this Jade, did you make any calls?

Jade: No, I think all my housemates were out. I can't remember if I used my phone. Probably not.

4: THE SILENT VIGIL

Sunday 30th September 2018 -
Ethan

A s Jade stepped into the derelict building, Ethan stood still under a lamp post
on the corner of the street. He wondered
what on earth she wanted inside the boarded-
up shop that hadn't sold anything for at least
twenty years.

He hadn't planned to follow her there. He'd
sat on a bench in the park opposite her house, to
see if she'd told him the truth about going out
later. He'd seen her crying through her bedroom
window before she'd drawn the curtains. Then
he'd been curious about where she was going,
dressed in clothes he'd never seen her wear before. He hadn't meant to scare her by the dust-

bins - he was only keeping an eye on her, making sure she was safe.

He stumbled towards the small card that Jade had dropped outside the building and picked it up with shaking hands. It seemed to be a business card of sorts, but the colours and words seemed to blur in the dusk; the sun had just set.

Ethan crept back towards the lamp post and it all became clear. The card had a white background with the word 'Princesses' printed in pink italic letters on it. On the right, a fluffy white cartoon cat winked. On the left, there were more words: 'Good fun guaranteed. For men. The Castle. Central Croydon.'

His mind raced. The card had come from Jade's pocket. She had just entered an old building called The Castle in the centre of Croydon. He thought of her constant tiredness and how irritable she had become. The phone calls that she wouldn't answer in front of him and her strange choice of clothes. Her run-down house-share and low, part-time, salary.

He stood still in shock as the world spun around him. He hadn't breathed in a while and, as he gasped, he felt winded. He grabbed the lamp post and turned away from the building.

He felt furious with himself for not realising what was happening and angry with her for doing something so disgusting. Surely, he thought, she was being forced into it. But then why hadn't she asked him for help? His family had plenty of money, and he would have emptied his bank account for her if she'd asked.

Another bitter thought entered his head, more disturbing than any others he had: Maybe this is what she wants? Perhaps she likes doing this?

He turned and ran away, each thought that entered his head more harrowing than the last. He didn't know where he'd been or how far he'd run. It could have been minutes or hours, but he finally arrived at his front door, and let himself in. Thankfully, his parents were already in bed.

He collapsed onto his bed and tossed and turned as he thought of the ways he could save Jade. Eventually, he fell into a troubled sleep, full of dreams of her in danger.

A soft, repetitive knock on his door woke him the next morning. He felt dizzy and nauseous, as the memories of the previous night came flooding back to him.

"Ethan, I've brought your breakfast. You were so late back last night."

His mother poked her head around his bedroom door and glanced at him, her eyes wide with concern, and her lips pursed. He accepted the breakfast tray with a weak smile but didn't offer any explanation.

He forced himself to eat the omelette, the cereal and toast. It tasted dry and bland in his mouth, but he needed energy.

He had a plan. There was no point in being angry or upset, that wouldn't help or save Jade. And going to the police straight away wasn't an option. If he did that, it could put Jade in danger with the people behind this 'Princesses' organisation. Or, she might even have to enter police protection and move away, with a new name and life away from him. That wasn't an option.

Instead, he would investigate. He'd find out who was behind it and then go to the police himself. No-one would be watching him, or know it was him who had informed. A few hours before he went to the police, he would tell Jade what he was about to do. He'd keep her safe at his house while the police arrested the people who'd exploited her.

No one would ever know she had been a part of it, and she would be free. He could lend her money, put her up in his parents' spare room. Perhaps then, she may even see him in a new light.

The little business card was his first piece of evidence. He retrieved it from his coat pocket, where he'd scrunched it in rage the night before. He felt a creeping heat and redness rise up his chest, emanating from a bubble of anger in the pit of his stomach. With a deep breath, he suppressed it. Jade needed him.

"Princesses," he whispered to himself, as he looked at the pink slanted writing along the top.

"'Princesses' in The Castle," he mumbled, as he

re-read the address underneath.

"And what have you got to do with anything?" he asked as he looked at the cartoon fluffy white cat with a pink collar. It winked up at him from the right-hand side of the card.

Ethan turned to his laptop and grimaced as his search for 'princesses escorts' returned over 38 million results. He narrowed the results down to London, but there were no 'Princesses' based in Croydon. He couldn't find anything with the same pink writing or white cartoon cat.

All he managed to find was a more detailed history of the building itself, which had been a B&B, a barber's and a sweetshop. The front of the building was listed, which explained the presence of the old signage. There was no owner or leaseholder mentioned, apart from Croydon Council.

He closed his laptop and grabbed his coat; there was no time to lose. Within half an hour, he was queuing to speak to one of the officers in the Town Hall Records department.

"I'm sorry, sir," said the tired-looking lady behind the desk. "All I can tell you is that the front of the building is listed. And that no-one has successfully applied to rent it for over twenty-two years."

"Why haven't they been successful? Don't you, I mean, doesn't the Council want the rent money?" asked Ethan, and the woman sighed again.

"To be honest, I don't think the Council is letting anyone rent premises on that road. They're hoping to empty them all and sell the whole row to a big buyer."

"So, it's Council owned then?"

"Yes. Well, sort of, sir, judging by the records I'm looking at here. It's complicated, but it is our responsibility."

"Do you inspect it, make sure there's nothing dodgy going on there?"

"I do know a few people in building control. They are stretched because of the cuts, you know. I'm afraid they prioritise making sure nothing dodgy is going on in buildings which aren't abandoned. And let me tell you, sir, that keeps them busy enough."

Ethan paused, taking in the information. The woman looked at him, her eyebrows narrowed.

"You know, if there's something you're worried about, you could tell the police. It'd still be quicker than waiting for a Council inspection."

"N-No," stuttered Ethan. "I'm just curious about whether the building could be used again. School project."

He turned and walked away before the printout of the record had finished. The woman sighed again and threw the sheet of paper into the bin, then turned to her next enquiry.

Feeling let down by the internet and the authorities, Ethan decided to hang around The Castle. It gave him an odd sort of satisfaction to watch over it. He took hundreds of pictures and noted down any patterns he spotted.

Over the next few days, he noticed that the girls tended to arrive before sunset. Often, they came alone. But a couple of times, they appeared in small groups, chatting away in a language Ethan didn't recognise.

Sometimes there were other people on the street when the girls entered and exited the building, but they didn't seem to notice or pay any attention. What happened behind the listed shop front was well and truly hidden in plain sight.

After darkness, the 'customers' appeared. Some of them loitered around the building until the street was clear before entering. Twice he saw a larger group of younger men appear. They too waited on the road with bottles of beer, entering the building one by one.

On the first night, Ethan saw Jade again. She looked so small against the broad street and tall lamp posts. She paused outside, lit a cigarette and entered the building. Horrible images tormented him, and he almost ran away. But he endured and sat on the flat roof of one of the opposite buildings for hours until he watched Jade leave.

He thought he saw Jade again on the second night, but it was another young girl with blond hair. He craned his neck and looked through the dirty window of a late-night greasy spoon, across the road from The Castle. He was sure he recognised the girl, but he couldn't get a good enough look before she entered the building.

On the third night, a Wednesday, the air was much milder. Ethan sat once more in the best watching place he'd discovered so far - the flat roof of the opposite building. He squinted through the dwindling sunlight as a young girl hurried down the street, her eyes fixed on the road beneath her. She had brown hair, so he knew it wasn't Jade, but she still looked familiar to him. As she got closer, he took a deep breath in dismay. He recognised her, and at the same time, he realised who the other familiar-looking girl was.

His head spun as he fumbled to activate his camera. He needed to capture a picture of the girl to prove he hadn't imagined it.

Surely, he thought, this couldn't be a coincidence. Jade and the two other young girls he'd recognised all worked at the Melwood supermarket.

Excerpt: Interview with Ethan Hutchins. Tuesday 4 September 2018, 15:00

Officer: Thanks for talking to us, Ethan. I'll cut to the chase. How well did you know Janice Locke and Caitlin Murphy?

Ethan: Not well at all, sir. I only started working at the supermarket in June this year, after my exams. They were sometimes supervising the department when I was working, but we didn't speak.

Officer: Did you speak to them socially?

Ethan: No, I never socialised with them. They're a bit older than me.

Officer: Do you know any reason why anyone would want to harm Janice or Caitlin?

Ethan: No, I didn't know anything about them.

Officer: Ethan, we have to ask this as a matter of course. Where were you on the evening of Friday 3rd August?

Ethan: It's OK. I was at the pub, the `Spoons by the supermarket, with some of my cousins and their friends.

Officer: You were there all night, Ethan? You didn't go out at any point?

Ethan: No, I got there around 5 pm and my cousin helped get me home at about midnight. I'd had a few too many.

Officer: Thanks, Ethan. Anything else comes to mind; please call me.

Post-interview officer's notes: Pub landlord confirms Ethan's story; he advised Mr Nicholas Hutchins to escort Ethan home just before last orders at 11:30 pm. Will provide CCTV if necessary.

5: LOST AND FOUND

Thursday 4th October 2018 - Debbie

D ebbie Gomez awoke with a start, ten minutes before her 6 am alarm. She was out of breath, and the back of her neck felt damp with sweat.

As her breathing returned to normal, she tried to remember the nightmare. There was a gun and lots of blood, and there were two bodies on the ground. But were the bodies Janice and Caitlin, or Karen and Dawn? The details slipped away from her as she sat up and rubbed her face with her hands.

Debbie's husband Joe slept silently, unaware of how deeply the death of two colleagues and friends still affected her. She hauled herself out of bed, careful not to wake him, and tiptoed past her children's rooms towards the stairs.

She paused to look at herself in the small hallway mirror and sighed. Every time she looked in it, an older, more tired person looked back at her. Her skin was paler and puffier than usual and her long, dark bob lacked its usual bounce. She turned to the kitchen to make her children's lunches, hoping it would distract her from her thoughts.

An hour later, she returned to her bedroom and opened the blinds, letting the dim morning light enter the room.

"What time is it?" asked Joe, as he stirred in the bed.

"Almost seven. But don't worry, the kids are having breakfast and I've left their lunches in the fridge."

"You're a star," he mumbled, and she kissed his forehead in return.

"Are you OK to drive the kids to school before work?" asked Debbie, "I have to start at opening time again."

"Of course, but you're working too much, love. Remember, you took the supermarket job to have more time with the kids and a less stressful life."

"Yeah," laughed Debbie humourlessly, "and look where that got me. It just feels like there's this dark cloud hanging over me, over the supermarket."

Tears welled up in her eyes, but then she

looked at the clock and realised she was running short of time.

Debbie put on her uniform, brushed her hair, and kissed her husband and two teenage children goodbye. It was a routine Debbie now insisted on since the murders. A shiver ran down her spine as she thought about Janice's husband and children. They didn't get a chance to say anything before their wife and mother died on their doorstep.

She travelled to the supermarket, zombie-like. She only emerged from her daze once she'd climbed up the stairs to the staff area.

"Stinks around here, doesn't it?" a voice croaked behind her, disrupting her thoughts.

"Oh!" gasped Debbie with a small jump, as she pushed her jacket and bag into the locker. "Yes, Edith, it sure does. I'll see you downstairs."

"Maybe you will," chided Edith, with a smile.

"What's that supposed to mean?" sighed Debbie. She wouldn't put it past Edith, the store's oldest employee, to go on strike without good reason.

"Well, the police are here again. They went in there two minutes ago." Edith pointed at the Manager's office with a proud grin. "They're with Steve and Gillian now, so I suppose they might want to talk to you next."

"Right," said Debbie as her mind raced. Her palms felt sweaty, and her shoulders tensed.

"I don't suppose you've heard anything then, any updates on the case," queried Edith, eagerly.

"No, I haven't. And even if I did, I wouldn't be able to tell you," replied Debbie, with her eyes fixed on the door to the Manager's office.

"Oh, keep your sodding secrets then," croaked Edith. "Bloody supervisors won't tell us anything even after thirty-five years of service," she muttered as she shuffled away.

Debbie followed Edith down to the shop floor. There was no sign of her best friend, Karen, who was due to work alongside Debbie. Instead, the shorter, rounder Marie stood at the Supervisor's desk, scribbling over Debbie's schedule.

"What are you doing here?" asked Debbie with a frown.

"Good morning to you too, Deborah," replied Marie. She didn't look up from the schedule, to which she'd applied liberal amounts of Tipp-ex.

"You and Karen might be a bit busy today, so Gill called me in. Lucky, really, given the state of this," Marie muttered.

"Where's Karen then?" asked Debbie, as her fists curled.

"I don't have a tracking device on her. Though, come to think of it, someone should."

Before Debbie could retort, another voice spoke behind her.

"Deborah Gomez?"

"What?" she replied through clenched teeth,

her arms raised in the air as she spun around.

"Deborah, I'm Detective Sergeant Joanne Harris. I'm here with Detective Chief Inspector Okafor. He'd like to talk to you upstairs. Both Steve and Gillian are aware."

"Oh, yes, of course, that's fine," mumbled Debbie, as Marie smirked to herself.

DS Harris directed Debbie into the staff training room next to the Manager's office. DCI Okafor was already seated, his large hands raised to his receding hairline as he looked down at a stack of papers in front of him.

"Hello," he said, looking up at Debbie as she sat down. He had a reassuring voice and a kind, trustworthy face. But, the lines around his eyes and mouth told their own story; he was under a lot of stress.

"Thank you for agreeing to speak with me today, Deborah."

"No problem. Please, it's Debbie." She clutched her hands together.

"And thank you again, for answering our questions at the beginning of this investigation. You gave us really useful information, even though you were grieving for your friends."

"Have you found them, the people responsible?" asked Debbie. Her voice shook as her body trembled.

"No, we haven't," Okafor sighed, raising one hand back towards his head. "I'm afraid that's not why I'm here. Let me cut to the chase. We have pursued several potential leads and lines of inquiry in this case, but they have not yet yielded results. This false start is not uncommon in out-of-the-blue cases like this, though of course, it is very frustrating for the families and friends of the victims. Now, we're not back to square one, but we are refocusing our efforts to catch the person or persons responsible, which rest assured we will do.

"Debbie, I want to talk to you on a more informal basis. You are not under any kind of suspicion here. I wanted to talk to you because you are the person in this building who seemed to know these women best. You share my desire to catch the perpetrator as soon as possible. I need a little more insight from you on your colleagues and their behaviour."

He paused to let his request sink in. Debbie shifted in her seat and her muscles tensed.

"Can we do this, Debbie? This is no more than an informal chat at this stage. Though, I must ask that you keep everything we say between these four walls."

"OK," whispered Debbie, trying to steady herself so that she could be as helpful as possible.

"Excellent, Debbie. So, I'm right in thinking that your departmental team consists of Gillian, Renee, Karen, Dawn and Marie. And, more recently, following the murders, Jade and Ethan."

"Yes."

"Do you get on with them? It's OK if the answer is no; honesty is the most helpful response here."

"Well, Karen is my best friend, we've known each other since high school, our children get on, and we're fortunate to work together. I get on with Dawn well enough too, though she is a very private person. I've dropped her home a few times, but we don't go out together. Gillian is a bit of a machine. She's married to the job, you know, as well as Kevin. But she's tolerable once you get over the bossiness. She gets things done, you know. Jade and Ethan, I barely know them. They seem like good, smart kids. But I'm old enough to be their mother, so I wouldn't say we were friends."

"Thank you, Debbie," said Okafor, ticking off some names. "There are still two remaining," he added with a hint of a smile.

"Well, Renee, as I'm sure you've seen, is a bit of a character. She appeared in January this year, transferred from another store. She's created a lot of division, I'm afraid. Either she thinks she's better than us, or just enjoys causing trouble. Or both. She is quite funny sometimes; she's efficient when she puts her mind to something. Perhaps, if we didn't work together, we could be friends. But we do, and we're not. I do not have time for Marie. I'm afraid difficult doesn't begin to cover it," continued Debbie, as DS Harris scribbled opposite her.

"She seems to idolise Renee and has no qualms about stirring and gossiping. She's mean and lazy. I know Jan and Caitlin felt the same about all the people I've mentioned."

"OK, that's good, thank you. Now, these behaviours you've mentioned: bossiness, privacy, stirring, meanness. Did any of them start shortly before or after the murders?"

Debbie paused for thought. Renee and Marie were annoying before, and their indifference to the murders wasn't out of character. Gillian had always been bossy. Dawn quiet, and Karen a bit absent-minded, aloof.

"I'm sorry, I can't think of anything now, can I take some time to think about it?"

"Of course. I have one more thing to ask if I may?" Okafor paused and waited for Debbie to nod. "Does the name 'Princesses' mean anything to you?"

"No," she replied honestly. "Should it? Does it mean something to you?"

"Not yet, Debbie, but I hope it will soon."

Okafor smiled enigmatically and picked up the papers in front of him.

DS Harris accompanied Debbie back to the shop floor. As they reached the end of one of the aisles, Debbie found Marie in the same position she'd left her in.

"Can we speak to Karen Goldman too, please?" asked DS Harris.

"Oh, I'm sure you can," replied Marie, "but I'm afraid she disappeared about fifteen minutes ago after I told her you were here."

Debbie felt the anger towards Marie bubbling up again. Before she could act on it, Gillian appeared from underneath the Supervisor's desk.

"Karen missing?" she asked, in her high voice. "Shame, I was going to ask her to clean the lockers with you, Debbie. You had better find her and get going."

Marie snorted as Gillian held up two flimsy pairs of rubber gloves and a bin bag.

"I can see you have work to do," interjected DS Harris. "We're running late anyway, and I can catch up with Karen another time. I have her phone number."

Debbie traipsed back upstairs again. As she reached the staff area, Karen stepped out of the Manager's office in front of her. Her usual tight ponytail was slightly loose, her cheeks flushed.

"Where the hell have you been?" whispered Debbie.

"Oh, here and there, you know," Karen replied, breathlessly. "What's that in your hand? Why have you got a bin bag?"

"We have to do the locker cleaning, Gillian's orders. I need to get the master key from Steve then let's get it over and done with."

"I'll get it!" said Karen with a smile. She re-entered the Manager's office and closed the door behind her. Debbie stood outside, perplexed.

They began opening and closing lockers, searching for rotten food and wiping down the insides. After fifteen minutes, Debbie turned to Karen with a mischievous look. "The police were here, Karen," she whispered.

"I know. Mardie said."

"You've got to stop calling her that," giggled Debbie. "They were looking for you after they spoke to me."

"Me, why?" asked Karen, as she pulled out a mouldy lunch box and rotten banana with a grimace.

"Same as me, I expect," whispered Debbie. "I'm not allowed to say anything at all, so don't tell anyone. But they think the murderer could have been someone who works here."

"No way," gasped Karen.

"Shh. And, Okafor asked if I knew about any-thing called 'Princesses'. What do you think that could be?"

"Isn't that Renee's cat's name, 'Princess'?"

"Oh God, you're right, I forgot," hissed Debbie. "Do you think Renee has something to do with it?"

"Well her cat certainly doesn't. Now don't go running away with this Deb. I know we don't like her, but... come on!"

But Debbie was frozen to the spot, her eyes wide in shock. Inside the locker she'd just opened was a small designer bag. The owner had shown it to Debbie around three months ago after her new boyfriend had given it to her.

She unclipped the clasp, revealing a mobile phone and a small purse. She opened the purse and took out the credit cards, which all had the same name on them: Caitlin Murphy.

Excerpt: Interview with Deborah Gomez. Thursday 9 August 2018, 12:30

Officer: Thank you, Debbie, that was a thorough interview, very helpful indeed. I have just one more question, which I'm afraid I have to ask. Where were you on Friday 3rd August, between 9.30 pm and midnight?

Debbie: I was at home. The children were in their rooms upstairs. Joe, my husband, and I had two of our neighbours over for drinks. They left around 10 pm, Joe and I cleared the kitchen and went to bed ourselves.

Post-interview officer's notes: Alibi confirmed. Joseph Gomez has been interviewed and has confirmed his wife's whereabouts.

6: ANYTHING FOR YOU

Friday 5th October 2018 - Marie

A repetitive, high-pitched beeping sound woke Marie at 9 am on the dot. She turned towards the noise, stuck her short arm out from under the duvet and hit the snooze button.

Her head was fuzzy, her mouth paper dry. She shuddered as she opened one eye and saw the near-empty wine glass and full ashtray on her bedside table. She was very thirsty, so she hauled herself out of bed and shuffled on heavy legs into the kitchen.

The mess made her heave. Piles of soiled pans and plates were stacked next to the sink, and the bin was full to the brim. She grabbed a bottle of water from the fridge and some paracetamol from a drawer.

Light streamed in through the windows of her converted loft flat. Usually, this brought the artwork covering the walls to life. But this morning it reflected off the surfaces into her eyes and worsened her headache. Back in bed, she gulped the water and swallowed three painkillers.

She picked up her phone and saw three missed calls; one from Gillian, two from Renee. A message from Renee appeared.

I can't work today. Don't say you'll cover my shift. Jade can do it - I've already asked her. I need you to come over and help me with something.

Marie smiled to herself. Spending time with Renee was the only thing she enjoyed as much, if not more, than her painting. Before she could respond to the message, the phone vibrated.

"Hi, Gillian," answered Marie brightly.

"Marie, hello. Renee has decided not to come in today. Can you cover?"

Marie took a deep breath and made a hissing sound through her teeth.

"Sorry, Gill. I'm looking after one of my elderly relatives, to give the usual carer a break."

"I see," Gillian replied coldly. Marie wondered whether her boss had somehow detected her lie.

"I've spoken to Renee, and she said Jade was

able..."

"Yes, yes I know about that," said Gillian, cutting across Marie. "I was checking if you were free too. More experienced pair of hands, you know."

"Sorry, Gill."

"OK. I'll see you over the weekend."

Marie turned back to Renee's message and responded.

Told G I can't cover. She's not happy. When and why do you need me? Hope all OK xxxx

The reply came straight away, which was a pleasant surprise. Sometimes it took Renee days to respond to her messages, and at other times she didn't respond at all.

Soon as you can, like now! Need some help with something.

Marie rolled her eyes. Asking for 'some help with something' was vague. Perhaps the cat had gone missing again.

She gulped down some more water, showered and blow-dried her hair. She rarely bothered to wear make-up, but when she saw Renee, she tended to add a bit of lipstick and mascara. Today, she added a spray from a perfume bottle she'd had on her dresser for over ten years.

Marie left the flat, pausing only to grab a croissant from the fridge, and hurried down to her car.

Ten minutes later, Renee Beck flung open her front door to let Marie in.

"Ohhh my God, Marie," cried Renee dramatically. "Thank goodness you're here at last. I am having the most terrible time and I desperately need a favour. A big favour."

Marie took in the scene. Renee didn't look or sound ill at first glance, but her usually tidy house looked as though someone had rifled through it. Drawers and cupboard doors were open, DVDs and books had been removed from the shelves and piled on the floor.

Renee had no make-up on and was wearing leggings and a baggy old jumper. She beckoned Marie further into the living room.

"Renee, what's going on?" asked Marie with trepidation.

"Sit down, Marie," ordered Renee, and she ushered her into the armchair. Princess the Persian cat appeared from behind the chair and jumped onto Marie's lap. She pawed at her shoulder and looked back and forth from Marie to Renee.

Renee remained standing and turned to address Marie.

"Marie," she announced, with the look and tone of a Shakespearean actor ready to break into a monologue. "I am afraid I am ill. I do not feel well at all, and I am very sick."

Princess tilted her head slightly as Marie's eyebrows narrowed.

"You don't look very ill, Renee, what's wrong? Not something serious?"

"Well, no Marie, I'm not dying," answered Renee, and Marie breathed a sigh of relief. "But trust me. I am ill, and I need to sort things out."

"OK, so what can I do to help? Do you need a lift to the doctors?"

"I need you to go shopping for me, Marie. I am going to be quite ill for around three days."

"How do you know?" asked Marie, as Renee paced around the living room.

"Write this down, Marie, I need healthy things. Fruit, you know. Smoothies and one of those vape things."

"Juice and a vape?" asked Marie, incredulously, as she lifted an anxious Princess off of her lap. "Renee, can you please sit down?"

"And comfy things," continued Renee, ignoring Marie's request.

"A blanket, new books, because none of these are suitable," Renee added as she kicked over a pile of them on the floor.

"OK...OK! I'll go shopping. I need to pick up some bits too. But will you promise to rest while I'm gone? Whatever is wrong with you, this," Marie gestured at Renee, "can't be good for you."

Renee stopped mid-pace, allowing Marie to stand up and grab her arm.

"Come and sit down for a minute. Has something happened with Kevin? Or, I'll tell you about work yesterday and the police coming in?"

"No, Marie, I don't have the time. I need to go out, you see."

"Out? But you're ill, that's why I'm here, and I'm going out for you."

"Oh, Marie, won't you just do as I say and stop questioning me!" shouted Renee as she raised her hands to her head and closed her eyes.

Marie raised her eyebrows, sat back down with her arms crossed and sighed.

"Sorry. I'm so sorry!" purred Renee, as she wedged herself into the armchair next to Marie and put her arm around her.

"You know I wouldn't ask if it wasn't urgent. I promise we'll do something fun together soon."

Marie could smell Renee's perfume and as she turned around to look at her, their faces were quite close. Close enough for Marie to notice the dark shadows under Renee's eyes, which seemed a little bloodshot.

"Fine," agreed Marie. "Of course, I'll go then. Anything for you."

"Marvellous!" exclaimed Renee, jumping out of the armchair and pushing her long hair away from her face. "We've both got our little missions then. Drop the shopping back off here when you're done. Oh, and here's some cash," she added, and handed Marie a couple of £20 notes with a smile.

Marie raised her eyebrows and pursed her lips. Renee quickly rearranged her face into a frown and coughed unconvincingly.

Marie drove past the supermarket towards the town centre with her shopping list. Her head was starting to hurt again. She felt like there was an elastic band around her temples, tightening against the dull ache behind her eyes. Marie wondered where her frantic friend was going. Renee had taken a different turning at the Melwood Junction and sped off into the distance.

Marie had heard stories about Renee's behaviour on her nights out. Her affair with Kevin was the tip of the iceberg, considering her history. But Marie had never seen her like she was today. She was usually so happy and confident, the life and soul of any party.

She parked the car in a little-known car park and walked up towards the High Street, past a row of tatty, boarded up shops. She noticed Ethan sitting in a café as she passed it, but didn't stop to say hello. Small talk wasn't her strong point and she wanted to get started on Renee's shopping straight away.

She reached the end of the High Street two hours later and sat down in a café with heavy bags of healthy food and drinks, new books, cat food and art supplies. She'd also bought Renee a few gifts, including perfume, aromatherapy candles and bath oils. If Renee was in the midst of a mental health crisis, they might help.

As she ate her panini and chips, Marie ran through Renee's list to check she hadn't forgotten anything. She remembered Renee saying something about comfy things, so she decided to make one final stop.

It was another warm day outside and it was far too hot inside the large department store. Marie felt the heat inside her jacket, and she struggled to keep hold of all the bags. She grabbed a couple of plain knitted jumpers in size ten and headed towards the pyjamas.

As she bustled through the underwear section, she looked up at the skinny mannequins dressed in matching sets. She started to imagine Renee in them and began to feel even hotter. She turned away and bumped into a tall, thin woman, with very straight, shoulder-length blonde hair.

"Marie?"

"Oh, hello," she mumbled. Her face reddened as a smartly-dressed Karen gazed down at the jumpers.

"I'm not sure they'll fit you," commented Karen, with a smirk.

"They're for Renee, not me."

"Doing her shopping too?" asked Karen, as she looked down towards Marie's many bags.

"Bloody hell Marie, have you won the lottery or something?"

Marie shuffled the bags between her hands and shook her head. She was desperate to get away from her least favourite colleague.

"If you must know, prints of my paintings have been selling well, and I sold an original last month. Now I had better get on."

"I didn't know you painted," said Karen, who seemed unable to take the hint.

"You've never asked. Now, I really must go."

Marie's face was burning red, and her arms ached from the strain of the bags. She turned away from an intrigued looking Karen and hurried towards the till to pay for the jumpers. She hated getting caught off-guard, especially by the likes of nosy Karen. She and Debbie both seemed incapable of thinking before they spoke or keeping anything to themselves.

Back in the car park, Marie loaded the bags into her boot, caught her breath, and drove back towards Renee's. However, when she reached the house, Renee's car wasn't in the drive, and nobody answered the front door. Marie sighed and returned to the car. She lit a cigarette and cracked open a can of gin and tonic from one of the shopping bags.

Excerpt: Interview with Marie Webster. Monday 13 August 2018, 16:00

(nb the interviewee has requested legal representation for this interview)

Interview resumed 16.18

Officer: Thank you for agreeing to continue Marie. Of course, it was not my intention to upset you, though I recognise this is a very distressing time. *Pause* Now, I only have a few things to clarify. Earlier, you said you weren't particularly close to Janice and Caitlin. *Pause* So I'm a little surprised that talking about what happened has prompted such a strong reaction from you. Were you friends with these women?

Marie: No, we were never close; that was true. I didn't know them outside of work and at work they were just thick as thieves with each other. Over the last year, we didn't get on at work. But I'm still upset they're dead.

Officer: Of course. Do you know anyone who would have wanted to cause them harm?

Marie: No, but then as I said, I didn't know them. Who knows what they had gotten themselves into?

Officer: OK, I only have one more question, Marie, then we're done. Where were you on the evening of Friday 3rd August between 9.30 pm and midnight?

Lawyer: Ms Webster is not a suspect in this case, or under arrest. Marie, you do not have to answer.

Officer: I am aware, thank you. Marie, all of these questions are voluntary, but the answers may be beneficial in terms of ruling you out of any further inquiries.

Marie: I don't know why I should tell you my whereabouts, I didn't do it, I didn't know them well, I didn't even know where they lived!

Officer: I'm aware of that Marie, and I repeat, you are not under suspicion here. This interview is just standard procedure to build a picture of events. I am fully expecting you to rule yourself out of involvement, and for this to be our last conversation.

Marie: *Pause* I was at home.

Officer: The whole night?

Marie: Yes.

Officer: Was anyone else there?

Marie: No.

Officer: Did you use your phone, send any texts?

Marie: *Pause* I don't think so.

Officer: Home alone, not on your phone. What were you doing then?

Lawyer: This is an aggressive line of questioning against my client, who is not a suspect and is clearly very distressed. She has now provided you with voluntary information on where she was last Friday night, and what she does in her own home is not your concern. I suggest this completes the interview.

7: THE AMATEUR DETECTIVES CLUB

Friday 5th October 2018 - Karen

Karen left the town centre shortly after her encounter with Marie. Of all the people to bump into, she thought, as she meandered back up Croydon High Street. She couldn't wait to tell Debbie about it later that evening. They'd agreed to meet so that Karen could give the low down on her imminent meeting with the police.

She had looked forward to her meeting with Okafor ever since Debbie's discussion with him.

She had pictured the event in her mind; the handsome DCI leaning over the table and looking deep into her eyes. He'd share his suspicions and ask her to help him solve the case of two murdered women. She'd even dressed up for it, in a smart short skirt and her best silk blouse.

It was darkly glamorous, and she couldn't wait to tell him her opinions about her colleagues. It was high time she delivered some payback to Renee and Marie. After all, they'd recently engineered all the complaints against her at work.

Karen pulled up outside the police station and rushed inside with a smile.

"I'm here to see Vincent Okafor, I'm Karen Goldman," she announced to the young receptionist.

"OK Madam, you and everyone else today!" he replied.

"I'm a little late; I hope that's not a problem?"

"No Mrs Goldman, not to worry. As I said, he's busy himself. I'll let his team know you're here and they'll come down when they're ready. Please, take a seat." He gestured at the busy waiting area.

Karen grudgingly took the last remaining chair, between two people who looked like they were from the New Grange estate. She lifted her nose and took out her phone to distract herself from them.

Twenty minutes later, a uniformed officer escorted Karen to a small, dank room with no windows. In contrast to the warmer autumn breeze outside, the air in the room was cold. A fluorescent light flickered above her head. There were two chairs and a table covered in unplugged recording equipment. Karen crossed her arms, tapped her feet on the floor and took in her surroundings. It was hardly the interview location she'd anticipated. She waited another five minutes until DS Joanne Harris entered the room and closed the door behind her.

"Karen Goldman?"

"Yes, that's me. Where's Vincent?"

"DCI Okafor is away on urgent business, Karen. It's been a hectic day. He's asked me to have this quick conversation with you in his absence."

"Right," replied Karen tersely, not hiding her disappointment.

"It won't take long, and we do appreciate you coming in to help us with this investigation. Are you OK to proceed?" asked DS Harris, removing a pen and notepad from her jacket pocket.

"I suppose so."

"Great. We wanted to pick up something from your original interview with us. We asked about your whereabouts on Friday 3rd August, between 9.30 pm and midnight."

"You did," replied Karen as she tried to recall the conversation.

"And do you remember what you said?"

"I said I was at home, I think."

"It's fine, I have the transcript here," replied DS Harris. "Yes, you said: 'I think I was at home'."

"Yes, how is this relevant?"

"We wanted to ask whether you did go and check your whereabouts. This question isn't about any kind of suspicion, Karen. We just need to dot the 'I's and cross the 'T's, you know." DS Harris smiled at Karen, awaiting a response.

"Oh, right," sighed Karen. "Well I did check, and yes, I was at home all evening with my husband, Pete. It was just the two of us; the kids had a sleepover that evening at a friend's house."

"Perfect, thanks, Karen. We'll get that checked with your husband and add that to the case notes."

"Check with Pete? Is that necessary?"

"Yes, I'm afraid so. As this case continues, we must have all our paperwork in order. Thank you for your time today, and sorry we missed you at your work yesterday. I know it would have been more convenient to talk to you there."

DS Harris rose from her chair and picked up the papers in front of her. Karen, however, remained seated.

"Is everything OK, Karen?" asked DS Harris.

"Is that all?" Karen replied, and she looked up at the detective in disbelief.

"Yes, it is, unless you have anything to add. Was there something else you wanted to discuss?"

"Well, Debbie said you discussed more with her, asked her something about a Princess," Karen mumbled.

"We also asked Debbie to keep the contents of that conversation private."

"It's just Debbie mentioned it, and I remembered that our colleague Renee has a cat called Princess."

There was a brief look of surprise and interest on DS Harris' face, but she covered it with a smile.

"Thank you, Karen, now let me see you out."

Thoughts raced through Karen's mind as she stomped out of the police station and into her car. Did they trust Debbie more than her? Was she a suspect? And how come the police weren't grilling Renee or Marie? It would have been different if Vincent was there, she thought, as she kicked off her high heels and replaced them with a pair of old pumps. Her anger rose as she thought of DS Harris' smiling face.

"Patronising bitch," she muttered to herself, as she started the engine of her black Range Rover and drove towards Debbie's house.

"Karen, you're early!" Debbie looked surprised as she swung the door open.

"Yes, I am, sorry, it didn't take as long as I expected. Vincent wasn't even there."

Debbie led the way down towards the conservatory. It was bright and heated by the autumn light streaming through the glass panes. Debbie's demeanour seemed to have changed. She seemed much more hopeful and happier than she had done over the past few months.

"I have something to tell you," said Debbie with a mischievous grin, as she poured them both a glass of wine. "But first you have to tell me about the police, what did they say to you?"

"Well, Vincent wasn't there, he got called away. So, I don't think his deputy was able to talk as much. But she asked me about a few things in my original statement, and then about the Princess."

"Princesses?" corrected Debbie, her eyebrows raised.

"Yes, 'Princesses'. I told her about the cat."

"Good," grinned Debbie. "I wonder if it means anything to them?"

"Who knows. Anyway," sighed Karen, keen to change the subject from her underwhelming police visit. "Guess who I saw today, out in town?"

Debbie picked up her wine and looked at Karen with interest.

"Mardie! I was browsing, and I turned around and bumped into her. She was staring at these two mannequins in underwear." Karen laughed out loud, and Debbie snorted into her wine glass.

"She was doing Renee's shopping for her; can you believe it? She had so many bags, Deb; it was like she'd won the lottery or something. Expensive perfume, candles, and bags of other stuff."

Debbie was staring at Karen, eyes wide.

"Well," said Debbie with the same grin as before, "Renee was too busy to do her shopping today."

"What do you mean?"

"I saw Renee driving through the Melwood junction by the store today. She almost caused a big accident at the traffic lights. And she ended up at Gillian's, you know, in Fair Lawns."

"How do you know she went to Gill's?" asked Karen, though she had a feeling she knew the answer.

"I followed her," replied Debbie casually, as she took another sip of her wine. "After my chat with Okafor yesterday and the thing about the cat, I was curious. And anyway, it paid off."

"Debbie, you can't go around following people! Renee's from that awful council estate, she might know dodgy people. What do you mean, it paid off?"

"Well, I pulled up around the corner from Gill's, but I could see her front door. I knew Gill was at work, so I couldn't figure out why Renee was there. Anyway, she knocks on the door and Kevin answers."

"Kevin!" Exclaimed Karen, "Gill's husband?"

"Yes. He lets Renee in, and she's there for like half an hour. I was about to go, but she comes out of the house and Kevin gives her an envelope. It looked like one of those brown ones stuffed with cash."

Karen couldn't believe what she was hearing.

"And then," continued Debbie feverishly, "she speeds off out the gate, scratching her car on it as she goes. By the time I got back on the road, I'd lost her. No idea where she went."

"Bloody hell Deb. It could have been anything in the envelope."

"I know. But it's too much of a coincidence, isn't it? Marie is splashing the cash in town, Renee is getting envelopes of cash or something from Kevin. They're up to something, and they have a secret."

"Oh, come on," challenged Karen. "They're vile, but you don't actually believe it was them who killed Janice and Caitlin, do you?"

"I do think it's possible," asserted Debbie. "And what proves it, is us finding Caitlin's bag in the lockers yesterday. The killer must have put it there to hide it, and therefore, the killer must be someone who works in the store."

"Caitlin could have left it there by mistake on the night she died," ventured Karen, though she felt like she was fighting a losing battle. There was no stopping Debbie when she was in this kind of mood.

"No, Karen, I doubt it," replied Debbie, rolling her eyes.

"What have you done with the bag then? Have the police picked it up, seeing as it's evidence?"

"I haven't told them about it yet. And don't

look at me like that, I just wanted to take a closer look first."

Debbie's eyes drifted to the table at the end of the conservatory, where a phone lay charging.

"You can't be serious, Debbie!" gasped Karen as her shoulders tensed. "Do not turn that phone on."

"Don't you want to know what's on there? There could be a clue about why they died. The police will have had access to her and Janice's messages from Jan's phone anyway. We're not withholding anything they don't know."

"What is this, the Amateur Detective Club?" hissed Karen, as Debbie leant over to see if the phone had charged. "I say we throw it all away, bury it somewhere and pretend we never found it. We could be in danger if anyone knows we have it."

But Debbie had already turned the phone on. Please let there be a passcode, thought Karen.

"Passcode. Let's try 2412," said Debbie. "Her birthday," she added as the phone sprung to life.

"There must be something on here Karen. They knew something before they died. You remember how they were, always talking to each other in whispers."

"Jesus," whimpered Karen, with her head in her hands. She peered between her fingers at her friend. No wonder Debbie looked so invigorated, she thought, she believes she'll solve the case herself.

As the phone sprung to life, new messages popped up. Debbie scrolled through and then stopped. Her eyes flitted back and forth over one message in particular. She glanced at Karen and beckoned her round. Karen reluctantly peered over Debbie's shoulder to read.

Sorry, Cait – I know you won't get this till 2m morning. Sorry I didn't come back in with you and for being so down. We know something dodgy is going on at work, linked to Princesses. It must all be run by someone at the store, they're pulling the strings, must be to make money. We just need a bit more proof it's who we think it is – then we report it to protect the vulnerable ones. Good luck tomorrow, you will smash it. J xxx

"Oh God, I didn't think we'd find anything. What is 'Princesses'?" whispered Debbie.

They scrolled down through the messages to find more clues, but there were none.

"I have no idea, and neither do the police," replied Karen. "But it sounds like Jan and Cait knew something about it."

"Yes," replied Debbie gravely, "and it may have cost them their lives."

Excerpt: Interview with Karen Goldman. Thursday 16 August 2018, 17:30

Officer: Thank you for making time to see us, Mrs Goldman, I understand you have a busy schedule.

Karen: Sorry it's taken so long. I've had to rearrange so many appointments, it's just been difficult.

Officer: I understand, this shouldn't take long. Now, how well did you know Mrs Janice Locke and Ms Caitlin Murphy?

Karen: We worked together. I've known them since they joined the store. I used to go out with them for drinks, Debbie would arrange it.

Officer: Were you friends?

Karen: I suppose, yes, we were.

Officer: And were you ever aware of any problems they had, any situations they were uncomfortable with?

Karen: No, not really. Caitlin was younger than us; she was just happy and laughed when the three of us complained.

Officer: What about?

Karen: Our husbands mostly.

Officer: What did Janice say about her husband?

Karen: Oh, nothing too bad. I just think he didn't really like her working full-time. She never said anything terrible about him.

Officer: So, there was no-one you can think of

who'd want to cause either of them harm?

Karen: No.

Officer: I have to ask this Karen, where were you on the evening of Friday 3rd August between 9.30 pm and midnight?

Karen: I think I was at home.

Officer: You think?

Karen: I mean yes, I was at home with Pete, my husband, I think.

Officer: Are you sure of this, Karen?

Karen: Well, perhaps let me go and check, sorry I meant to say yes, I was at home, but now I've confused myself.

Officer: OK, Karen, please do check for us and let us know as soon as you can.

8: THIN BLUE LINE

Saturday 6th October 2018 - Vincent

DCI Vincent Okafor arrived at the police station shortly before 8 am. He wasn't meant to work on Saturdays, but he'd felt compelled to read through the Melwood murder files again. He hated long, drawn-out cases, preferring to close them as soon as he could and move on. That attitude had helped him rise through the ranks in the police force to Chief Inspector.

After a very bumpy six months in the role, the last thing he'd needed or expected happened; an unfathomable double murder in the more leafy, suburban part of the borough: Melwood. The inevitable media circus began, with all the reporters asking the same question. Why were two well-liked and decent women, with no criminal connections, shot dead in cold blood on the same summer's night, after their shift at the local supermarket?

Over two months had passed since those murders, and he was feeling the pressure acutely. He only remained the Senior Investigating Officer because no-one else wanted the job. They all knew they couldn't have done any better, and that the case would likely remain unsolved.

Okafor hadn't put a foot wrong. First, he'd considered the 'how' of the crime. The killer murdered the women at point-blank range, with no signs of a struggle. The perpetrator used a vehicle with its number plate obscured. They drove it off-grid and torched it, leaving no trace of evidence.

It wasn't a crime of passion, an accident, or a random occurrence. It was planned and premeditated. Okafor was sure that the women had known their assailant. After all, Caitlin had let them into her flat without any sign of a struggle.

His first hypothesis was that the women were secretly involved in organised criminal activity. After all, such executions were not uncommon in that world, and the women could have led a double life. His team worked under his guidance to seek out a link, but they found none. The friends and families of the two women seemed confused about why he had even considered it.

He was sure that, had the situation not been so grave, they would have found it laughable.

He moved his team onto more familiar ground. They started a deep dive into the men in Janice and Caitlin's lives. Here, the working theory was broader; that one of the men had, for some reason, decided to kill his partner and her close friend. Shortly after they began investigating, they caught a strong lead. Janice's devastated husband clearly didn't have the means to kill his partner and her friend. But the same could not be said for Caitlin's new boyfriend, Christian.

He was a wealthy trader in the city and had swept her off her feet. He'd showered her with gifts and promises of a fantastic future together. He hadn't told her of his two juvenile convictions for assaulting young women, or his dismissal from military training for theft of a firearm. By the time they'd uncovered this, Christian had left the country. Then, after two wasted weeks, he presented himself to the UK Embassy in Spain. He returned with extensive evidence of his innocence, in the form of a video alibi and witness statements. He knew he'd be a suspect given his background, and he'd preferred to compile his defence from a sunny villa than the inside of a holding cell.

Okafor re-focussed. 'Don't lose heart,' he'd told his team. 'We haven't even scratched the surface of people our victims have come into contact with.'

A re-examination of the Janice's phone had revealed only one message of interest, sent from Janice to Caitlin just moments before someone shot her.

"We know something dodgy is going on at work, linked to Princesses. It must all be run by someone at the store, they're pulling the strings, must be to make money. We just need a bit more proof it's who we think it is – then we report it."

The team should have passed it on to him when they first saw it. But he understood how they'd missed it. At first, they'd been looking for signs of organised criminal involvement, violent partners or stalkers. This message contained no such indication. All it told them was that the victims thought someone at work might be up to something' dodgy.' It wasn't clear whether they'd report something to the police, or the Human Resources team. As for the link to 'Princesses,' no-one knew what that meant at that time.

But, he'd thought, at least it gave his team another lead to follow. It was a mystery to solve, which may or may not help in the grander scheme of things. And it was better than nothing. They'd come close to having no leads at all, which would have taken some explaining to the Superintendent.

Okafor hung his jacket over the back of his chair and switched on his computer. He opened a folder full of the transcripts from interviews with Janice and Caitlin's colleagues.

DS Duncan Hill, who had since moved onto investigating a series of violent crimes committed in the north of the borough, had conducted the interviews. His replacement, DS Joanne Harris, seemed far more energetic and ambitious than her predecessor. She was the one who'd spotted the text message, giving them the crucial lead they'd needed.

Okafor's eyes scrolled over pages of Renee Beck's interview transcript and slid out of focus over her long-winded answers to some very straight-forward questions. He'd watched part of this interview live. He thought Renee rather liked the sound of her voice and was probably capable of talking her way out of anything.

There was a knock on his door and DS Harris appeared, with two coffees and a bag of croissants.

"DS Harris,' Okafor smiled and beckoned her into the office.

"Morning sir, I suspected I wouldn't be the only one working this case today." She handed him one of the coffees.

"Quite. This one isn't going to solve itself. Thanks for this," Okafor gestured to the coffee, "and I appreciate your coming in. Why don't you bring me up to speed on the last few days? I've seen you with your head down."

DS Harris sat down opposite her boss.

"Sir, I've been through the papers from this investigation so far. I've tried to find a gap or a slip-up, but there isn't one. The team did everything they should have."

Okafor nodded.

"So, that brings us to the text message and the supermarket. Does that mean anything to you yet, Joanne?"

"No, sir. But Karen Goldman did come in yesterday. I took the interview while you were out. She is now sure that she was at home with her husband."

"But didn't think to confirm this sooner," replied Okafor, rubbing the greying stubble on his chin. "Did she have anything else to say?"

"Well, sir, I'm afraid Debbie spoke to her about our separate chat. She seemed to expect more from my conversation with her. At the end, she said she knew we'd asked Debbie about 'Princesses'."

"That is disappointing," Okafor sighed.

"Yes, but then she went on to say that her colleague, Renee Beck, has a cat called Princess."

"Something dodgy going on, linked to Princesses," he said, paraphrasing the text message. "That doesn't fit with a cat, but let's keep it in mind."

"Sir, should we assume what they discovered was serious. And that the colleague behind it found out they were onto them. To protect the secret, they killed the women, or arranged the murder?"

"Correct, Joanne, we have to work on that basis. And if it turns out not to be so, that it is something unrelated, at least we can rule it out and move on to other leads which may appear in the meantime."

"Do you have an instinct, sir, some thoughts on where to start?"

"Luckily, we have some semblance of a start already, as you've seen. Eight close colleagues, all interviewed and asked for their opinions and their whereabouts."

He placed the transcripts out on the table.

"We have Gillian, Debbie and Karen. All roughly the same age, early 40s, no previous offences. All at home with their husbands at the time. Two husbands, so far, have concurred. Please check in with Peter Goldman today to confirm the third."

"Sir."

"Then we have Renee, Marie, and Dawn, all claiming to be at home alone. This Dawn, I can believe it. We barely got a word out of her during the interview; I can't imagine she spends much time socialising. Same with Marie. But, you'll see how she reacted in her interview. She did not respond well to questioning on her whereabouts. I find it very difficult to believe that Ms Beck was home alone. People like her don't spend Friday nights in by themselves. But I suppose, if she was genuinely ill, she might not have had a choice. The two others, Jade and Ethan," he continued, as DS Harris scribbled down notes, "both nineteen years old. He was in the pub, and she was at home because she can't afford to go out. They barely knew the victims; they're new to the job and were promoted after the incident to cover the hours."

"We need to talk to more people in the store, sir. Get a clearer picture of who these women did or didn't get on with. And what they might have been suspicious about."

"Correct. Let's get some more opinions on this friction between Janice and Caitlin, and Renee and Marie. Was there anything other than professional rivalry involved in it? Focus on the shop floor workers first; they'll know more gossip than the managers. We need to know everything. Who's seeing who, who's complained about whom, who's had too much time off, who's working too hard. The full works."

DS Harris nodded, still scribbling in her notebook.

"No more mention of 'Princesses', unless someone else raises it with us. And no more discussions with Debbie Gomez. She can't be trusted not to blab to Karen and others."

"Yes sir," replied DS Harris, standing up from

her chair.

"One last thing, Joanne," said Okafor, as he felt a little jolt in his stomach usually associated with a hunch.

"If we can stretch to it, keep an eye on Renee and Karen. If I were a betting man, I'd wager they're lying about where they were that night. If you watch the videos, they have a similar look in their eyes. But whether that means they had anything to do with the murders, I don't know."

DS Harris gave one last nod of assent, then left Okafor's office. He sat back in his chair and took a swig of his coffee. He smiled and picked up the transcripts again, ready to give them his full attention.

9: INSIDE THE CASTLE

Sunday 14th October 2018 - Jade

Jade once again stood outside the dilapidated 'Castle' building on the old market street in Croydon. The autumn sunshine had finally given way to lower temperatures and a miserable grey drizzle, which dripped off the hanging shop sign. The off-white paint was cracked along the window and door frames. It reminded Jade of old, dry skin flaking away from a once-healthy body.

She approached the door with her usual uneasy feeling and wondered what lay ahead that evening. Most nights were quiet, and so were most of the men who snuck into The Castle. They, like her, wanted to get it over with and avoid eye-contact. How has it come to this? she thought, as she paused by the door.

She tried to remember the details of how she got involved in 'Princesses'. Someone she'd never met before had spoken to her on the estate and told her they knew an easy way to make money. They got her a job, working as a waitress in the evenings at a cash bar in town.

She'd ended up in trouble, though, because some money went missing on her shift and they blamed her for it. They'd asked her to cover shifts at The Castle to make up for it.

Her mother was in serious trouble at the time. So, against all better judgment, Jade agreed to switch to The Castle as a short-term measure. Months later, Jade knew that she'd lost control. She was blackmailed into staying and not contacting the police about her predicament.

She pushed against the heavy door, hearing the slow creak of the hinges and the scraping against the uneven floor below. A tall, muscular man in a bomber jacket raised his head to look at her, smiled and gave her a key to one of the rooms upstairs.

"Looks like a quiet night tonight love, call me if you get lonely," he leered.

She ignored him and climbed up the old wooden staircase, avoiding the exposed nails sticking out of the boards. As usual, she experienced a crushing inner conflict. On the one hand, she wished for no one else to walk through the door that evening; but then, no people meant no money.

On her most desperate nights, she found herself wishing more of them into The Castle. She even gave out the horrible little business cards to customers and encouraged them to pass them on. On those nights, she hated herself just as much as the man on the phone and the faceless boss.

She walked past three locked rooms. She never saw the other girls who worked there; they all arrived at different times. All the rooms were the same: old fashioned, dusty, with patterned wallpaper and carpets. They all had a small bathroom attached; she often wondered if the place had once been a hotel.

An hour later, Jade remained alone, sitting on the creaky double bed in the centre of the room. The man downstairs had it right; it was a quiet night at The Castle. She sat in the musty old room, dwelling on the awful day she'd had.

That morning, she'd arrived at the supermarket, a few minutes before 10 am. She dreaded a day working with Gillian, who seemed increasingly stressed about staff shortages and the rest of their team's behaviour.

She'd approached the Supervisor's desk, where Gillian was talking and gesturing at a scared-looking Dawn.

"Obviously, Dawn, I don't mind if people are ill, but I know she isn't. I don't know what Renee is up to, but I'll give her a written warning if she can't get a doctor's note."

Dawn had raised her eyebrows and looked at Jade over Gillian's shoulders. Gillian spun round, and then looked relieved that it was only Jade standing there.

"Jade, good morning." Gillian had greeted her with her usual sweet smile.

"Morning. I'm happy to cover the hours. You know, if Renee or anyone else is ill. I could work for the rest of this week?"

Jade recalled the look on Gillian's face. Her boss' eyebrows and lips had narrowed, and she'd paused before answering.

"Ah, yes that's good to know, Jade. I expect Renee will be better soon, and there won't be any extra hours for the foreseeable, but I will let you know.

"Now," she'd continued before Jade had a chance to respond. "We are short on the tills today; would you mind a shift on a checkout? Dawn and I can supervise, I don't have much office work to do."

Gillian held out a till key and Jade once again felt she didn't have a choice. Dawn had glanced at her apologetically, as Jade turned towards the till at the end of the row.

She'd served customer after customer, all with trolleys full of expensive alcohol and food. Few of them seemed worried about the cost of it all. They spent hundreds and hundreds of pounds, which Jade so desperately needed, without a blink of an eye.

One customer had spent the entire time complaining about the lack of organic hummus in the store. Anger had bubbled in the pit of Jade's stomach. Was that all he had to worry about?

At the end, he'd asked her if she had anything to say on the matter. She'd opened her mouth to respond, but all that came out was 'Sorry,' and he'd walked away with a sigh and his hands in the air.

The only thing that had broken the monotony of day was the sight of DCI Vincent Okafor. His team hadn't asked to speak to Jade again, for which she was thankful. It had been so strange to talk to them about murders she knew nothing about, rather than her horrible situation.

She had left the supermarket as soon as she could and walked the familiar path towards the New Grange estate where she'd grown up. Within an hour, she'd reached her father's place. He had bought the house next door to his own a few years ago and knocked down some of the connecting walls. His house was now the biggest on the estate, not that he ever invited her to it.

He had many small businesses around Croydon. However, rumour had it that he and his sons made their real money from selling drugs. Either way, Jade had thought, he owed her nineteen years worth of birthday presents. Perhaps, he would even give her enough money to run away with her mother.

Her stepmother looked down at her when she'd arrived at the door.

"What do you want," she'd asked bluntly, as her eyes looked Jade up and down. She looked less composed than usual and her dark roots were two inches long.

"Is my Dad here?"

"No, he's away. What did you want from him, Jade?"

"Just to say hello," she muttered.

"Yeah right, you want something from him - money no doubt?"

Jade had looked at the floor and didn't respond.

"Well let me tell you, he's got enough on his plate at the moment. This new Inspector is poking around his business, and he's got rivals popping up everywhere. Your father's priority is the boys and me. He doesn't owe you or your junkie mother anything. Don't come here again, I'm warning you."

Jade had wanted to cry and shout and punch everything around her. She thought about texting Ethan to ask for help, even though he'd barely spoken to her over the last few weeks. But she didn't, because her phone rang, and the man told her to go to The Castle.

A knock on the door to The Castle bedroom

interrupted Jade's thoughts and recollections from the day. She felt thankful, but at the same time nauseous, as if there wasn't enough air in the room. She opened the door with what she hoped was a smile and let the man enter. He was old, definitely old enough to be her dad. His eyes darted around the room, and he scratched his head.

"Come and sit down here," she said, as confidently as she could. The man smiled, grateful for the instruction.

"Are you ready?" she asked as she removed her vest. His hands shook as he tried to undo his zipper. She thought about starting a new life, far away from here, and made herself numb to anything else.

After he left, a few more hours passed undisturbed until the clock clicked round to 2 am. Jade took a scalding hot shower, in an attempt to wash away the grime of the day. She dressed and left her room to give her key to the man in the bomber jacket. From the top of the stairs, she heard two men chatting and laughing.

As she got closer, she recognised one of the voices; it was the cockney one she usually only heard over the phone. He was older and a bit heavier than she thought he would be, with squashed features and a bald head.

He turned to look at Jade, then looked back to the bomber jacket man with a smile. "Which one is this then?" he asked, in his strong East London accent.

"This is Jade," the other man replied.

"She doesn't talk much," he added as he took the room key from Jade and handed her a £20 note in return.

"No way, Jade! We've been talking for a while now, haven't we girl? Let me give you a lift home; I was only here to pick something up, the car is outside. I'm going back your way."

'No', said a part of her brain that didn't trust the man at all. After all, he'd threatened her mother after Jade tried to quit working for him and his boss. But she also felt exhausted and couldn't face a 45-minute walk home alone in the dead of night. So, reluctantly, she said "Yes."

She followed the man to the car and got in. He leaned over her and placed a couple of envelopes and some packages in the glove box, and locked it.

As they drove in silence, Jade stared out of the car window and thought about how much she hated the criminals behind 'Princesses' and the people who gave them money. She hated the police, who let them get away with it. She hated the inequality that led people like her into these inescapable situations.

"You OK, girl?" asked the man, looking over towards Jade, who sighed.

"I told you on the phone, I don't want to do this anymore," she whispered.

"I hear you. But you need the money right, what else are you going to do?"

"Maybe I don't need the money anymore," she lied.

"No? Come on, girl, if that were true, you'd already be miles away, not sitting in my car. Look," he continued as he steered the car into Jade's small estate, "I get that you want out. I understand, because sometimes I do as well."

She made eye contact with him and, for a fleeting moment, she believed he might be about to help her. But then, as he pulled up in front of her house, he reached over her and removed something from the glove box.

"Here's a little something to help you escape, girl. You have this first one on me."

He thrust a small plastic bag filled with a brownish powder towards her, along with a bigger brown bag containing a syringe.

Jade grabbed them, left the car swiftly and fumbled in her bag to find her keys. Without looking back, she entered her house and ran upstairs to her room, her heart beating fast. Her emotions and feelings from the day surged: the exhaustion, the rejection, the anger, the frustration, the inner turmoil.

She knew what the little bag of powder was; she'd seen her mother shoot-up enough times to recognise it. It would be madness to take drugs, she thought, but then she desperately needed some kind of release. Perhaps, she could do it once. Tears welled up in her eyes. Against her will, she started to recall images of the man who'd knocked on her door earlier.

She struggled to gather her thoughts. Her breathing quickened as she moved towards the sink in the corner of her room. She washed the powder away and threw the rest of the package out of her window as hard as she could.

She strode towards her desk and picked up her small kitchen knife. She drew the blade closer to her left forearm and pierced her skin. Then, she moved it backwards and forwards to create three deep cuts. For a moment, before the searing pain kicked in and the stream of blood appeared, she felt free.

10: JADE, LOUISA AND STACY

Monday 15th October 2018 - Ethan

Ethan lay in bed, struggling to shake off an uneasy feeling in his stomach. Last night, like most nights, he'd kept watch on The Castle until around 2 am.

Usually, he followed Jade home at a distance, to make sure she got back safe. But last night, she'd got into a car with a man who'd also been inside The Castle, and they'd sped off into the distance.

Who was he? Where was he taking her? Ethan added more frustrating, unanswered questions to his ever-growing list.

He thought about texting Jade to check on

her, but it didn't feel right. Over the last two weeks, he hadn't contacted her much at all. Instead, he'd kept a silent watch over the supermarket girls at The Castle. But, something wasn't right about that car, or Jade's fearful look as she got into it. Ethan put his phone down and decided to go straight to Jade's house.

He pulled his hoodie over his head to shield himself from the rain dripping down from the low grey cloud. He walked around piles of fly-tipped rubbish, strewn across the streets. As he approached Jade's house, he saw a bag with a needle poking out of it on the pavement. He picked it up and threw it in a waste bin.

He knocked on Jade's front door twice and gazed up at her bedroom window; he thought he saw the curtains twitch. He knocked again, louder, and looked through the letterbox. With relief, he saw Jade's legs coming down the stairs. She creaked the door open and held it ajar so that he could only see her face and the right side of her body.

His heart sank; Jade looked terrible. Her face was paler than usual, and there were dark shadows around her eyes, which he'd never seen so puffy before.

"Ethan, I didn't know you were coming over?" she said wearily.

"No, sorry, I was in the area, so I thought I'd say hi."

She looked at him, her eyebrows raised.

"Can I come in?"

She looked uncomfortable and nervous, and he didn't understand why. He wasn't like those other men; he would never hurt her.

"Or we could go out, and I'll get us lunch if you want. My treat."

"Ok, OK, fine. Wait here, I'll get dressed then we can go for lunch."

The large pub opposite the supermarket was open, so they stepped inside, out of the rain. While outside was cold and wet, the pub was warm, and it smelt of chip fat and stale beer. Ethan watched Jade reluctantly remove her jacket, to reveal a thick woollen jumper. He tried and failed to start conversations with her.

"I suppose I wanted to catch up because we haven't spoken much lately," said Ethan, once they'd finished their meals.

"I know. I thought you'd got a girlfriend or something, which would have been fine."

He shook his head

"Are you sure you're OK though, Jade? Is something happening?"

"No, I'm fine, honestly. Anyway, I should go."

Her voice wavered, and she looked as though she had the weight of the world on her small shoulders. Ethan felt a pain in his chest and a stinging sensation in his eyes.

Jade pushed her plate aside and reached over to her bag. At the same time, Ethan leant over and put his hand on her left arm, to stop her from leaving. She cried out and winced in pain and jerked her arm away from him.

"Jade, I'm so sorry, I didn't mean to hurt you. I didn't grab you, did I? Has something happened to your arm?"

For a flash of a second, as Jade threw on her coat, he thought he saw blood seeping through the cream wool. He took a deep breath.

"It's nothing Ethan, I fell and bruised it a few days ago. I'm not feeling too good, I had better go."

He watched her hurry out of the pub. He remained at the booth for some time, with his head in his hands, trying not to cry. Had the man in the car hurt Jade?

He wrenched his notebook out of his holdall and slammed it on the table. He pored over the pages of notes he'd made while watching The Castle building. He'd noted down the registration number of the car Jade had gotten into last night. It would be worth tracking down the vehicle, finding out the owner's name. Was he the person running 'Princesses'?

Ethan's eyes settled on two names: Louisa and Stacy. He was sure Louisa worked at the supermarket on Monday dayshifts, and he knew Stacy worked in the evening.

It was 3.45 pm; if he started his shift early, he'd be able to speak to Louisa when she finished her shift at 5 pm. He grabbed his holdall and jogged over the road, towards the supermarket.

He entered with his hood up and his head down. But despite his efforts to hide, someone called his name from the Customer Service desk. He looked up and saw Edith, Renee and another two women in a huddle. They were all looking at him with big, yet somehow intimidating, smiles.

"Ethan, you shouldn't get my hopes up like this," pouted Renee, with a twirl of her golden-brown hair. She stared at him with one eyebrow raised, and her hand on her hip. She was as tall as him, and he couldn't help noticing the glow of her skin and the fullness of her bright red lips. She'd framed her amber eyes with dark eyeshadow, and her shirt was slightly too tight across the chest.

He flushed and mumbled 'uh, whaddayamean?' in response. The women around Renee giggled.

"Well, I saw you, and I thought it must be 5 pm, home time for me. But you're an hour early. You do know Jade isn't here today, right?"

The other women dissolved into laughter. He didn't know what to say, so he was thankful when someone else broke the silence.

"Lucky he's here if you ask me," chirped Gillian from behind Renee's group.

"I could use some help with running the department. So please go and clock in Ethan," she continued, with a pointed glance at Renee.

Ethan turned away, but still heard Gillian's voice. "And seeing as you've so miraculously recovered from your illness, Renee, you can supervise the tills while I take a break."

He clocked in and approached the Supervisor desk, wondering if Jade would be at The Castle tonight. Gillian muttered to herself and flicked through the schedules for the rest of this week.

"No, no, this won't do," she moaned. "Ethan, I'll need you to pick up some overtime this week. Thursday night and Friday dayshift?"

"Sure," he agreed, absent-mindedly. He looked around the department in an attempt to spot Louisa.

On the schedule, Louisa's name was next to 'kiosk'. All seemed quiet on the checkouts, so he strolled towards it. He heard Renee before he saw her. When he turned the corner of the kiosk, there she was, talking to Louisa and another young girl. Renee was telling them a story; her arms waving around wildly, and her voice oscillating. The two girls smiled and hung off every word.

"And that, girls, is why you should always check if the man you're seeing has a brother!" The girls erupted with laughter as Renee turned to look at Ethan.

"Everything OK, Ethan? On the checkouts?" she asked, as her eyes bored into him again.

"Um, yes."

"Good." she replied, as she turned her back on him to resume her conversation with the girls.

He walked away, abashed, and had to wait until the very end of Louisa's shift to get her alone.

He saw her leave the kiosk just before 5 pm and took his chance to follow her to the staff area. Before she made it to the stairs, he touched her shoulder.

"Hi, Louisa."

"Ethan, did I forget something?" she asked, with a worried look on her face.

He instantly realised his mistake. He'd put no thought into how to broach the subject or to get the result he wanted. He looked at Louisa's young face, freckled nose and curly dark hair, and tried to compose himself.

"I just thought I'd ask, are you caught up in something you don't want to be? I wondered if you needed help or anything. I could even speak to the police with you?"

It was clumsy, and he knew he'd messed up when her eyes began to widen in fear.

"You don't know anything about me! Stay away from me!" Louisa whispered, her voice shaking. She turned away from Ethan and hurried up the stairs.

He stomped back down towards the checkouts. Gillian had handed over the Manager's keys to Marie, and Stacy was already seated on a checkout towards the end of the row.

Usually, Ethan and Marie got on well enough during their Monday night shifts. But this evening, Marie seemed to keep more of an eye on him than usual. Annoyingly, she kept disrupting him whenever he tried to venture over to Stacy.

After a couple of hours, he wandered over while Marie was on a break. Stacy couldn't have been more than seventeen years old. She'd fixed her dark blonde hair into a bun with hairspray and drawn on dark eyebrows over small pale blue eyes.

"Hi Stacy, are you doing anything after work tonight?"

"Um, no, why?" she flushed and looked down at her lap.

"I wondered if you fancied a drink, you know, with me?"

"Yeah," she replied coyly. She sat up a little straighter in her chair and smiled.

He walked back to the Supervisor's desk and saw Marie standing there looking daggers at him.

"What have I done?"

"You're here to work, and you're a Supervisor. You shouldn't hound the girls." she replied, her lips pursed and her eyes narrowed behind her heavy glasses.

At the end of the shift, Marie locked up and shuffled towards the car park without saying goodbye. Ethan jogged towards the pub, where he'd asked Stacy to wait for him.

He bought a beer for himself and a vodka and coke for her. He suspected she was underage but decided to overlook it. After all, alcohol might encourage her to open up to him and go along with his plan. He asked her about her family, her sixth form courses, and what she thought of people at work. She seemed quite shy and nervous and it occurred to him that she thought this was a date. He stifled the guilt. Jade needed him to do this; it was the only way to keep her safe.

"So, are you sure everything is alright with you, Stace? I've noticed sometimes at work you seem upset or distracted?"

"No, nothing's wrong, I'm fine," she replied as she folded her arms and sat back in her chair.

"Come on, Stace. If you're in trouble, I could help you."

She looked at him and then back down at her drink with a sigh. He let the pause hang in the air.

"Even if I told you, you wouldn't be able to help," she whispered, as her cheeks flushed.

"Try me," he encouraged, as he leaned over the table towards her. "I like you, and I want to help you. I could even come to the police with you if you want?"

She pulled away from him, and her eyes widened in fear, exactly like Louisa's had.

"No Ethan, you've got this all wrong, I don't

want to go to the police, please don't say any-thing to anyone." She downed the rest of her drink as the bell for last orders rang.

"Thanks for the drinks though, I enjoyed our chat earlier, perhaps we can do this again some-time?"

Ethan sighed as Stacy hurried through the pub doors without looking back, just as Jade had done earlier.

11: TROUBLE AND STRIFE

Friday 19th October 2018 - Debbie

"Joe!" shouted Debbie, for the third time in less than ten minutes. She stood by the front door, her coat and shoes on, hands on her hips and a sharp edge to her voice.

"Joe, we are so late," she hissed, as her husband appeared at the top of the stairs. She scowled as he grabbed his keys and ran towards the car.

She threw the last few bags into the boot of the car and slammed it shut. Inside, her fifteen year-old son Marco raised his eyebrows and turned his music up.

"What are you waiting for, Joe? Go!"

To her relief, Joe smiled, started the engine and pulled away from the kerb at speed.

"I suppose I had better text Karen, tell her

we're running late," Debbie tutted, breaking the silence.

"They might be running a bit behind too," Joe replied, hopefully. "I'm sure they won't mind."

Debbie raised her eyebrows. She was sure that both Karen and her rather grumpy husband, Pete, would mind.

"I don't mind being late," said their thirteen year-old daughter, Abbie, from the back seat of the car.

"Why's that, love?" asked Joe.

"I don't like Daniel anymore, he's weird."

Debbie glanced at Joe, who grimaced. Neither of them could argue with their daughter. Karen's son, Daniel, was moody even by teenage standards and had very few friends. Melwood High School had suspended him quite a few times.

"Are any of you looking forward to this?" asked Debbie. Her family fell silent and avoided eye contact with her.

Marco broke first under her gaze.

"We used to enjoy it, Mum. But now we only go along with it because we know you and Auntie Karen like to drink wine on the beach."

Abbie raised her hand to her mouth, and Marco looked a little nervous. Debbie opened her mouth in shock and looked towards Joe, who bit his lip. At the same time, they all burst into laughter, and the tension in the car evaporated. They were still joking and laughing as they pulled into the seafront car park half an hour later.

"There they are," said Joe, and he pointed over to the car park entrance.

Karen and her husband, Pete, stood a metre apart, facing away from each other with their arms crossed. Only their daughter, Rebecca, greeted Debbie's family with a wave and a smile.

"I'm sorry, so sorry," apologised Debbie as she approached them.

"Someone," she gestured towards Joe, "took an absolute age getting ready this morning. I honestly don't know how it took him so long."

"Men need to take care of themselves; that's what women always say, right, Pete?"

Pete, who was a foot shorter than Joe, bald, and about ten kilos heavier, shrugged his shoulders. Karen pursed her thin lips and turned away from her husband with a look of disgust.

"Right," Debbie broke the awkward silence. "Let's make the most of the sun. Straight to the beach?"

The eight of them headed towards the beach, Debbie and Karen at the front.

"Is everything OK with you and Pete?" Debbie whispered. She linked arms with Karen as they strolled towards their favourite spot.

"No, it's not," replied Karen with a frown. "We had a huge row in the car. He said he's stressed, that I haven't been there for him and that he wants us to spend more time together."

"OK, so that's fixable isn't it? We could call it a day this afternoon so you could have the evening together?"

"Well, the problem is I don't want to spend time with him, the fat lump," whispered Karen with a look of disdain. "He makes no effort. Look at the state of him, compared to Joe."

"Well, it does take him a long time to look that good," replied Debbie kindly. Privately, though, she agreed with Karen's assessment. Joe was ageing annoyingly well, whereas Pete increasingly resembled a potato.

"No amount of time would help Pete," replied Karen, bitterly.

Debbie's eyes widened. Karen often complained about Pete, but usually she laughed as she did so.

"Let's get rid of them and talk on the beach," mumbled Karen, "he's probably trying to listen in knowing him."

She turned her head towards Pete, who was huffing and puffing alongside Joe, weighed down by Karen's many bags and a parasol.

"Are you looking forward to the staff party on Sunday night then?" asked Debbie. "Who do you think is going to cause a scene this year? My money is on Renee."

"Oh God, that's this weekend? I completely forgot," replied Karen, slapping her forehead. "But I'll be there, don't worry. Any excuse to get out of the house," she added, with another glare in Pete's direction.

"Excellent lunch, Deb," said Joe as they set up on the beach. He peered into the cool box and pulled out two bottles of Sauvignon Blanc.

"Well, I thought you guys might take the kids to the pier and pick up some food on the way back. Nothing better than fish and chips on the beach, right?"

"True enough," said Joe with a knowing smile. "Pete, let's go. These two are desperate to open the wine and talk about us."

Pete frowned, and he remained mutinously in his chair, until Karen caught his eye. She hissed 'off you go' at him, through gritted teeth.

Karen poured a large glass of wine for herself and Debbie and launched into a rant about Pete. He'd taken her for granted, let himself go, and been a bad father to Daniel and Rebecca.

"You've not mentioned this before," said Debbie, when Karen finally paused for breath. "Has something happened recently to make you realise all this?"

"I've realised, recently, that I don't have to be stuck with Pete for the rest of my life," replied Karen. "I know I always make out that things are fine, that I'm happy, but I'm not. The kids are growing up, and it's time to put myself first and find a new partner."

"Umm, it sounds like you have someone in mind?"

"I don't know. Maybe," replied Karen with a wave of her hand. She looked away and took another gulp of wine.

Debbie looked at her friend and sighed. "Can I talk to you about something else?" she ventured and Karen nodded in return. "I've been thinking more about you know what."

"What, the evidence you've rifled through and hidden in your house?"

"About everything. About Jan and Cait, about what 'Princesses' might be, and which colleague they suspected. I've got a theory."

"Go on then, you're going to tell me one way or another, aren't you?" replied Karen with a roll of her eyes.

"OK, so I think someone at work is running a side business. Something dodgy that makes money. It could be selling drugs or something like that. Anyway, 'Princesses' is the name of the business and this person gets vulnerable people from the supermarket involved in it somehow."

Karen raised her eyebrows and shook her head as she pulled her phone out from her bag.

"That's not all," continued Debbie. "What if Jan and Cait found out about it, and they were going to report it. So, this person silences them."

Karen started typing a message on her phone, but Debbie pressed on.

"And they take Cait's phone, to check nothing is incriminating them. Once it's all clear, they put it in her bag in a random locker at work."

"You think it's Renee, don't you?" guessed Karen as she looked up from her phone.

"Yes, I do. Think about the cat."

"If she'd taken the phone and checked it, she'd have deleted the message you're obsessing over," argued Karen. "And as if she'd walk into the store with the bag after the murders, it's so risky."

"Sounds just like her. Anyway, Marie's involved too, it must be how she's getting all that money."

"Mardie! Come on now, she's hardly a criminal mastermind."

"And I suppose Kevin's involved or caught up in it too. Why else would he give Renee money?"

"Debbie, that is mad."

Karen was still typing away on her phone, to Debbie's growing annoyance.

"I don't think so, Karen." Debbie raised her voice to get her friend's attention. "Jan's message said they needed the final bit of proof to go to the police and protect people, and I'm going to find it. I'm going to finish what they started."

Karen, engrossed in her phone and message, didn't respond.

"Who are you texting?" asked Debbie, and she leaned over to peer at Karen's screen. "Who's Steph?"

Karen jerked her phone away from Debbie's gaze.

"No-one," she held her phone tight to her chest. "Now I'm sorry Deb, but whatever plan you have, I don't want any part of it. I think you should drop it and move on."

Debbie turned away from her best friend and sat back in her chair. She couldn't believe how disinterested Karen was. After all, Janice and Caitlin had been her friends, too. But it was like she'd forgotten about them already. She was more preoccupied with her marital dramas and messaging 'Steph,' whoever that was.

Karen typed in silence, oblivious to Debbie's moody glances, until Joe, Pete and the kids returned. They ate their fish and chips, as grey clouds started to gather above them. Debbie caught Joe's questioning eyes a few times but shook her head in return.

After an hour, the clouds darkened and the wind picked up. Debbie had the excuse she needed to propose an early end to the day. No-one objected, so they all gathered their bags and walked silently back to the car park.

"Well, sorry again for being late," said Debbie sheepishly, as they reached Pete's car. "I'll see you at the party on Sunday though, right?"

"What party is this?" asked Pete, looking from Karen to Debbie and back again. Karen rolled her eyes, and Debbie realised she'd put her foot in it.

"It's the supermarket staff party, Pete," said Karen. "I told you about it ages ago."

"First I've heard of it," retorted Pete, as he slammed the boot down.

"I wouldn't worry Pete," said Joe. "I've been a few times, but this year I'm avoiding it and you should do the same. It's messy."

"I'm not worried about going," replied Pete. "I'd just like to see my wife for an evening at some point."

Debbie smiled weakly and steered Marco and Abbie away from Pete's car, and gestured at Joe to follow them. The last thing they heard as they walked away was Karen shouting, 'Just get in the effing car, Pete!'

"Wow," said Joe, looking at Debbie as he started the ignition. "Did something happen with Karen while we were gone?"

"We had a little disagreement, yes. Karen wasn't interested in my theory about, you know, Jan and Cait. Said I should move on."

"Well, she might have a point, love," he replied. "But I know it's hard. They were your friends."

"They were hers too, though," Debbie pointed out. She looked out of the window and watched the rainfall over the beach. "I want to do right by them, why doesn't she?"

"I know love, but Karen seems like she's got a lot on her plate."

"She might divorce Pete."

"Wouldn't blame her," smiled Joe, "I bet she'd prefer someone who takes a long time to get ready."

Debbie smiled and pushed him gently on the shoulder as they joined the motorway and headed north towards home.

12: OLD KILLER KAREN

Saturday 20th October 2018 - Marie

"Caught!" Renee's husky voice sounded over the top of the Supervisor's desk, and her face beamed down at Marie. "Talk about slacking, Marie!"

"I've been working!" replied Marie as she hauled herself up from the floor. She'd perched down there to take some painkillers, after a sudden rush of customers.

"Yeah, yeah," smiled Renee as she adjusted the staff schedule. She chewed on the end of her multi-coloured pen, leaving bright red lipstick marks around the top. Her hair was loose, which Gillian didn't usually allow, and it shimmered brown and gold in the bright supermarket lights.

"Oh, at last!" muttered Marie. Karen had appeared from one of the aisles and was strolling towards the supervisor desk.

"Karen!" exclaimed Renee, wiping her forehead dramatically. "We were about to send out a search party for you."

Marie giggled at the sight of Karen's narrowed eyes and frown.

"I was taking my tea break. I'm sure you both coped without me," grumbled Karen. She'd been miserable all morning and no help to anyone.

"Well, we've seen off the rush now," said Marie, as Karen looked over Renee's amendments to the schedule.

"So," added Renee, "If you don't mind, Marie and I will go on a break together now. I'm sure you can hold the fort now it's quietened down, and I've fixed the schedule."

Marie had some misgivings about leaving the department in the hands of Karen. But then, Gillian wasn't around to check-up on them, and she loved taking her breaks with Renee. She grinned at Karen and strolled away from the desk, after Renee.

"So then," whispered Renee mischievously, as they sat down in a private booth in the canteen. "What's the big deal with the party tomorrow? Is it fun or tragic?"

Marie shifted in her seat. In truth, she always found the annual party to be an uncomfortable and awkward affair. But she didn't want to put Renee off from going with her.

"Well, everyone goes. Even Dawn went last year. There's a free bar, and often there are rows, and people kissing each other on the dance floor by the end of the night. I sit and watch it unfold."

"That sounds brilliant," grinned Renee. "You know I love a bit of drama."

"Of course, it might be a bit different this year, after, you know, what's happened."

"Of course," mused Renee, as she ripped up a croissant. "Especially as there have been no arrests, and the police are still talking to people here. You know what that means, right?"

There was a silent pause as Marie tried to work it out, and Renee rolled her eyes.

"Well they think it's someone here, don't they?" whispered Renee, between bites of her croissant.

"I know it's mad, but they must have a reason for thinking that, right? Has anyone said anything about it to you?"

"Not really," replied Marie, and she saw some disappointment in Renee's eyes. She urged herself to say something interesting. "I do have some suspicions myself."

"Go on," urged Renee, her eyes widening.

"Do you think Karen has been acting suspiciously lately? I know she's always been rubbish at her job, but at least she used to try. Now, she's always late, she disappears all the time and her mood is up and down. One minute she seems happy, then miserable the next."

"True," said Renee, as she spooned yoghurt into her mouth. "But what's her motive?"

"I don't know, maybe Janice and Caitlin found out something about her. Do you remember how the two of them froze out Debbie and Karen towards the end? Why?"

"I tell you what Marie, why don't we have a little fun this afternoon," suggested Renee with a grin.

"Let's ask around and find out what the police have been saying to people and see if anyone has the same suspicions as you."

It sounded like a terrible idea to Marie, as it involved her making conversation. But under Renee's excited gaze, she replied, "OK then."

"Marvellous! What a way to spice up a Saturday afternoon!" Renee jumped up from her chair, prompting Marie to do the same.

"Cigarette before we go back down?" asked Marie, as she removed a new pack from her fleece pocket.

"Oh, not now, thanks," replied Renee. "One of us had better go and check on old killer Karen, make sure she hasn't dumped Edith behind the chiller!"

"Renee!" Marie shook her head as Renee strolled back towards the shop floor, laughing to herself.

That afternoon, Renee floated around talking to customers and staff in hushed whispers. When Karen was present, she cast furtive glances at Renee and tried to listen in on her conversations. Marie wondered, ominously, whether Karen had some inkling about the subject matter.

As awkward as she found small talk, Marie didn't want to let Renee down. She took a quiet moment to prepare herself for it. Edith shuffled towards her, pushing a stack of baskets.

"Hi Edith," began Marie, and she tried to force a smile.

"Marie," replied Edith in her low croak. "Don't ask me to do anything else, Renee's just told me to do the baskets."

"Oh, no I won't, I thought I'd see how you were."

"I'm fine. Now tell me what you really want to talk about," replied Edith shrewdly.

Marie sighed; how did Renee find this so easy?

"Well, I wondered whether you'd spoken to the police yet. I've noticed they've been around a lot. Do you think they suspect someone?" The words tumbled out of Marie's mouth.

"Well, as you've asked, I have spoken to the police, yes," beamed Edith. "I'm helping them out a bit if you must know. Because unlike some, I am not a suspect."

"Helping them how?" asked Marie.

"They want to know the inside track, of course, on who hates who, who's screwing who, who might be capable of murder etcetera. So, you better not get on the wrong side of me," finished Edith with a cackle, that turned into a cough.

"Interesting," nodded Marie, "and have you given them any serious leads yet?"

"Couldn't say," replied Edith, with a wide grin that exposed her stained teeth. "Only things I've noticed. Like certain people acting strangely, and secrets I've discovered. You supervisors don't know it all, you know, even among yourselves."

"Right," continued Marie, "and this secret you discovered. Wouldn't happen to be about a lanky, blonde, stuck-up supervisor, would it?"

Edith took a deep breath and looked over Marie's shoulder with a grimace. Marie turned to follow Edith's gaze.

"Talking about someone?" Karen's voice had a discernible edge to it, and her hands had curled into fists.

Marie closed her eyes and willed the ground to swallow her up. She looked up at Karen and tried to arrange her features into an apologetic glance.

"What's that smirk for, Marie?" demanded Karen, shaking with rage. "You and Renee always complain about me gossiping, yet here you are bitching about me on shift."

Karen grabbed Marie's arm and pulled her away from Edith.

"And how dare you suggest that I had anything to do with what happened to Janice and Caitlin! They were my friends."

Marie wrenched her arm free and stared back at Karen. Months of tension and conflict were bubbling to the surface.

"If you don't want people to be suspicious, Karen, then stop behaving so weirdly. You always get here late, disappear, get cross at the smallest things."

"None of that gives you the right to call me a murderer," Karen raised her voice. "You know Marie; some people have actual lives outside of here. Husbands and children that cause stresses that you wouldn't know anything about."

Marie flushed, but she held Karen's gaze.

"If I ever catch you talking about me like that again," warned Karen. She took a step closer to Marie and looked down at her.

"You'll what?" asked Renee, who had run across the department to join the fray.

Karen stared at Renee for a few seconds and then, to Marie's relief, she stormed off without saying another word.

"Oops!" snorted Renee, once Marie had given her the lowdown.

Marie avoided Karen for the rest of the afternoon and decided against talking to anyone else about her suspicions. Just before 5 pm, Gillian arrived to cover the evening shift. Marie approached her at the Supervisor's desk, where she was deep in conversation with the Store Manager, Steve.

"Not like you to work Saturday evening," Marie said to Gillian, as she handed over the Manager's keys to her boss.

"I suppose not, but I'd rather keep an eye on Jade and Ethan for their first few Saturday nights," Gillian replied in a smug tone, with a glance at Steve. Perhaps she's hoping for a gold star, thought Marie.

"What happened today, with Karen?" asked Steve, before Marie could walk away.

"What do you mean?" replied Gillian, as her beady eyes swivelled between Marie and Steve.

"Karen seemed upset. She said she'd had a row with Marie on the shop floor. I'm sure they'll sort it out though," he added with a wave of his hand.

"Oh, they will," replied Gillian, with a stern look towards Marie.

Marie could think of nothing to say, so she turned away from her two bosses and trudged towards the staff area.

As she entered the staff area, she saw Renee talking to someone by the storeroom. Renee held out her hand, indicating that Marie should stop and wait.

"Are you sure you're OK?" asked Renee. "You're looking worn out, and I'm worried about you."

Marie shuffled forwards to hear the response.

"I'm OK," muttered Jade. "I've got a lot on with my Mum, you know. My Dad is in trouble too."

"I heard. But Jack will bounce back, with all those businesses. His name means something in New Grange. Now, what about Ethan?"

"Oh, he hasn't bothered me since the meeting, I think he's got the message. Anyway, I'd better go and start my shift. Thanks for the chat though."

Jade emerged from the storeroom and walked past Marie with a weak smile.

"Sweet of you to check in with her," commented Marie as they walked up the stairs to the staff area.

"She's a good girl from a bad family, same as me," replied Renee. "I want to make sure she's OK."

"I kept an eye on Ethan as you asked," said Marie, as she quickened her pace to keep up with Renee.

"The other night, he followed Louisa to the staff area after her shift, and then he kept trying to talk to Stacy. I think he asked her out."

"Interesting. Well, we had better keep a close eye on him for the foreseeable. Starting with the party tomorrow," replied Renee. She grabbed her coat and bag from her locker and checked her phone.

"Fancy a quick drink at the pub?" asked Marie, hopefully.

"Sorry, Marie, I can't tonight," whispered Renee with a smile.

"Oh, OK, I'll see you tomorrow then."

Marie watched Renee's expression soften as she scrolled through messages. Marie could guess who they were from. As much as Renee didn't like to admit it, her feelings for Kevin were obvious. Marie wondered what on earth would happen to the team when he finally left Gillian for Renee.

"Tomorrow," said Renee, breaking Marie's chain of thought. "The party. Yes, of course, I'll pick you up at seven."

"Oh, great," replied Marie, as she left the store, finally with a smile on her face.

13: PARTY TIME

Sunday 21st October 2018 - Renee

Renee stood in front of her full-length mirror, admiring her outfit. She twirled her hair and hummed to herself, as she thought about the night ahead. She wore fitted, ankle-length dark trousers, stiletto heels, and a V-neck pastel-shade cashmere jumper. It hung from her shoulders and chest and clung to her waist. Her hair was poker straight, and her make-up carefully done. Her eyeshadow was slightly more dramatic and her lips looked a little fuller than usual.

"What do you think?" she asked Princess the cat, who twirled herself around her legs. "I look pretty good, right?"

She picked up the fluffy cat and carried her down to the kitchen. It was 6.40 pm, almost time to leave. She kissed the cat on her forehead, leaving a red lipstick mark on the white fur, and put her down on the kitchen floor.

"I've left the treats Marie bought you in your bowl, and if you go out, don't do anything I wouldn't do!" Princess hissed and ran out of the cat flap, leaving Renee alone. "Which doesn't rule much out," she muttered to herself.

She sprayed some more perfume on her neck and chest and left the house with a spring in her step. She revelled in nights like this. Groups of people, all with histories and rivalries, forced into a room together with free-flowing alcohol. It reminded her of the night she and Kevin met at a regional supermarket awards ceremony over a year ago. That was before Renee had transferred to Melwood and started working with his wife.

Renee arrived at Marie's flat at 7 pm and took her phone from her bag. She then remembered the many messages Marie had sent her last night to which she hadn't replied. She grimaced, put her phone in her pocket and pressed her car horn instead.

Two minutes later, Marie appeared beaming and waving. Renee returned the wave but sighed at the sight of her friend. She'd chosen an unflattering and outdated outfit, even by Marie's standards. Her make-up was overdone and garish. Her dress was too tight around the middle and hung down to her ankles, exposing a pair of walking boots. As Marie got into the car, Renee caught a whiff of Chardonnay mingled with a sweet-scented perfume.

"You look great!"

"Thanks," giggled Marie. "Just threw something on, didn't want to put too much effort into a work party," she added, as Renee raised her eyebrows.

"You're driving," commented Marie as they pulled away from the flats. "Are you going to leave your car there?"

"Nope," replied Renee with a wink. "I plan on having a couple of drinks and watching others abuse the free bar. That way, I'll be able to remember every little detail of what I see and hear!"

They arrived at the venue, a local hotel, shortly after 7.15 pm. A crowd stood on the veranda terrace, clouds of cigarette smoke billowing around them. At the main entrance, a short woman in a fitted black dress and chunky gold jewellery greeted people. Her curls remained fixed in place, even as she laughed and chatted with those arriving.

"Typical," muttered Renee. "Looks like Gill has decided to be the official greeter. She's pretending it's her bloody party."

Ahead of them, Gillian ushered two women from HR through the door. As she turned around to face Renee, her smile faded.

"Ah, Renee, Marie. I see you're making a habit of arriving fashionably late these days," she remarked. Her eyes met Renee's, then moved downwards towards Marie's.

"Through you go then," said Gillian after a moment's silence, gesturing towards Marie.

As Renee attempted to follow Marie, Gillian stuck out her stubby arm and blocked her way. Renee looked down in shock. Gillian looked up at Renee and lowered her voice to a whisper.

"I'll be keeping an eye on everyone tonight, including you. I don't want any stirring, gossiping or trouble. So, for your own good, behave!" she threatened.

Renee raised her car keys and waved them in Gillian's face.

"Designated driver, Gillian. You won't have any trouble from me." She skirted around Gillian's arm and entered the party without looking back.

The scene inside was reminiscent of a high school disco. Everyone sat in small groups at tables around the empty dance floor. The DJ was playing 'Everybody Dance Now,' but the only people standing were those waiting at the bar.

Marie was in the queue, looking agitated between two groups of younger people. Renee scanned the tables and spotted one close by, occupied by Jade and Ethan. They seemed to be having an intense conversation and, as he reached out to touch her arm, she recoiled.

"Hello, you two," interrupted Renee. Jade exhaled and looked up at her, a large gin and tonic in her hand. Ethan folded his arms and sat back in his chair with a roll of the eyes.

"Ethan, get me a lemonade, and another drink for Jade, too, will you?"

Renee sat in Ethan's vacated seat and leaned across to Jade.

"Everything OK? What was he saying?"

"We were talking about work and he said he'd been doing a lot of overtime, which is weird because I asked for some and didn't get it. Does Gillian think I'm rubbish?"

Jade's cheeks flushed pink, and her eyes were glazed; the gin clearly wasn't her first drink of the evening.

"Don't take it personally," replied Renee with a wave of the hand. "She's a cow to everyone. I thought you had another job, anyway?"

Jade reclined in her seat with a sigh. She took another large sip of her drink, then tugged on the long sleeves of her plain pink polo neck.

Renee scanned the room again, considering her next move. Gillian remained at the entrance door, though she was staring over at her and Jade. Karen, who was wearing too much make-up and not enough clothing, was with Steve by the bar. Across the hall, Debbie and Dawn sat on their own.

Ethan and Marie arrived back at the table at the same time. Renee took her lemonade from Marie, who was also holding a full glass of white wine.

"You take my seat, Ethan; we're going for a mingle."

Renee left Ethan and Jade in an uncomfortable silence and worked her way around the tables, Marie in tow.

By 9 pm, the queue at the bar had grown, and the laughter and conversations were louder. The opening chords of a Cyndi Lauper song prompted a surge towards the dance floor. Renee dipped out of the crowd and sat down next to Debbie and Dawn.

"Phew," sighed Renee as she plonked herself down with them. "Getting pretty lively now, did you two not fancy joining in?"

"We're just fine here," answered Debbie, with a quick, furtive glance at Dawn. "Are you OK, Renee?"

"Oh fine, but I needed a break from all the chatting and dancing. I'm happy to sit and watch for a bit," replied Renee with a wink.

Debbie smiled but then looked away from Renee. There was something strange in Debbie's expression and body language. She was tense, nervous and agitated about something.

"I hope you're keeping an eye on Karen," offered Renee, breaking the silence again.

All three of them looked at Karen, who was dancing with her eyes closed and arms outstretched. Her very full glass of red wine sloshed onto the dance floor.

Debbie sighed and rolled her eyes at the sight of her friend, and Renee noticed Marie on the dancefloor nearby. Unlike Karen, Marie had her eyes open and didn't have a drink in hand. But she looked just as merry as she attempted to throw shapes around the dancefloor.

For the next fifteen minutes or so, Renee felt like she was watching the party in slow motion, as the laughter and music got louder.

The DJ played 'Don't Stop Me Now', which got all but a few stragglers onto the dancefloor. Stuart, the night shift Manager, danced with Gillian on the periphery of the group. Steve took Edith by the arm and twirled her around. Jade and Ethan swayed among a group of younger people, all smiling with drinks in their hands.

The guitar solo kicked in, and everyone jumped up and down, bumping into each other and laughing. Gerard, the Duty Manager, grabbed Marie by the arm and swung her around, sending people running to get out of the way. As he let Marie go, she hurtled across the floor and collided head-on into Karen.

Renee raised her hand to her mouth, as wine flew out of Karen's glass and into her face. Karen awoke from her daze as Marie stumbled and fell onto her hands and knees. The music continued, though everybody had stopped dancing. In one swift movement, they all stepped away to create a circle of space around the two women. Karen stood still, her pale face, blonde hair and white dress soaked with red wine, while Marie scrambled to get up from the floor.

Debbie and Renee stood up to peer over the crowd. Gillian shouted, 'What's going on?' repeatedly from the back of the group.

Karen wiped the wine from her eyes and stared venomously at Marie.

"You stupid bitch!" she hissed, as mascara ran down both sides of her face.

"My fault, Karen," interjected Gerard with a nervous laugh, extending his hand to help Marie up. "No harm done."

"No bloody harm done?" shouted Karen, her eyes fixed on Marie. "I'm soaked! That cow did it on purpose. She's got it in for me," she slurred and swayed on the spot.

"As if I'd touch you on purpose," shouted Marie, pink-faced after her fall.

"You should be so lucky, you fat dyke!"

There was a collective gasp from those on the inside of the circle. Renee, Debbie and Gillian all struggled to make their way through the crowd.

"You know what we all call you?" Karen continued, to a now red-faced Marie. "Mardie! Lazy Mardie," she taunted, and she tilted her head back to laugh.

Renee had almost reached the centre as Marie stepped forward and shoved Karen forcefully on the shoulder. Karen stumbled but regained her composure. She reached out an arm and slapped Marie hard around the face.

The crowd gave another collective gasp and suddenly, things seemed to speed up again. Steve broke through the crowd and grabbed Karen's waist, restraining her. Gerard did the same to Marie and dragged her back through the circle of people. The crowd dispersed, eagerly discussing what had happened.

Renee reached Marie and relieved a mortified Gerard from his duties. On the other side of the room, Steve passed Karen over to Debbie with an angry look on his face.

"Come on, Marie," giggled Renee, as she grabbed her shell-shocked friend by the arm, "time to leave!"

As they reached the door, Renee caught sight of Gillian, Debbie and Karen a few metres ahead. Gillian had both hands on her hips and a thunderous expression on her face.

"Why should I leave," slurred Karen.

"I'll tell you why," hissed Gillian, who had turned purple with rage. "Because you have both disgraced our department and ruined this party."

They actually made it, thought Renee, but for once she bit her lip.

"Yesterday," mumbled Karen, as she grabbed Debbie for support, "Mardie said I killed them, Janice and Caitlin."

"Did not," sulked Marie. Renee grabbed hold of her friend, who now looked and sounded like an overgrown toddler.

"Enough!" shouted Gillian. "I do not want to hear any more about this! You are both too drunk. We will deal with this tomorrow. You'll both be lucky not to get fired."

Debbie tugged Karen towards the door, and Gillian held her hand up to stop Renee and Marie. Once Debbie's car engine started, Gillian lowered her hand with a sigh. Renee hauled Marie towards the door and stopped as they reached Gillian.

"And you thought I was the one to watch," said Renee, with a smile.

"Get out of my sight," replied Gillian through gritted teeth. She glared at her so fiercely that Renee dropped her gaze, taken aback. She rushed out of the door, dragging Marie along with her.

She shoved Marie into the passenger seat and got into the car. She reached into her bag for her phone and sent a quick message to Kevin.

Sorry I've not been in touch. Good luck with G tonight. It all kicked off at the party between Marie and Karen, and she is livid! Never seen her so angry! X

The reply, as usual, came straight away.

Oh great. Don't suppose you fancy eloping with me in the next 30 mins? I hope you're ok, Ren. I miss you.

Renee felt something strange in her stomach, like a flutter. Her heart was beating faster than usual. Her face felt very hot, as she imagined a life far away from this one. A life where she and Kevin were happy together, free from Gillian and Melwood.

She wasn't quite sure how long she sat in the car, for once lost for words, as her thumb hovered over the keypad. But at some point, Marie broke the spell by leaning forward and vomiting profusely onto the floor of the car.

14: EDITH'S TALE

Monday 22nd October 2018 -
Vincent

DCI Vincent Okafor stretched his legs onto the top of his desk, rubbed his eyes and stifled a yawn. He'd been awake all night at the police station on the graveyard shift. He'd used the quiet time to review the research into local gangs that pushed drugs.

He'd focussed on South Croydon and the surrounding areas: Homestead, Melwood and the New Grange estate. Thanks to some newly acquired informants, he was progressing well. On the wall in front of him were four faces; Jack Dimont and his three very similar-looking sons.

All evidence so far pointed to the Dimonts as the primary drug pushers in the south of the borough. Local businesses fronted the operation - the Dimonts owned a car wash, a garage, and a few beauty salons.

Okafor was confident that further investigation would unveil all sorts of wrongdoing. Money laundering, drug dealing, and maybe even human trafficking or modern slavery.

Of course, Jack Dimont wasn't the top dog; more likely a middleman in a much larger operation. But Okafor was keen to test how much information Jack would trade in exchange for a reduced sentence. He was optimistic; his new sources had also informed him that Jack was struggling to keep rival sellers off his turf.

'Dimont,' he thought, as he rubbed his temples. He'd seen the name before, he was sure of it. An image of a short, thin, blonde-haired young woman floated into his mind - Jade Dimont, the young girl who worked at the Melwood supermarket.

His team had interviewed her in connection with the murders of her two colleagues. It's a small world, he thought, and he made a mental note to check her relationship to Jack.

He checked the clock: 7.45 am. It was almost time to hand over to the Superintendent. With a sigh, he packed away the files and pictures of the Dimonts, then sat down to complete his hand-over email. A soft knock on his office door interrupted him.

"Come in," he yawned.

"Sir," said DS Harris as she entered the office, coffee in hand and a bemused look on her face.

"Good morning, Joanne. Unless you're here to tell me that a major incident has occurred, in which case, piss off!" he replied with a smile and a wink.

"No major incident, sir," she laughed. "But I thought I should tell you about an interesting phone call I received first thing this morning."

"Go ahead, and please take a seat," he gestured to the chair opposite his desk.

"Thank you, sir. The call was from a lady named Edith Coaker, who works at the supermarket in Melwood. She rang because I'd asked her to keep me briefed on anything unusual that happened there. She seemed well suited to the task."

"I know the lady you mean, Joanne, and I fully agree with your assessment."

"Well, sir, she was at a party last night, a store staff party, and it all ended in tears. Marie Webster knocked a glass of wine over Karen Goldman, and Karen slapped Marie around the face in return."

"Right," chuckled Okafor, as he pictured the scene in his head.

"Now here's the interesting part, sir. Renee Beck got hold of Marie, and Deborah Gomez got Karen, you know, to take them home after it happened. But on the way out, Gillian told them all off. At that point, Karen said that Marie had started it, by accusing her of murdering Caitlin and Janice."

"Edith heard this herself?" asked Okafor, raising his eyebrows.

"Yes, sir, she followed them all to the door, hoping to see some further fireworks. When Gillian was having a go at them, she listened from around the corner."

"Naturally," mused Okafor, rubbing his chin and pausing for thought.

"If what Edith says is true, then it would be good to know why Marie made that accusation, wouldn't it, sir?"

"Quite. But first, let's get a second opinion on events. It doesn't quite make sense for Marie to make the accusation and throw the first punch, so to speak."

Okafor picked up his mobile and found the contact.

"Sir?"

"I've always found Gillian, the Manager, to be straight-talking and succinct. And by Edith's account, she's the only other witness to this claim from Karen."

He pressed the dial button and switched to speakerphone.

"Hello," an impatient high voice answered.

"Gillian, hello, it's DCI Okafor here." There was a pause at the end of the line, so he continued. "Is now a good time to speak?"

"Yes, yes, of course. It'll have to be quick

though, we have a store inspection a week today and I'm already busy preparing for it."

"This won't take long. I'm following up on reports of an incident at your store party last night, concerning Ms Webster and Mrs Goldman."

Gillian exhaled heavily.

"News travels fast doesn't it!" she tutted. "Oh, please don't tell me they've pressed charges?"

"I wonder if you could share your recollections with me, Gillian. I hope not to have to bring you in for an interview, but I would like to build a picture, should one of them make an accusation."

"It was a misunderstanding," replied Gillian with another sigh.

"Both of them were drunk. Marie clattered into Karen on the dance floor, and a glass of wine ended up all over Karen. Karen thought Marie had done it on purpose, you see, and she called her a name. 'Mardie,' some people call her. Anyway, Marie pushed Karen, and then Karen slapped Marie. It got broken up, and Debbie and Renee took them home."

"Thank you, Gillian," said Okafor, keeping his tone light as DS Harris scribbled down the notes. "And did you speak to any of them, after the incident?"

"Yes, I did. I told Marie and Karen that they'd disgraced the department, they'd let me down, and that we'd deal with it in the morning."

"OK," said Okafor. "And did either of them say anything more about the conflict between them? Another reason why the fight had started?"

"Not that I recall; they were both incoherent. And I won't be asking them, either. I have too much to do today. I'm going to amend the schedule to keep them apart for the week, then deal with them both after the inspection."

"Right, thank you, Gillian. You'll call DS Harris if anything further comes back to you?"

"Yes."

Okafor said goodbye and ended the call, then turned to a puzzled looking DS Harris.

"Why would Edith make it up? Why would she say Marie had accused Karen of the murders if it never happened?" Joanne pondered.

"Or, why would Gillian leave it out of her account?" asked Okafor with a sigh.

The case continued to frustrate him. Both he and his officers had spent a fair chunk of time at the supermarket to gather information. They'd learnt a lot. The Head of HR and the Head of Accounts hated each other because of a disagreement over two years ago. The husband of one staff member had made sexual approaches to young men working at the store. And Colin was one to watch because he disappeared behind the stockroom crates around the same time every day for some 'alone time.'

Although much of the gossip was intriguing,

none of it had given them a further lead or insight into the murders. Not one person had mentioned anything to do with a princess or princesses. Well, apart from Karen's comment about Renee's cat.

He'd considered asking Renee why she chose that name for the cat. But how on earth would that look in the press? He could see the headline now: 'Desperate cops pussyfooting around in double murder case.'

His gut instinct told him loud and clear that they were missing something. The store and some of the people within it were guarding a much bigger secret that would unlock the motive behind Janice and Caitlin's murders. Yet, resources were tight, media interest was waning, and serious organised crime was the new priority.

Pressure was mounting on him to declare the Melwood case cold and direct all resource onto the Dimont investigation. His diligence and progress on that front would at least mitigate the internal criticism he might receive for an unsolved murder case.

"I know what you're thinking," sighed DS Harris.

"Frustrating, isn't it?" replied Okafor with a shake of his head.

"But we've been over the files, and there are no clear next steps, no more leads to follow unless we re-interview. But that is resource-intensive and won't reflect well on us. No-one has emerged as a clear enough suspect to warrant surveillance, and the Dimont investigation is heating up."

"Will you close the case then, sir?"

"Close the case? No, Joanne, we won't be closing this one yet. I want you to keep half an eye on it when you can spare it."

Her shoulders relaxed and a small smile appeared on her face.

"These 'princesses' may crop up again at some point, and when they do, we want a flag raised on this case. So please set that up today before you continue on the Dimonts. And don't hesitate to note down any thoughts or other reports from people within the supermarket. Something tells me this one will heat up again, and I want us to be ready when it does."

"There was something, sir, that both Edith and Gillian agreed on that I thought was quite odd. Well, worthy of note anyway."

"Go on," encouraged Okafor, curiously.

"Well, does Renee Beck strike you as the designated driver type?"

Okafor sat back, surprised that he'd not thought of it himself. It was extraordinary that renowned party girl Renee, who usually thrived on being the centre of attention, had played a supporting role.

"No, Joanne, she does not. Be sure to note that down. And one last thing, please. Can you find out the relationship between Jack Dimont and Jade Dimont from the Melwood store?"

"She's his daughter, sir."

"His daughter?" he replied, in shock. "She looks nothing like him."

"She's illegitimate, sir, for want of a better word. After Jack's sons were born, he had a brief affair with a woman in New Grange, and Jade was the result. Spitting image of her mother. She doesn't live with the Dimont family, but even so, it might be too risky to talk to her. We don't know what the relationship is like, and she might tip him off."

"You've thought about this, Joanne?" asked Okafor, impressed with her diligence.

"Yes, I have, sir. I haven't been neglecting the Dimonts. I know quite a bit about them."

"Good work."

Okafor locked his files away with a smile, and they both left to attend the Super's morning briefing.

He nodded to his team on the way out of the office, then took a route home through Melwood, past the supermarket. Images of Janice and Caitlin, Jade and Jack Dimont flicked through his head.

After two decades in his line of work, he didn't much believe in coincidences.

15: ISN'T IT OBVIOUS?

Monday 29th October 2018 - Debbie

D ebbie put on an ironed uniform and brushed through her thick hair, which stubbornly refused to stay flat. Today, nothing less than perfect would do. Gillian's preparation for the inspection had been meticulous, and Debbie didn't want to let her down.

Her phone beeped over and over again from the bedside table. She put the hair straighteners down to read the stream of messages from Karen.

Renee has gone sick today.
Can you believe it?!
Inspection day of all days.
Gill rang me, says I have to come in.
Can't really say no after last week.

You're in, right?

Please tell me Mardie isn't working, I can't face her.

Debbie?

Debbie carried her phone over to her dresser and responded.

Absolutely can believe it – typical Renee. Will be me, you, Gill and Dawn today – Marie and Ethan always do Monday night shift together.

Despite her best efforts, Debbie was running late again. As she got into her car, her tights snagged on the wall of the driveway. She prayed the damage was minimal and drove towards the supermarket at speed.

As she entered the store, she could sense the change in atmosphere. There were no cheery 'hellos' or quick chats as she walked through the store and staff area. Everyone, especially the managers, was cleaning and preparing their departments.

When Debbie reached the Supervisor's desk, she found Gillian muttering to herself. She also spotted Dawn sweeping the area around the checkouts in a lacklustre fashion, casting furtive glances at Gillian.

"Morning," said Debbie tentatively.

"Debbie. Have you heard? Renee!" replied Gillian. The stress seemed to have rendered her incapable of forming proper sentences.

"Yes, I did hear, Gill. But Karen is coming in, so we're all covered."

"Right. Tills, change, now Debbie!"

Debbie took this as an instruction to fill all the tills up with loose change. She didn't hesitate or ask any further questions; it was, at least, a better job than sweeping. As she reached the basket-only tills at the end of the row of checkouts, Gillian barked further orders at her.

"You stick to the schedule Debbie. Dawn will focus on swaps and returns, and you make sure every member of staff is where they need to be. Give any angry customers what they want. Today must go without a hitch."

At that exact moment, the first customer of the day lost control of his trolley. It swung into the Halloween display at the front of the store, sending pumpkins rolling. Debbie almost laughed, but she stopped herself when she saw that Gillian's face had turned a deep shade of red.

Unfortunately, the pumpkin incident seemed to set the tone for the day ahead. At 10, an angry customer loudly returned a tin of rotten beans, not due to expire until 2025. At 10.45, an elderly customer fainted in the biscuit aisle. It shortly became clear that there were no first aiders on shift. At 11.30, a hungover trolley boy crashed a long trail of trolleys into a customer's Jaguar.

Worst of all, the Inspector had decided to poke around the storeroom in the early afternoon. He'd bumped into Colin behind the tins. Shortly afterwards, Steve escorted Colin from the premises with a P45 and a face of thunder.

The Inspector reached the checkout department at 3 pm. It was busy enough, but to Debbie's relief, there were no long queues, and everything was running smoothly. Gillian beamed as she ran the Inspector through various folders and schedules.

It was all going a bit too well until around 3.45 pm, when Debbie heard a loud crash from the basket till area. A bottle of vinegar had smashed and covered a customer's white trousers in flecks of brown. Debbie looked at Gillian and saw a vein twitching around her temple. She put down the staff schedule and ran towards the incident.

"You stupid girl!" the customer shouted at Louisa, who didn't respond.

"I'm so sorry, sir," Debbie apologised, as she skidded to a halt next to the puddle of vinegar.

"Cleaner to basket-only tills immediately." Karen's voice sounded over the store announcement system.

"Sorry won't fix this!" shouted the customer. He jabbed his finger towards his cheap-looking white trousers.

"Come with me, sir, let's take you around to Customer Services. We'll replace the vinegar and give you the money towards dry cleaning. Follow me."

To Debbie's relief, the offer seemed to appease him. But as they turned away, Louisa burst into tears. Gillian and Dawn both walked towards the scene but didn't know what to do with Louisa.

"Gillian," called Debbie, "take the gentleman to Customer Services. Dawn, jump on this till while I take Lou upstairs for a little break."

Under the gaze of the Inspector, Gillian nodded. But she then whispered, "Calm her down and bring her back, Debbie. No long chats."

Debbie nodded and put her arm around a sobbing Louisa.

"That man was an arse," tutted Debbie, as they entered the canteen. "Please don't let him upset you."

He had upset Louisa, though; huge teardrops seeped from her eyes and ran down her freckled nose. Close up, Debbie noticed how the girl's uniform hung off her. Her eyes, though puffy, had dark grey circles underneath them. She was only a few years older than Marco, but she looked so different, so uncared for.

"Has something else happened?" asked Debbie, as she stroked Louisa's back.

"I, I c-can't do this anymore," stuttered Louisa through her sobs.

"This job?" asked Debbie.

"Everything. I c-can't do it."

"Now then, what do you mean? Are you in

some kind of trouble?"

Louisa nodded, but then her eyes widened in fear, and she raised her hands to her face and covered her mouth.

"Lou, I could help, you can talk to me," urged Debbie, but Louisa shook her head and bit her lip.

"N-no you can't help, no-one can. Can you give me a few minutes, Debbie? I'll be OK. I don't want Gillian to be cross with me. I need this job."

By the time Debbie returned, the Inspector had moved to another department. Gillian still looked stressed though.

"Well?" she squeaked as soon as Debbie approached her. Her eyes were a little bloodshot, and the vein in her temple was still pulsing.

"Well nothing," replied Debbie. "The man was rude to her, and it upset her. She was a bit shook up, but she'll be fine."

"Anything else?"

"Oh, no, nothing else," said Debbie calmly, though her mind was racing.

Louisa was in some kind of trouble. Someone was making her do something she didn't want to, and she couldn't escape. Debbie's mind wandered to the text on Caitlin's phone.

'Something dodgy is going on at work… we report it to protect the vulnerable.'

The evening shift staff arrived and broke her chain of thought.

"Right," said Debbie, as she tried to concentrate on the people in front of her. "Julia, you take Edith off the till early, it'll make her day. Simon, go to the Customer Service desk please and send Karen back round here. Stacy, can you clear the baskets and tidy the tills for half an hour please."

Stacy nodded and turned around with a yawn. Debbie watched her slink away. She also looked the wrong side of thin and always seemed tired and nervous. And, now that Debbie thought of it, so did Jade.

"God, that vinegar man was a pain," moaned Karen as she approached the Supervisor's desk. "I'd pay him not to wear those hideous trousers."

"Karen," whispered Debbie, looking around to check no-one was listening. "Do you think there's something up with some of the young girls that work here?"

"The teenagers?" replied Karen with a look of surprise. "Well they're teenage girls Debbie, I expect there's plenty up with them."

"No, I mean something serious. Have you noticed Louisa and Stacy, and even Jade? They all look too thin, don't they? Dark bags under their eyes, bad skin, miserable? It's not healthy for people that age."

"Well, I'm not being funny," replied Karen, "but they're all from New Grange, aren't they?

They're poor, Deb," she added.

"No, there's something dodgy going on," whispered Debbie, with a pointed glance at Karen.

"Oh no," muttered Karen after a moment's pause. "Not this again. No, Deb, I don't want to hear it."

Debbie tried to protest, but Karen put her fingers in her ears and said "la, la, la" over and over again.

"Where do you think Renee is, then?" asked Debbie, after a short silence.

"How should I know? At home ill, I expect. It's not like we needed her here anyway. Speaking of which," she added before Debbie could interrupt, "you don't need me here for the next fifteen minutes, do you?"

"Well, no, but…"

"Great! I'm leaving early then. Don't want to bump into Mardie."

Typical, thought Debbie, as she watched Karen turn and walk away from the checkouts. She saw out the remaining shift in a daze until Ethan and Marie arrived to take over.

Debbie reached the staff area shortly after 5 pm, feeling exhausted from the day. As she opened her locker, she looked over and saw Dawn standing still, staring into space.

"Dawn?" asked Debbie, making her quiet colleague jump with a start. "Are you OK?"

"Yes," Dawn replied with a sigh as she pulled

her coat from her locker.

Dawn had worked at the store since before Debbie joined. Yet, apart from a few more grey hairs and wrinkles, she hadn't changed at all. She'd always been private. She got on with her job without complaint and blended into the store itself.

Debbie felt compelled to move closer to Dawn, to confide in her. Unlike Karen, she hoped Dawn would take her seriously.

"Hey, Dawn, have you noticed that some of the girls who work here don't seem right. You know, the younger girls," she whispered.

Dawn's eyes widened as she looked over Debbie's shoulder. She swept the locker area to ensure no-one else was there, listening in.

"Like, they're depressed or something?"

Dawn shook her head.

"They're not depressed, Debbie," she whispered back, "isn't it obvious what's going on?"

"What do you mean?" asked Debbie, but Dawn didn't respond.

"What's going on, Dawn?"

Dawn grimaced and swept the locker area again. In the distance, Debbie heard a door close. "Something is happening to these girls. Someone at the store is forcing them into something they don't want to do?" ventured Debbie, and Dawn nodded.

"Did Janice and Caitlin find out?" Debbie whispered, praying that no-one would interrupt them. Dawn shrugged her shoulders but gave a short nod.

"Who is it, Dawn?"

They heard footsteps in the distance, and Dawn swiftly turned around to face her locker again.

"Not here, Debbie," she replied, under her breath. "I'm going to the police at the end of the week to tell them what's going on. I just need another few days to double-check things. Keep your head down and don't say a word. The more you know, the more danger you'll be in."

Dawn rushed away, leaving Debbie standing at the lockers, shell-shocked. Her head span as adrenaline coursed through her veins. It wasn't only her who had suspicions. She wasn't being paranoid or getting carried away. Dawn had joined the dots too. Janice and Caitlin were right. There was something dodgy going on, affecting young girls from the New Grange estate. Were the girls forced into other jobs and made to sell drugs?

Or, Debbie thought, as a chill ran down her spine, could it be prostitution? The word 'Princesses' definitely suggested prostitution, rather than a criminal gang.

Either way, someone else within the store was behind it all, pulling the strings. Janice and Caitlin were onto them, but they were killed to protect the secret.

Debbie fought the urge to run away from the

supermarket and go to the police herself. If she made a rash move now, the culprit might have time to cover their tracks. She could put everyone in danger. She'd have to sit tight and wait for Dawn to go to the police with the evidence. Then, finally, the police would make a breakthrough in the investigation, and there would be closure at last.

So, instead of running, she strolled back through the store. She smiled and waved goodbye to her colleagues, many of whom she now thought of as suspects.

16: FRIGHT NIGHT

Wednesday 31st October 2018 -
Debbie

Debbie gazed out of her kitchen window at the darkening sky. Her eyelids dropped, and her head nodded downwards, before snapping back up with a start. She'd barely slept following her conversation with Dawn two days before.

Debbie wished Dawn would reply to her messages. She had texted her four times in the last two days but hadn't received a response.

"Mum, it's time to go to the party," shouted Abbie from the doorway, breaking Debbie's thoughts.

She turned to her daughter, jumped in fright, and dropped her phone on the floor. Abbie was wearing a white angel costume for the Homestead Community Halloween party. And, she'd added blood spatter to her outfit, and a bullet wound to the side of her head.

"Oh my God, Abbie," gasped Debbie, steadying herself. Her stomach turned. "Where on earth did you get that from?"

"It's Halloween, Mum," she stated, as though she was talking to a small child. "I can't be just an angel, can I? Dad got me it as a present."

Debbie grimaced and clenched her fists.

"Abs, get rid of that thing on your head, or I'm not taking you. No arguments," she ordered, and Abbie stomped away with a whimper.

Debbie's legs felt like lead and when she walked, the floor felt soft beneath her. She put the kettle on and made a strong coffee.

"Come on them, Mum," urged Abbie, fifteen minutes later, with Debbie's car keys in her hand. "Marco is ready, too."

Debbie sat down in the car and turned the key. The coffee had worked, and she already felt sharper.

"We are a bit early Abs. It starts at seven, right? It doesn't take twenty-five minutes to drive to Homestead."

In the back, Marco snorted with laughter and Abbie folded her arms, her face cross and flushed.

"We'll go a long way around, have a look at the decorations," suggested Debbie, though she had another plan in mind.

When she reached the Melwood junction, she turned off towards South Croydon. This route through the back roads would take her past Renee Beck's house.

Renee. She had been so radiant at the staff party, and so full of life at work since. Yet, she'd phoned in sick on the day of the inspection and taken today off as annual leave at short notice.

Debbie reached Renee's house and pulled up on the opposite side of the road, giving her a clear view of the front door. Renee's car was on the drive, and her front window lights were on, the blinds half down. A group of dads and young children in costume were almost at Renee's door with arms full of sweets. Debbie turned off her engine.

"Mum, why have we stopped?" asked Abbie from the back seat.

"Shh, Abs, we're too early anyway. Let's just stay here for a minute." Debbie pretended to check her phone.

A minute later, the group of children scurried up to Renee's front door, which opened after the second knock. Debbie did a double-take; Renee didn't look terrible, but way below her usual standards. Her hair was wavy, her face was pale, and she looked exhausted. She reappeared at the door with a bar of chocolate. She passed it over, then slammed the door in the scared-looking children's faces.

"Was that the fit woman from your work?" asked Marco, curiously.

"No," lied Debbie as she sped off towards Homestead. "And trust me, it's not all about looks, Marc."

They arrived ten minutes early, which didn't stop Abbie running in ahead of Debbie and Marco.

"Debbie," sang a familiar voice from the edge of the hall. "Come and give me a hand with this."

"Oh no," muttered Debbie under her breath, as she recognised Gillian. Her boss, dressed in a fitted red dress and a pair of flashing devil horns, was attempting to unfold a picnic table.

"I didn't realise you helped organise this," said Debbie, as she grabbed a table leg.

"I do it most years," replied Gillian. "This is the area I used to represent," she added, bitterly.

Debbie bit her lip as the memory came back to her. Earlier this year, Gillian had been a local Councillor for Homestead. But she'd lost her seat in May to an independent candidate who opposed supermarkets. Debbie and Karen had found it funny at the time, though Gillian had been quite distraught.

Debbie bit her lip as Gillian fussed over the table display. She neatly lined up each craft item and hummed to herself as more people entered the hall.

Debbie wondered if Gillian, who was so meticulous and organised, had noticed what she and Dawn had. She was the Manager, after all, and as a former Councillor, she might know the best way to handle the situation. Perhaps, even better than her and Dawn.

"Gillian," said Debbie tentatively. "Could I have a private word with you some time, outside of work?"

Gillian raised her eyebrows and opened her mouth to respond, but Marco interrupted her. He'd run through the growing crowds towards Debbie.

"Mum," he gasped, "Abbie's crying."

"What, why?" asked Debbie as she turned away from Gillian. "Where is she?"

"She wanted to get here early because a boy she likes said he'd meet her here," replied Marco. "But he told her he's not coming, cos there's riots in Croydon, and his Mum won't drive him here. She's by the toilets."

Debbie apologised to Gillian, then rushed through the crowd. Everyone was checking their phones, so she reached for hers and saw two messages from Joe.

There's trouble by work in Croydon, riots by the looks of it. People in Halloween masks running around – police not here yet. I can't leave work, so I won't make the party.

Deb, it's all over Twitter, trouble is heading south towards you. Take the kids home.

"Oh God," muttered Debbie. She remembered the last riots in Croydon back in 2011. Rioters burnt department stores, looted smaller shops and broke into homes.

She spotted Abbie sitting behind the pumpkin table, pouting and wiping her eyes. Her daughter's fake bullet wound had reappeared, which made her stomach churn again.

"Come on, kids. We're leaving."

"But the devil lady says everyone should stay," said Marco. He pointed towards Gillian, who was standing on a chair, barking orders at everyone.

Typical, thought Debbie.

"Stay put everyone," Gillian shouted over the chatter. "We can lock the doors and wait until the police have rounded the rioters up."

"She's not my boss at the moment, Marc," said Debbie, "and your Dad says we should go home."

That was good enough for Marco, so the three of them ran out of the hall. As they got in the car, Gillian pulled the doors to the entrance closed and locked herself and everyone else inside.

"You better get a move on, Mum," hurried Marco, as he scrolled through a social media feed on his phone. "People in Melwood say that groups are smashing up cars near our High

Street."

Debbie sped towards the main junction by the supermarket and got held up at the lights. Ahead, cars were making three-point turns, as boys in dark clothes ran around them. They were wearing masks, and some of them had cans of spray paint in their hands.

"Oh no," groaned Marco, and Abbie started crying again.

A few of the rioters ran in Debbie's direction. One of them, a skinny teenage boy, paused by Debbie's car to catch his breath. She recognised Karen's son immediately and wound down her window.

"Daniel!" she shouted. "What are you doing? Wait until I tell your mother."

"Tell her if you can find her! She doesn't give a shit about us," Daniel replied through deep breaths.

Ahead, a car window smashed, and someone cried out in fear. police sirens screamed in the distance. The masked figures ahead were moving closer; one of them wielding a baseball bat.

Debbie pulled her car onto the opposite side of the road and entered the supermarket car park. She swerved past the recycling area and took a slip road marked with a large 'Do Not Enter' sign.

"Mum," said Marco as he held onto the dashboard. "What are you doing?"

"Deliveries don't come at this time," she replied as she swung into the loading bay for lorries.

"So, I can take their entrance slip road onto the other road, cutting out the junction."

She knew the way through the back roads to her house on the other side of Melwood. She had taken the route a few times when she'd dropped Dawn off after work.

Dawn. With all the drama of the evening, Debbie hadn't thought any more about their conversation. Now, the memory of it crept back into her head, as she rushed through Melwood's peaceful back roads. Without thinking too much about it, she turned into Dawn's road.

Just as she'd done at Renee's earlier, Debbie pulled up across the street from Dawn's house. It was an old fashioned semi-detached that Dawn had lived in her whole life. Her car was in the driveway and the front curtains undrawn. But, strangely, all the lights were off which made it difficult to see inside.

"Mum," Abbie and Marco shouted at the same time.

"Shh," hushed Debbie, as she reached for her phone. "I thought we could stop here, and check the next few roads are OK," she lied.

As the kids scrolled through their phones, Debbie looked over at Dawn's house. She contemplated her next move. Could she knock on the door and pretend they were seeking shelter from the riots? Dawn would hate the intrusion, and she wasn't too far from her own home.

"There's nothing on the next few roads Mum, but the police are clashing with people on our High Street."

"OK, OK, let's go," replied Debbie. She started the ignition and turned on her headlights. They exposed a tall, slender figure dressed all in black, coming out of the side gate of Dawn's house.

Their hood was up, and they wore a black and white Guy Fawkes mask, which shone back at Debbie. For a second, the person froze in the glare of the headlights. They turned their head from side to side before running back through the side gate.

"Did you see that?" whispered Debbie to her children, but both of them had their heads down, looking at their phones.

"See what?" replied Marco.

"I thought I saw someone in a mask, run out of that gate and then back through."

"Uh, sounds like a burglar, Mum, so just drive, and then call the police at home."

"Come on, Mum," pleaded Abbie from the back seat.

Debbie lowered the handbrake and drove home. The kids ran inside as she opened the garage door and locked her car inside. An uneasy feeling crept over her as she entered her living room and sat down on the sofa. Something wasn't right about Dawn's house; especially the dark rooms and open curtains. She had definitely seen someone run through the side gate.

It could, of course, have been a rioter who'd broken off to run away from the police. That would explain why they were running through gardens and had fled at the sight of headlights. But Debbie's gut feeling told her that it was something altogether more malevolent.

Her hands shook as she picked up her phone to message Dawn, who still hadn't replied to any of her calls or messages. She typed another.

Big trouble in Melwood tonight. Please let me know you're OK, I'm really worried.

Debbie sat there, her heart pounding against her ribcage. She felt nauseous and tired, but she still stared at her phone, willing something to happen. After a couple of minutes, 'online' appeared next to Dawn's name on the messaging app. Debbie focused her eyes as Dawn typed back.

I'm fine, all OK, do not worry. See you at work.

Debbie breathed a sigh of relief and used her last ounce of energy to pull herself up the stairs to her bedroom.

"Dad'll be home soon, kids," she yawned.

She entered her room, changed into her pyjamas, and collapsed into a deep sleep.

17: ANOTHER ONE DAWN

Monday 5th November 2018 -
Vincent

"Sir, the surveillance team are reporting optimum conditions."

"Excellent, thank you. Let's begin the operation as per the plan. Team briefing in ten minutes. Round everyone up," replied Okafor, with a smile that reached his bloodshot, tired eyes.

It was the moment he'd been waiting for, that would make the recent sleepless nights worthwhile. Surveillance of the Dimont family businesses had produced enough evidence to secure a search warrant of the house. Okafor also had enough evidence to bring in Jack's sons, Jack Junior, Joey and Jonny, for the handling of stolen goods.

It all fitted into Okafor's plan. He'd bring the sons in, leaving Jack sweating on the outside. He'd use the investigation into their minor crimes to search for evidence of Jack's bigger ones. Once he'd found it, he'd bring Jack in and offer a deal. If Jack exposed the people higher up the chain, he would avoid jail and be offered witness protection.

As his team assembled outside, Okafor checked that everything was in order. The next forty minutes would be crucial. He stepped out of his office with his head held high to address his team and kick it off.

"Everyone," he bellowed, and silence fell. "It's time. We have the best conditions for the Dimont search and arrests. As you know from your briefings, this means that they – Jack, Junior, Joey and Jonny – are at their house in New Grange. Tricia, the mother, is there too. You all know the plan and have your positions?"

There was an encouraging chorus of "Yes, sir!" from the team, so he pressed on.

"We aim to execute a search warrant on the house and arrest the boys for handling stolen goods. Nothing else at this stage, unless they resist arrest. We expect them to come quietly, but we'll cover all exits from the house, and armed support will form part of the convoy. All ready?"

The team nodded eagerly.

"Then let's go," he ordered, and he clapped his hands together.

Okafor notified the Superintendent and climbed into his car, towards the rear of the convoy. Uniformed officers drove him and DS Harris through South Croydon. As they got closer to New Grange, he willed the circumstances not to change. If Jack and the boys disappeared, it would raise questions about the integrity of his team. That would slow down the entire operation and tarnish his work to date.

"Sir," the surveillance team sounded through the crackle of the radio. "We have a problem."

Okafor closed his eyes and took a deep breath.

"Go ahead," he sighed.

"A girl has turned up at the house, sobbing, banging on the door. Tricia Dimont opened the door, they had a brief conversation, and then she slammed the door in the girl's face. But she's not leaving."

"Description of the girl?" requested Okafor with a sideways glance at DS Harris.

"IC1, short, thin, blonde hair, teenager."

"We think it's Jack's daughter, Jade," replied Okafor. "We can proceed as intended, but keep me informed of developments."

As the convoy reached the turning for New Grange, Okafor saw a group of hooded teenagers gawping back at him. They all had their phones out, taking pictures of the convoy. He expected they were sending them to friends on the estate who were up to no good, including the Dimont boys.

Okafor shrugged it off. There was only one main road in and out of the New Grange estate; his team had already cornered Jack and his sons.

"Approach slowly," he radioed, as the vehicles took up their respective positions.

The arresting officers crept in front of the Dimonts' house, followed by Okafor and DS Harris.

"Identity confirmed as Jade Dimont," whispered Okafor into the radio. The young girl was still banging on the door, oblivious to the two cars behind her.

"Dad, I know you're there, you need to help me!" she sobbed.

A slight movement caught Okafor's eye. He looked up and saw Tricia Dimont's face peering from behind the front bedroom curtains. Her eyes moved from Jade towards the two police cars. He squinted and saw her mouth move; he was sure she'd shouted 'Jack.'

"Officers at the garden alleyway and rear door, confirm your position," radioed Okafor.

"Confirmed."

"They know we're here. Easy now. Arresting officers, exit your cars now with DS Harris. DS Harris, take Jade to one side, and then officers can proceed as planned."

Okafor felt his entire body tense in anticipation. He'd set the trap, and the next few minutes were critical.

Jade turned around as the car doors clicked open. Her face was pink in the cold air, and tears streaked her puffy cheeks. Her eyes widened in shock, then narrowed in confusion at the sight of the officers.

"Tricia, what have you done?" she shouted, her voice and body shaking.

Okafor understood the situation from Jade's perspective. She must have thought that Tricia had called the police to remove her.

"We're not here for you, Jade," explained DS Harris, as she extended an arm to the troubled-looking young girl. "I'm sorry to interrupt you, but I need you to step aside and not obstruct our business here."

Okafor sighed with relief as Jade sloped towards the edge of the front garden, and sat down on the wall, head in her hands. DS Harris placed her hand on Jade's shoulder and nodded towards the arresting officers.

Jack answered the door after the second knock. A smile spread across his tanned face, framed by slicked back dark hair and a greying dark beard. He wasn't the tallest of men, but there was a certain aura around him, and a twinkle in his dark blue eyes.

"Fellas," he greeted, with a faint Dublin twang. "To what do I owe the pleasure? My little girl here making a bit too much noise?"

"Mr Dimont," stated one of the arresting officers. "We have a warrant to search your premises. We also need to speak to your sons."

Jack's jaw clenched, and he cast a look back at the door, where Tricia had appeared.

"Why?" he asked, with a forced smile. "Can you talk me through this warrant line by line, son?"

Okafor sighed; Jack was playing for time. To his relief, the arresting officer realised this too.

"It's a lawful warrant and we'll talk you through it later. There are officers stationed around your house. We will be entering your house, Mr Dimont, and your sons will come to the station with us. Whether we do this the easy way or the hard way, is up to you."

Jack's jaw clenched again, and his fists curled into balls. Okafor held his breath and prepared to issue further orders. But, after a tense ten seconds, Jack stood aside and called his sons to the door.

One by one, the officers arrested the them. They were helped into the cars in handcuffs, as Jack, Tricia and Jade looked on from the front garden. Jack tried to keep his demeanour light, but Okafor spotted the stern glances he gave his sons. He was sure he detected some non-verbal orders to keep their mouths closed.

Once the police cars and half the convoy had driven away, Okafor stepped out of his car.

"Vincent, isn't it?" called Jack. He stood confidently, still smiling, with his arms firmly around Tricia and Jade's shoulders. Okafor ignored him as he authorised the Search Team to proceed.

"Once we've cleared up this little misunderstanding, Vincent, we could try and get along." Jack heckled from the side-lines. "We'll have you and the wife over for dinner. Vivienne, right?"

A shiver ran down Okafor's spine, and he tried not to let it show.

The search continued throughout the afternoon, and a healthy haul of evidence bags left the house. Okafor enjoyed the souring of Jack's expression, as the team discovered more and more hiding places.

Jack paced around the garden many times and made a few hushed calls away from police ears. Jade had disappeared, leaving Tricia sitting alone and miserable on the wall.

Okafor terminated the search at around 5 pm. He felt incredibly tired; the earlier adrenaline had evaporated. He only needed to return to the station to check in on the questioning of the Dimont boys and congratulate the team, then an early evening beckoned. In the distance, the first fireworks of the evening whizzed and banged for bonfire night.

"Sir," said DS Harris, as she approached him with a concerned look.

"Yes, Joanne?" he replied as he rubbed his eyes.

"Sir, I've received a voicemail from Debbie

Gomez. Her colleague, Dawn Smith, didn't turn up for work today."

"Hardly a police matter," replied Okafor with a roll of his eyes. He stifled a yawn as he signed some paperwork from the search.

"Dawn's not had a day off in fifteen years, apparently, and she didn't phone anyone to say she'd be absent. Sir, Debbie sounded pretty concerned. She was whispering and crying. Here, listen."

Okafor reluctantly leant towards Joanne's phone.

"Joanne, DS Harris. It's Debbie here, Debbie Gomez from the Melwood supermarket. My friend Dawn didn't come to work today. I know that it sounds silly, to call you, but she's never been off before. And if she was sick, I know she'd call in. Her phone is off, I'm worried about her, and I don't know what to do. Please call me when you get this."

Okafor sighed. Now that he'd heard it, he felt obliged to at least check up on Dawn, if only for peace of mind.

"You have an address?" he sighed.

"Yes, sir. It's in Melwood, en-route back to the station."

They drove at the rear of the convoy out of New Grange, then peeled off when they reached Melwood High Street. They took the back streets to Dawn's house and pulled up outside the semi-detached house. There was a car parked in the drive and the curtains were open, but the lights were off despite the falling dusk.

Perhaps, thought Okafor ominously, Debbie Gomez had a good reason to be concerned. They approached the front door and knocked twice without response. There was no sound or movement from behind the door. Okafor shrugged, and DS Harris gritted her teeth.

"There's something not right," she muttered, and Okafor nodded in agreement.

"There's not enough here to justify forced entry, though," he said, moving his hand down towards the plastic door handle. To his surprise, he was able to push it down, and the unlocked door clicked open.

"Dawn," he shouted. "Ms Smith, it's the police, are you here?"

The house remained silent. Okafor reached a hand inside the door and switched on a light. It illuminated a hallway lined with old pictures and peeling wallpaper. Everything was neat apart from a collection of odd shoes, scattered on the floor. It looked like someone had kicked or tripped over them.

Okafor picked up his radio, gave the operator the address and requested back-up on standby. He wiped the sweat from his palms and stepped inside the house, followed by DS Harris. A rotten, acrid smell reached his nostrils as he stepped over the shoes towards the living room and kitchen. His hand moved instinctively towards the weapon concealed in his belt.

He heard a creak to his right and saw DS Harris creeping up the stairs, her jaw clenched.

"Dawn," she called tentatively.

Okafor swept the living room, as a cry from the upstairs broke the eerie silence. He immediately retraced his steps to the hallway and ran up the stairs.

DS Harris stood on the landing outside the door to the main bedroom. Her face shone with sweat, and she was as white as a sheet. The smell was pungent now, permeating the air and making Okafor feel as nauseous as DS Harris looked. Joanne didn't need to say it; Okafor already knew what was behind the bedroom door.

"She's d-dead, sir," she stuttered.

Okafor stepped forward, reached towards her arm, and urged her gently away from the door.

"Her wrists, they're b-both cut, and there's a knife in her h-hand. So much b-blood." She swayed on the spot and clutched the railing.

"Come on, Joanne, we need to preserve the scene," instructed Okafor. It wasn't Okafor's first dead body, but it may well have been his sergeant's. He supported DS Harris back down the stairs and picked up his radio.

"Cancel back-up, we need forensics here now."

Police Media Statement: Tuesday 6 November 2018, 07:00
DCI Vincent Okafor

At 17.45 on Monday 5th November, the body of a woman, Dawn Smith, 49, was discovered by police officers at her home in Melwood. Next of kin have been informed.

Ms Smith worked at the same supermarket in Melwood as both Janice Locke and Caitlin Murphy. However, Ms Smith's death is not currently being treated as suspicious or linked to those crimes.

We will not be taking any further questions until the forensic examination and coroner's reports have been completed in full.

18: LIAR

Tuesday 6th November 2018 -
Gillian

illian's hands shook as she put down her house phone. Her breath quickened as she stumbled into the nearest seat in her living room. The call was from Vincent Okafor, to inform her that he'd found another member of her team, Dawn Smith, dead at her home in Melwood. She rubbed her temples as she grasped at the details from the conversation.

Okafor had said 'not suspicious,' and that it looked as though Dawn had taken her own life. Then, he had suggested that Gillian speak to the Store Manager, Steve. Okafor had already informed him and recommended that they announce the news to the staff before they read about it in the media.

It was a good suggestion, thought Gillian, yet

she remained frozen on the sofa. She stared into a mirror, as a crushing feeling descended on her. Her chest was tight, her stomach felt like lead, and her thoughts raced.

What would people think and say? Three deaths in three months, all from the same team within the same supermarket. Would anyone honestly believe that Dawn had killed herself?

"Gill," said Kevin, nervously, from the living room doorway. "Did someone call?"

"Yes, it was the police," she whispered, her eyes fixed on the floor.

"And?"

"It's Dawn," she replied, turning to face her husband, who'd raised his eyebrows. "They found her yesterday evening. Suicide, they think," she added, as she brushed some dust from the sofa armrest.

Kevin exhaled and shuffled forward, moving his hand towards Gillian's shoulder. Before he could make contact, she shrugged.

"Not now, Kevin," she snapped. "I have things to do. Okafor said I should call Steve. He'll have to make the announcement. But I'll need to be there as soon as possible."

Kevin withdrew his hand and nodded. Gillian shuffled up the stairs, in a daze but with a sense of purpose.

In the privacy of her bedroom, she picked up her mobile phone and dialled Steve's number.

"Gillian," he answered straight away. "You've spoken to Okafor?"

"Yes," she replied with a sigh, "it's terrible, terrible news."

"I'm sorry Gill, I'm not sure if you and Dawn were close?"

"I suppose we'd known each other a long time," replied Gillian, as the crushing feeling returned to her chest.

"And so soon, after, you know..."

"Quite, yes. But Okafor said he doesn't think they're linked. They're not treating it as suspicious."

"Well, not yet," sighed Steve, and Gillian's heartbeat began to speed up again. "Anyway, what are we going to do about the staff, your team?"

"Okafor was right," replied Gillian. "You should announce it this morning to anyone on shift, before the media coverage. Renee and Marie are working this morning, and I could call Debbie and Karen and get them to pop in for it. They can cascade the news."

"OK, good idea, but, Gill," he paused, "can you do it, the announcement?"

Gillian froze again. It was the very last thing she wanted to do, and her face flushed red at the thought of it. But then again, she had been Dawn's boss; people would expect her to break the news.

"Steve, I really don't..."

"Please, Gill, I barely knew the woman, and you've done loads of speeches, you're good at this stuff," he pleaded.

Gillian closed her eyes and sighed.

"Fine, fine, let's do it together at 8.20 am. Before the store opens."

"See you then, Gill, and thank you."

Gillian's hands shook again as she created a new group message: herself, Renee Marie, Debbie and Karen.

Please come to the store for 8.20 am – I'm making an urgent announcement.

As she got ready, she heard her phone vibrating. She expected the messages were all coming from the new group. She could just imagine the speculation and questions. She didn't bother to check the messages, let alone respond. They'd all have to turn up and hear the news along with everyone else.

She took a fresh, ironed uniform from her wardrobe; it felt baggier than usual. She removed her hair curlers, did her best to cover her pale, blotchy skin and dry lips with makeup. The stresses of the last three months had undeniably taken their toll on her. She glared at the impatient clock, which told her she only had moments left before she had to go.

"Take it step by step," she muttered to the

mirror. "You're a leader, you've made a hundred speeches before, it's not another murder, it's suicide."

She breathed deeply, then willed herself to the front door. She glanced into the study; Kevin was sitting at his desk, looking down at his phone and typing.

"Kevin, I'm leaving now. Everything OK?"

"Yes," he jumped and dropped his phone on the floor. "Good luck, you know, making the announcement."

"How do you know I'm doing it instead of Steve?" she queried, her eyes narrowed.

"Oh, um…"

His eyes darted around the room, landing on the phone on the floor in front of him.

"I didn't, I just thought, you know, you're her manager," he mumbled.

"Liar," muttered Gillian, as she left the house. As she closed the door, she noticed that some of her plant pots had fallen over, and that soil had spread onto the driveway. She picked up a broom and swept until it looked perfect again. For about ten seconds, it made her feel much better. But then she remembered all her other stresses, and that time was ticking by impatiently.

Thirty minutes later, she sat in the store canteen. How could she get up and speak to all these people, when her muscles felt so tense and her breath was caught in her throat?

At 8.20 am, Steve knocked on a table to get everyone's attention, his face solemn. Silence fell, and dozens of pairs of eyes swivelled in her direction, in anticipation of the news.

In front of her, Debbie and Karen sat close together, looks of concern on their faces. Marie stood towards the back, with Renee perched on a table next to her. So, she's well enough to come and hear the announcement, thought Gillian, dryly. She took a deep breath.

"Good morning," she paused, her breath caught in her throat. "I-I'm afraid we have some terrible, terrible news to share with you this morning. Yesterday, our colleague Dawn was found at her home, and she had passed away."

There was a collective gasp; hands flew up to mouths and eyes darted around the room. The colour drained from Debbie's face; her hand twitched and grabbed Karen's arm.

"Now," said Gillian, though it was almost inaudible over the din of noise. "Now, this is not being treated as suspicious," she shouted, and silence fell again.

"What do you mean, not suspicious?" cried Edith from the middle of the canteen. "It's only been three months since Janice and Caitlin. And Dawn wasn't ill, was she?"

There was a murmur of agreement around the room. Gillian's head throbbed with pressure, and she struggled to catch her breath. Steve stood up.

"Everyone!" he shouted. "I know this is a shock, but you have to listen to Gillian, to the whole announcement."

"Not suspicious," Gillian spluttered, as everyone fell silent again, "because the signs, the investigation, the evidence points to suicide. It wasn't a murder, it was suicide."

There was an audible gasp again, followed by silence. In the front row, Karen had her arm around Debbie, who whispered, "no, no, no," over and over again.

"This may well be in the news today. I ask that you tell as many of your other colleagues as you can," said Steve, who had now stood up at his table.

"We'll share funeral details and contribution arrangements when we know them. But for now, the show must go on. The store opens in three minutes."

"I'd like a quick word with my supervisor team," shouted Gillian, as the room descended into smaller chats. She leaned down towards Debbie and Karen.

"I'm going to speak to Renee and Marie first because they have to open up. Wait here."

She sat down with Renee and Marie at a table towards the back of the canteen. They were both silent, for a change, and Gillian felt less tense. It was like she'd awoken from a bad dream and was becoming herself again; in control.

"I understand this might be quite a shock," commented Gillian, as she tried to make eye contact with the two women in front of her. Marie stared down at her lap; Renee raised her head.

"Uh, just a bit, Gillian, yeah. I mean, what happened? How did she do it? Did you know she was depressed?"

"No, of course I didn't," replied Gillian, ignoring the rest of Renee's morbid questioning.

"Now, we don't have long because you have a department to open, but as you can imagine, this is going to be a tough time for us. Christmas is coming, and we're already short-staffed."

"Jade wants more hours," mumbled Marie, coming out of her daze.

"I'll sort out the staffing, thank you," replied Gillian, and she held her hand up to prevent further interruption from Renee.

"It is important, now more than ever, that you set an example to the team: no fights, no gossiping, no bitching. You're going to get along with everyone, including Debbie and Karen. And you are going to reassure people that this isn't related to Janice and Caitlin. If you don't, there will soon be two more full-time vacancies for Jade to cover. Do I make myself clear?"

The corners of Renee's mouth twitched, but she nodded and left without further comment.

Gillian turned her attention to Debbie and

Karen. Debbie whispered and gesticulated frantically at Karen, who shook her head in return. As Gillian approached them, they both fell silent.

"Debbie, Karen," sighed Gillian as she sat down next to them. "If there had been any more time, Steve and I would have told you separately."

Neither of them responded.

"I know you were the closest to her, Debbie," offered Gillian, as she leant forward over the table. "Did she say anything to you, in the week or so before she died?"

Karen looked at Debbie nervously.

"No," replied Debbie as she wiped her eyes with her sleeve.

"I spoke to her on inspection day, of course, but only about the usual stuff. And then I sent her a few messages this week, but she didn't reply. During the riots, I asked if she was OK, and she said yes. Then she doesn't show up for work. Now, this…" Debbie trailed off into tears again.

"It is just terrible, really terrible," repeated Gillian. "But we must all pull together now and set an example for the team. Renee and Marie have agreed to reassure others that this isn't linked to Janice and Caitlin. We all need to try and move on."

Karen nodded, but Debbie's head remained fixed in place, tears dropping from her eyes.

"I'll take her home," said Karen, putting her

arm back around her friend. "We need a bit of time for the news to sink in, you know."

Gillian watched as Karen supported Debbie out of the canteen, exchanging meaningful looks with each other. Something compelled Gillian to stand up again and follow them. She wondered what they were saying now, and before she'd arrived at their table.

She closed the door to the canteen softly behind her and crept towards the locker area. Debbie and Karen were there, putting their coats on. She stopped around the corner of the lockers, hoping to hear a few words of their conversation.

"Gillian is right," hissed Karen. "We all need to move on with our own lives. It's awful, but people kill themselves all the time. She was lonely and miserable. You knew that."

"She's always been lonely and miserable," retorted Debbie. "But recently, she was onto something, and now she's dead."

"She killed herself, Debbie. And if she didn't, isn't the fact she's dead reason enough for you to stop nosing around?"

Gillian couldn't help agreeing with Karen's point, and Debbie didn't seem to have a counter-argument, either.

"Promise me, Deb, promise me you'll drop this now," whispered Karen.

Gillian couldn't see Debbie's non-verbal response. But the fact that Karen's next word was 'good,' suggested that Debbie had nodded in agreement. Gillian slunk back to the canteen as her colleagues made their way back downstairs.

19: OVERHEARD AT THE FUNERAL

Thursday 6th December 2018 - Joanne

O ver a month after she'd discovered the body, DS Joanne Harris dressed for Dawn's funeral. Each day since, she'd woken up and checked her emails for the final forensic and coroners' reports. Until they had them, they couldn't determine their next steps, if any, on the case.

But, despite the delay, the images of Dawn's bedroom, her body, and the blood were still crystal clear in Joanne's head. According to her in-force counsellor, she'd never entirely forget them.

The coroner had released his report a few days ago; a copy of it lay open on Joanne's dressing table, in front of her. He'd determined the time of death as Wednesday 31st October, between 7 pm and 9 pm. The body had been in the bedroom, undisturbed, for a whole five nights before Joanne discovered it.

It could have been there longer, had one of Dawn's colleagues, Debbie, not reported her absence to the police. Joanne felt a familiar pang of pity for the woman whose body she'd found. She glanced down at the report for what felt like the hundredth time. As always, the word 'suicide' stared back up at her, in bold black ink on the white page. She shook her head; this incident wasn't black and white, as the report seemed to suggest.

She remembered the shoes knocked out of place in the hallway. She knew that the team had failed to find Dawn's phone, which was last used at 8.30 pm on Halloween to send a message to Debbie. And buried in the forensic report was a reference to unfamiliar clothing fibres found on Dawn's body.

Of course, there had been plenty of evidence for suicide too. Indeed, the coroner had found the weight of evidence in favour of that verdict. Yet, that did nothing to quell the uneasy feeling in Joanne's stomach. She strongly suspected that Dawn, like Janice and Caitlin, had been murdered by someone she knew. She was also sure that DCI Vincent Okafor privately shared her suspicions. But then, Inspectors couldn't run around challenging Coroners' reports. He couldn't neglect investigations into organised crime and drug distribution to chase ghosts.

Indeed, that was why Okafor was leading the latest drugs raid today, while Joanne was off to Croydon crematorium for Dawn's modest funeral.

She took her time driving her car slowly through the town centre. She wanted to arrive only just on-time, to avoid awkward conversations with the supermarket workers she knew from the Janice Locke and Caitlin Murphy case.

Outside, it was a bland kind of day, neither warm nor too cold, neither sunny nor overcast. It struck Joanne as somewhat apt for Dawn's funeral. She passed the queues of cars outside the shopping centre and arrived at her destination a few minutes early.

Outside the crematorium, roughly twenty people were gathered, in black clothes and coats. Closest to the entrance were an elderly couple and a woman who bore some resemblance to Dawn. Beside them, staff from the supermarket chatted in huddles.

At the rear, Gillian stood on her own, shuffling Orders of Service. Joanne willed herself to approach her.

"Hello. Gillian, isn't it?"

"Hello," chirped Gillian. "Lovely of you to attend," she added, with a pursed smile.

It didn't take a detective to spot the change in Gillian. DS Harris had only ever known her to be visibly irritable and stressed. Yet now, she looked relaxed and content. Her short, dark blonde hair shone and held its shape. She'd put on a little weight, which filled the wrinkles on her face and suited her. It made her appear a bit less stern.

"Not at all, I'd like to pay my respects," replied DS Harris. "You're looking well, how is everything at the supermarket?"

"Oh, yes, we're doing OK. It's been tough, of course, after these terrible, terrible events, but we've pulled together. Things have been a lot calmer in the last month, you know."

Gillian's eyes swept the groups in front of her with the same tight smile. Joanne followed her gaze. Renee Beck and Karen Goldman were deep in what looked like an amicable conversation. Debbie Gomez was close by with her husband, engrossed in discussion with Marie Webster.

The only person who still looked miserable was Jade Dimont. She stood next to two other young people but wasn't taking part in their conversation. That was no surprise, though, given what had happened to her father and brothers in the last month.

"Good," said Joanne in reply, "and your husband, Kevin, is it, he's not here today?"

For a fraction of a second, Gillian's smile slipped. Yet, she recovered in a flash and looked back at Joanne with the same twinkle in her eye.

"No, why would he be? He didn't know Dawn, and he runs a very busy company." She wrinkled her nose and stared at Joanne, her lips pursed into a smile again.

"Of course," nodded Joanne. She breathed a sigh of relief as the vicar appeared and invited everyone inside for the ceremony.

Joanne sat alone near the back of the hall; her eyes fixed on the pamphlet in front of her. It was a short affair; the vicar cantered through the usual readings and a few standard hymns. Towards the end, he asked whether anyone would like to say a few words. The gathering exchanged nervous glances, as the three family members shook their heads.

The vicar looked somewhat taken aback as Debbie Gomez stood up with a start and marched to the front of the hall. Debbie's husband and Karen glanced at each other with concern from either side of the empty seat. Debbie cleared her throat and tucked her hair behind her ears. She clasped her hands together in front of her.

"I knew Dawn for almost fifteen years," she started, her voice shaking.

"Well, as well as you could know Dawn, I suppose. She was a very private person, very happy in her own company. Some of us need to be around other people all the time, to be the centre of attention. Dawn was the opposite of that, but it didn't mean she wasn't content."

There were nods and murmurs of assent from around the room.

"When she was at work, I suppose it forced her out of her comfort zone. But in those situations, she was always polite, and hard-working, and compassionate."

Debbie paused and looked as though she was weighing up her next words carefully.

"She noticed things," she spluttered.

Joanne noticed that Debbie's knuckles had turned paler, from grasping her own hands.

"And...and she wanted to do right by everyone. If she were here, you know, still alive, I would say to her that I knew the truth. And that I am so sorry that I didn't do anything to stop what happened."

Debbie's breath caught in her throat, and she gave a short sob before returning to the stunned audience.

Joanne could feel the tension in the room. After all, Debbie had just referred to someone who had apparently committed suicide as 'content'. Debbie's husband stood up and put his arm around her. Karen glanced at Dawn's parents and sister apologetically.

"Thank you," said the vicar, "for those kind words. Of course, it is common for us to find words for those who have passed, that we could not find in their life..."

The service continued a little longer until finally, the plain coffin rolled away. Karen hurried to escort Debbie, who was still crying into a tissue, to the toilets.

Joanne's detective instincts kicked in, and she sloped out of the hall after Debbie and Karen. After all, Debbie had chosen some rather curious and ambiguous words in her speech.

The door to the ladies' toilets hung ajar. Joanne loitered outside with her phone in her hand. She was close enough to hear the conversation within.

"What on earth was that all about?" demanded Karen.

"It's her funeral and nobody else was going to speak. She deserved at least one person saying something nice about her," replied Debbie.

"You know what I mean," hissed Karen. "You said, 'I know the truth, I'm sorry I didn't prevent it'. It has been such a good month, and things are getting back on track, please don't dredge all this up again."

"I can't help it, I feel like a fraud sitting here, everyone believing that she killed herself."

"She did!"

"We both know she didn't, Karen!"

Joanne couldn't believe what she was hearing. How could Debbie and Karen know Dawn's death wasn't suicide? Before she could gather her thoughts, the toilet door swung open. Karen marched out, looking paler than usual behind her black fascinator.

"Excuse me," Karen pushed past Joanne without looking at her. Debbie came out of the toilets a few seconds later and offered Joanne a teary smile and a nod. She shuffled over to Joe, who ushered her out of the main entrance after Karen.

Joanne hung back beside the toilets as Dawn's family and colleagues started filing out. She heard chairs scraping and muffled voices from inside the main hall. She leaned around a pillar to look back inside and saw Marie clutching Renee's arm.

"Jesus Renee, are you OK, you almost fell..."

"Yes, yes, I'm fine. I'm light-headed, that's all. Will you stop fussing over me," muttered Renee, as she stood up to her full height. She also looked pale and a bit clammy, underneath a long black jumper dress.

"Please, let me help," begged Marie, her voice strained.

"I don't need help!" snapped Renee, as she bent over to collect some items she'd dropped.

"Yes, you do. I know what you're hiding."

A red flush returned to Renee's cheeks, and she glared ferociously at Marie.

"Whatever you think, Marie, you don't

breathe a word of it to anyone!"

"I won't, I promise. But I can help."

"I mean it. Remember, I know your little secret too, don't I?"

Joanne hid as they stomped out of the building in silence, oblivious to her presence.

"Wow," she muttered to herself.

She took her notebook from her pocket and scribbled down what she'd overheard. One thing was for sure: Debbie, Karen, Renee and Marie were all hiding something. She couldn't wait to tell Okafor.

Once the final car had pulled away, Joanne skipped out of the building, keen to get back to the station. As she approached her car, she saw a small figure sitting on the ground next to the driver's door. At first, she thought it was a child. But as she got closer, she recognised the blonde hair and thin, pale face of Jade Dimont. She stopped in her tracks. The last time she saw Jade was the day of her three half-brothers' arrests. After that, her brothers, her father and stepmother had entered witness protection. Jack had taken a deal and given Okafor volumes of information on his suppliers and their network.

During the negotiations, Jack Dimont had not once mentioned his daughter. He didn't seem concerned about her wellbeing, or to want her to come with them.

"Hello, Jade," greeted Joanne. "What are you

doing down there?"

"You're the policewoman, you were there on that day, in New Grange," said Jade, as she got to her feet. She was wearing an old black jacket and a short black skirt that wasn't entirely appropriate for a funeral.

"I was."

"I wondered if I could talk to you alone?" asked Jade. She folded her arms across her chest, and her bottom lip trembled.

"I'm sorry, I can't discuss your family's case with you. Did the liaison officer explain what's happened to them?"

"Yes, but,"

"Well, I'm afraid I can't tell you more than that. If you like, I could get my colleagues to give you another call?"

Jade nodded and bit her lip.

"Is there something else, Jade?"

Joanne sensed that Jade had something on the tip of her tongue. But instead of saying it, the young girl shook her head and turned away. Joanne felt a tinge of guilt, though she couldn't quite put her finger on why.

She got into her car and dialled Vincent's number. She willed him to answer, and grinned as he picked up. She kept her voice as calm and level as possible as she reported everything she'd overheard at the funeral.

"Well, well," said Vincent. "I want you to talk

to Dawn's supervisor team. One by one, ask them where they were on Halloween evening. Keep it as casual as you can, as though you didn't hear those conversations. Then, we'll put their answers to the test. Anyone who doesn't pass will face some very tough questioning."

"Understood," confirmed Joanne, and she couldn't help but smile. Janice, Caitlin and Dawn deserved justice, and she would get it for them.

Excerpts: Saturday 8 December 2018 – Melwood Interviews

<u>Karen</u>

DS Harris: Can you recall your whereabouts on 31st October 2018, between 6 pm and 10 pm?

Karen: Umm, what day was that?

DS Harris: It was a Wednesday, Karen. Halloween evening, the night of the riots.

Karen: What's this about?

DS Harris: A review of Dawn Smith's case.

Karen: Right. What does Halloween have to do with Dawn?

DS Harris: It was the night she died, Karen.

Karen: *Laugh* Well, what are you asking me for?

DS Harris: It's helpful for us to place people who knew Dawn, on the night she died. You don't have to answer, but you will be helping us if you do.

Karen: Oh, fine. I was at home.

DS Harris: With your husband?

Karen: Yes, yes, and the kids. We had a family night together. But for God's sake, please don't go asking them. We're struggling a bit, me and Pete, and this will stress him. You've already wasted my time, don't waste his, too. The woman killed herself, and we all just want to move on.

<u>Gillian</u>

DS Harris: Can you recall your whereabouts

on 31st October 2018, between 6 pm and 10 pm?

Gillian: Why are you asking me this? You said it was suicide.

DS Harris: We are reviewing the case file, Gillian. You're under no obligation to answer, but it is helpful for us to place everyone who knew Dawn.

Gillian: Well, I was at the Homestead Community event, OK? I went straight there after work for 5.45-ish to help set up. Dozens of people saw me there. When we heard the news of the riots, I locked everyone, including myself, in the hall. We were there until about 9 pm. When the situation was under control, I packed up and drove straight home. I'll be on the Fair Lawns' gate camera coming back in at 9.30ish, no doubt.

Jade

DS Harris: Can you recall your whereabouts on 31st October 2018, between 6 pm and 10 pm?

Jade: I remember it because I was working on my own that night. I mean supervising the department on my own, from 5.30 pm when Gillian left. Steve wasn't there, but the Duty Manager, Gerard, locked the doors when we saw the rioters outside. We opened them again at 8.45 pm to let people out, and then we closed on time. I cashed up and walked home down Melwood High Street at about 9.30 pm.

DS Harris: You walked back alone?

Jade: Not like I can afford a cab! And I'm not scared of boys rioting, what's the worst they could do?

Ethan

DS Harris: Can you recall your whereabouts on 31st October 2018, between 6 pm and 10 pm?

Ethan: Halloween? The night Dawn killed herself?

DS Harris: Yes

Ethan: I was at home with my parents all night. Why, what else happened that night?

DS Harris: That's all, Ethan. Thank you.

Marie

DS Harris: Can you recall your whereabouts on 31st October 2018, between 6 pm and 10 pm?

Marie: No. *Interview refused*

Renee

DS Harris: Can you recall your whereabouts on 31st October 2018, between 6 pm and 10 pm?

Renee: Oh God, Halloween. I remember it because I just felt so awful. Really sick and weak all day. You know when you have chills and a fever at the same time? I just couldn't leave the house.

DS Harris: You booked the day off work, I heard?

Renee: Yes.

DS Harris: Rather than taking a sick day? You couldn't have predicted being sick, could you?

Renee: Well, no, I suppose not.

DS Harris: So why did you book it?

Renee: I never work on my birthday, that's why I booked it, not because I knew I'd be sick.

DS Harris: Your birthday is on Halloween?

Renee: Yes, it is. I usually have the best birthday parties. I'm not lying! Check my bloody birth certificate if you like.

DS Harris: So, were you sick, or out for your birthday?

Renee: Well, obviously, I had planned an evening out with my cousin, Claire, and some friends. We'd booked this table at this new cocktail bar in town. Great reviews. But because I felt so awful, I cancelled it and stayed at home. That was for the best, really, given what happened that night with the riots. I mean can you imagine, if I'd gone and got stuck in that! It would have been awful.

DS Harris: Thank you. So, you were at home all evening. Can anyone confirm that?

Renee: Princess was with me.

DS Harris: The cat?

Renee: Yes! How did you know she's a cat?

DS Harris: Anyone else, Renee? A human?

Renee: Ohhh, yes. I had a knock on the door from trick or treaters. I gave them my last chocolate bar.

DS Harris: What time was that?

Renee: Oh, no idea, sorry. It was getting dark.

Debbie

DS Harris: Can you recall your whereabouts on 31st October 2018, between 6 pm and 10 pm?

Debbie: I was at the Homestead community event until about 7.30 pm – then I drove the kids home when I heard about the riots.

DS Harris: Are you OK, Debbie?

Debbie: Um, yes, sorry, I'm still very upset about Dawn's death. Well, you saw me at the funeral.

DS Harris: What time did you get home?

Debbie: I – uh – had to take a longer route home, because of the riots, I can't remember exactly.

DS Harris: Are you sure you're all right? You've gone very red, Debbie. Can I get you something?

Debbie: No, no. I got in, texted Dawn as I told you before. And when she replied, I fell asleep. I felt exhausted. Why are you asking, do you think something else happened?

DS Harris: We're reviewing the case, Debbie. No stone unturned, you know.

Debbie: Good, good. You should do that.

DS Harris: Is there anything else you want to tell me, Debbie?

Debbie: *Pause* No.

20: RIVALS
AND ALIBIS

Monday 10th December 2018 -
Vincent

Okafor's phone rang towards the end of another late evening shift. He picked it up and accepted the transfer through to Jack Dimont.

"Vincent, how the devil are you?"

Jack's voice sounded lighter, refreshed. Okafor envisaged Jack sitting in a remote picturesque location, away from harm. For a fleeting moment, he felt envious of him.

"Very well thank you, Jack, and you? New place working out?"

"Well, there are pros and cons. Witness protection isn't five-star Vincent, but it's better than prison. And that's where I was heading if we hadn't made our little deal. Speaking of which, what can I do you for?"

"I need more information on your local competitors, Jack. You mentioned them briefly during our previous discussions," sighed Okafor.

His initial conversations with Jack focussed on his suppliers and those higher up the chain. The information was enough to link Jack's contacts to a much bigger, South London gang. It had led to some high-profile arrests in the north of the borough.

The Commanders recognised Okafor for his contribution, which buoyed his team. But in the south of the borough, drug-related crime seemed to be rising. To Okafor's frustration, this indicated that someone else had already moved in to fill the gap.

"Ah," chuckled Jack. "I guess the penny's dropped, then? I expect they're already covering the whole turf?"

"Come on, Jack, give me the information," replied Okafor. It was late, and he was in no mood for Jack's guessing games.

"OK, OK. So, there's something I didn't tell you a few weeks ago, Vincent. You were doing me an even bigger favour than you thought with this deal. As I told you, when the boys and I got involved in all this, we were only warehousing boxes for the big guys. We didn't even know it was drugs and stolen goods.

"Before we knew it, we were laundering money through the businesses and distributing drugs. And we got on with it, but we didn't have big ambitions, we didn't want any trouble. We stuck to our turf and kept it all plodding along. I suppose you could say we were complacent, not keeping up with the times.

"Now earlier this year, some of the lads tell me that the addicts are buying from other sellers. People are selling drugs that aren't ours, for a lower price. By the time you'd picked me up, I'd already lost about half my trade to this rival group."

"You can't be serious? How did you square that with your suppliers, Jack?" asked Vincent, stunned by this new admission. He knew that Jack wasn't the only local player, but he had no idea that he'd lost half his trade.

"I told them another group was on the patch, and they told me to sort it out myself. And they said that if I didn't, they'd remove me. Well, the boys and I tried, but we didn't know where to start. As I said, we'd got complacent."

"What did you do to keep them off your back?"

"So, we were in a pickle; had to pretend to the suppliers that we'd sorted it out. Then we pretended we'd made the sales and gave them our own money, so they didn't suspect anything. We didn't have a plan for when that ran out, though."

Okafor sighed again. He dug the tips of his fingers into the side of his head.

"What can you tell me about the rival group itself, Jack?" he asked, his voice strained.

"Well, they have their supply of drugs coming in, which they sell cheap. Rumour has it that an operation from Surrey has pushed up into New Grange, Melwood and South Croydon. And they don't only sell drugs, mind. They're in the sex trade, running brothels, trafficking women so I've heard, though I never saw any of it myself. Unlicensed bars too, to launder money through. You know yourself how many of those have cropped up recently."

"Who's running it in our local area, Jack? Who's pulling all the strings? You must have tried to find out?"

"Well, wouldn't I like to know!" Jack laughed down the phone. "We did try, but no-one knew anything, or they wouldn't say anything, at least. They call her 'The Boss,' that's all I know."

"Her?"

"Yes, Vincent, 'her.' It's the 21st century; women can be baddies too."

"So," replied Okafor, "we have a woman in Surrey selling drugs, running brothels, laundering money through cash bars. She saw your turf in Croydon as a weak spot and muscled in as a rival."

"Yes, Vincent, that's right. And now I'm gone, I suppose it's her turf until the big boys from London come down to reclaim what's theirs."

Assuming they don't come for you first, thought Okafor bitterly. He ended the call and resisted the urge to throw the phone against the wall.

By removing the Dimonts from the area, he'd opened up the remaining turf for another group, who sounded slicker and more resourceful than Jack's. Now, he faced a new battle against a faceless, nameless enemy. An impatient knock on the door broke his thoughts. He beckoned DS Harris in.

"Sir, the team have completed the review of the alibis from Janice and Caitlin's colleagues."

"Joanne," he stopped her and rubbed his eyes. "Do you mind if we pick this up tomorrow morning, it's been quite a day."

"I'm afraid I do mind, sir. I need to debrief you on this immediately."

DS Harris gripped the report tightly; her knuckles had gone white.

"Sit down, Joanne, and talk me through it. And at least give me the good news first."

"Sir, we've looked into the whereabouts of the seven colleagues, on both the 3rd August and 31st October. We spoke to Peter Goldman. He confirms that Karen was at home on both evenings. There isn't CCTV on her road, but we don't see her car on any other roads on either evening. On both nights, she receives but doesn't answer calls from Pete, though. He says she'd lost her phone both times, he was just calling to help locate it. The phone triangulation does put the phone at home."

"Not watertight, but pretty close," muttered Okafor.

"Second, the Manager, Gillian. Her husband Kevin provided her alibi on 3rd August, and we have a neighbour confirming him at home. There's one camera at the Fair Lawns Estate front gate; neither Gillian nor her car leave all evening. On 31st October, she's seen by dozens of people at the Homestead Community Halloween event. She's there from 6 pm, and locks herself and others in, between 7.45 pm-ish and 9 pm. There are no cameras in Homestead, but the estate camera picks her up at 9.30 pm, and she doesn't go back out."

Okafor nodded; that seemed watertight unless Gillian could be in two places at once.

"Next, Jade. She lied to us about the 3rd of August; she wasn't at home. A camera catches her walking up Melwood High Street at 7 pm, then she turns towards Croydon. We've tracked her to the town centre at 8 pm-ish, and then we lose her off the main High Street. She reappears at about 2 am walking the same route back home. Now I know that raises questions, but on the 31st she was the one working the evening shift at the supermarket. She didn't leave until 9.30 pm, then walked back down Melwood High

Street to her home."

"Good. We should ask Jade why she lied about the 3rd, though. She might have seen something. Now, the next ones?"

DS Harris took a deep breath and looked down at the table.

"Ethan Hutchins, the young guy. On 3rd August, he told us he was in the pub, and the landlord confirmed this. Now we've looked at pub CCTV, and we see Ethan stumble to the toilets at around 9.30 pm. He only reappears at 10.30 pm. So, either he was in the bathroom for an hour, or he slipped out the back door and went somewhere else. On the 31st, he emerged from the Melwood backroads at 9.20 pm and loitered outside the supermarket. Then, he followed Jade at a distance back down Melwood High Street, then went home."

"Weird, very weird. Add Ethan to the list to bring in. Next one?"

"Renee. She said she was at home ill on 3rd August. But, that was a lie. We have her car popping up at 8 pm in Melwood, driving up towards Homestead, where she goes off-grid. She returns, via the same route, at about 10.45 pm. No phone data for the entire period, she'd switched it off."

"Jesus, that would give her time to park up, switch the vehicle, commit the crime and switch back."

"In theory, sir, yes. But she's harder to pin down on the 31st. We asked her a couple of days ago, and she said she was ill again. Her phone puts her at home, and her car stayed there all night. She gets a load of messages and calls through the evening from known contacts, which she picks up, at home. Curiously, though, there is one call, unanswered, from an unknown number at 8 pm. The caller triangulates to the area around Dawn's house."

Okafor rubbed his head.

"Let me go to Marie. On 3rd August, her phone puts her at home in east Melwood. She messages Renee a few times, including once at 10 pm. Now, if that's her sending the message, she couldn't have killed Janice. But, on Halloween, we pick her up leaving her house at 6.15 pm, driving to a road near Dawn's, where we lose her. Her phone is off, and she reappears the next morning, driving straight out of the backroads and into work."

"So, what on earth was she doing all night?" Okafor's mind raced. Were Renee and Marie responsible for the deaths of three colleagues? Did Renee commit the first murders, and then send Marie to kill Dawn? The evidence certainly pointed towards that.

"We need to bring Renee and Marie in immediately, to explain themselves. We should get access to the content of the messages, too. And Jade and Ethan, call them in, too."

"I'm afraid not, sir," said DS Harris, her hands shaking. "There's someone else we need to bring in before them."

"Who?"

"I haven't given you the debrief on Debbie Gomez, yet."

"What do you mean?" asked Okafor, as the blood drained from his face. He thought of Debbie and her helpful, thorough interviews, her remorse and sadness. Surely she wasn't involved?

"On the 3rd of August, sir, she told us that her friends were at her house in Melwood until 10 pm. There's no CCTV, but we checked with them, and they said they definitely left by 9.40 pm. That would have given Debbie ample time to leave and commit the crime."

"But her husband confirmed she stayed at home after they left, and there's no motive. What about Halloween?"

"We have her car driving through Melwood. She sped through the store lorry park, exited onto the main road then turned into the backroads. She told us about that. What she didn't tell us was that she turned into Dawn's street at 8.07 pm," Joanne paused as Okafor's mouth dropped.

"There isn't CCTV on Dawn's road, but Debbie exits it again at 8.15 pm, and drives around the corner into her road."

"It's not enough time to kill someone and stage it in that way, is it? What about the text, between her and Dawn and 8.30 pm? It doesn't make sense, Joanne."

"It doesn't, sir, I know. But why on earth didn't she tell us she was there? Has this concerned and mourning friend thing just been an act? It would explain her behaviour at the funeral; saying she knew the truth and apologising to Dawn."

Vincent took a deep breath and tried to take it all in.

"There are huge holes in this Joanne, huge holes. The person who killed Janice and Caitlin so professionally wouldn't drive their own car into Dawn's road on CCTV. Would both Karen and the husband both turn a blind eye to it? I don't believe Debbie Gomez is capable of this unless she's the world's best actress." Okafor rubbed his eyes and temples again.

"But you're right. Debbie's alibi doesn't stand up for the 3rd. She's at the scene of the crime on the 31st. You heard her saying she knew Dawn's death wasn't suicide. She has a lot of explaining to do, even more so than the others. Arrange surveillance on her house overnight to make sure she stays indoors. We'll bring her in first thing tomorrow under caution and secure a warrant to search her house."

"Yes, sir."

21: IT WASN'T ME

Tuesday 11th December 2018 - Debbie & Vincent

D ebbie's incessant alarm woke her up to dark, damp fog swirling outside the window. She ran through her schedule for the day: packed lunches, school runs, Christmas shopping, wrapping presents, chores. It wasn't glamorous, but it was the kind of day she preferred at the moment; busy but not too challenging.

It had been a strange month since Gillian announced Dawn's death in the cold and crowded staff canteen. In the week after the announcement, Debbie's sense of grief had consumed her. The shock came in waves every time someone mentioned Dawn's name.

Another week passed, and she found it slightly easier to tell herself that Dawn was at peace. After three weeks, she felt a little lighter. Life was much less scary when she wasn't pursuing the truth about Janice and Caitlin. Of course, nagging feelings still emerged at quiet moments of the day, and they often kept her awake at night. She felt a particular pang when she saw a young girl from New Grange looking tired or sad. Debbie knew something terrible was happening to them, yet she was too scared to get to the bottom of it or go to the police.

She was frightened of the masked figure she'd seen outside Dawn's house on Halloween night. She was sure they'd killed Dawn to protect the same secret that Janice and Caitlin had discovered. She was also sure they'd stolen Dawn's phone and then sent her a reassuring message, pretending all was well.

She had just finished the lunches when the doorbell rang twice, followed by a short sharp knock. Joe ran down the stairs and opened the door before her, as Debbie zipped up her tracksuit and ran to join him.

"Mrs Gomez," said the uniformed officer. "We need you to come to the station to answer questions about the murder of Janice Locke and Caitlin Murphy, and the death of Dawn Smith."

"Oh no, I really can't," replied Debbie as Joe rolled his eyes. "I've got such a busy day. Why didn't you call me to arrange an appointment?"

"Mrs Gomez," said the other uniformed officer, "we have the authority to bring you in under caution. It's your decision whether we invoke that or not."

"What?" Debbie and Joe gasped at the same time. They looked to DS Harris, who nodded gravely to confirm. Joe started to protest further, but Debbie held her hand up to him.

"There's been some kind of mistake," she sighed. "Joe, take the kids to school and don't worry. I'll see you when you get home," she continued, as she followed DS Harris into the police car.

An hour later, she sat with a tape recorder ahead of her, and a mirror on her right-hand side. Two empty chairs were opposite her, nearest to the door, and there was another one to her left. She'd declined the offer of legal representation because, after all, why would she need it?

DS Harris entered the room with an older colleague who Debbie didn't recognise. DC Jameson, an embattled fifty-something from the Violent Crime Unit, introduced himself in a broad northern accent.

"Why have you forced me here and then left me sitting alone for an hour?" demanded Debbie, as she drummed her fingers on the table edge.

"We're questioning you in connection with the murders of Janice Locke and Caitlin Murphy," DC Jameson answered. "And the death of Dawn

Smith. You have waived your right to representation. For the tape, please state your name."

"Oh, right. It's Debbie," she said and then saw him roll his eyes. "Oh, Deborah Anne Gomez, sorry. Can I just ask…"

"We'd like to start, Deborah, on the 3rd August," he said, cutting her off. "Where were you between 9.30 pm and 10 pm?"

"I've told you this! I was at home. I had my neighbours, the Millers, around for dinner and drinks. They left at, I don't know, 10ish, then Joe and I tidied up and went to bed."

"We've spoken to your neighbours, Debbie," said DC Jameson, leaning forwards towards her. "They say they left at 9.40 pm."

"Oh, well, perhaps they did. We'd had a few glasses of wine, and I could have got the timing wrong, what does it matter?"

"What exactly were you doing Deborah, after the Millers left?"

"I've told you, tidying up and then we went to bed. You can't think I sent the neighbours home and then dashed off to kill Janice and Caitlin?"

Debbie's heart sank as she looked at DS Harris and DC Jameson and realised that was exactly what they thought. Her leg began to shake under the table.

"No, no, I was their friend, I would never…" she spluttered, feeling a rising panic in her chest.

"Ask Joe, he'll tell you. I was at home with him after they left."

"We will ask Joe," said DS Harris. "Let's move to last week, Thursday 6th December, though we may return to 3rd August later."

"The 6th, Dawn's funeral," muttered Debbie, and DS Harris nodded.

"You said a few words at the funeral, Deborah, why was that?"

"Well, I felt awful that no-one, not even her family, was going to say anything. I wanted to say something nice about her."

"You said 'I knew the truth, I'm sorry I didn't prevent it.' What did that mean?" Asked DC Jameson in a stern voice.

The soles of Debbie's feet and the palms of her hands began to tingle, and a cold shiver ran up her spine. She fiddled with a hairband on her wrist.

DC Jameson sighed and looked at DS Harris, who nodded.

"Why, Debbie, at the same funeral, did you say to Karen Goldman: 'We both know it wasn't suicide'?"

Debbie recalled the conversation with Karen after the service. She'd said exactly that, and then she'd seen DS Harris outside the toilets when she left. She took a deep breath. It was time to come clean about her suspicions.

"Yes, I said that because I think someone killed Dawn," she whispered, as tears welled up in her eyes. "I've been too scared to say anything. I'll tell you everything I know, but you have to protect me, and my family, because I can't end up like Janice and Caitlin."

The detectives raised their eyebrows.

"Start at the beginning Debbie," urged DS Harris, with a small glance at the mirror on Debbie's right.

"Back in September, you asked me about my colleagues and something called 'Princesses'. Afterwards, I looked out for any strange behaviour, like you said. I noticed that some of the younger girls on the checkouts looked tired and upset all the time. I knew something awful was happening to them. I told Karen, but she wasn't interested, so I spoke to Dawn on inspection day. She said she'd noticed the same thing."

"What did Dawn say to you?"

"She said it was obvious what was going on. I asked her whether this thing with the girls was linked to something called 'Princesses'? She nodded, and she told me she knew who was behind it all. She was going to come and talk to you later in the week, she said. She told me not to say anything, so I didn't. Next thing I know, she's dead."

Debbie heard the desperation in her voice. She'd not explained events very well, and she hadn't told them what she saw at Dawn's house on Halloween. But then, should she mention that? Her trip to Dawn's road on the night of the murder could incriminate her further. She felt her heart pounding against her chest; it was too hot in the room, and it felt like the walls were closing in on her.

"If this is true, Debbie, why not come forward to us in the last month?" asked DS Harris. "If these girls are in danger, and your friends have been murdered, why not come and speak to us?"

Debbie grabbed two tissues from the table and wiped her eyes and face with her shaking hands.

"I was scared that I'd end up like them, dead. I told Karen what Dawn had said to me, and Karen said to forget it and protect myself and my family. So that's what I did, even though I felt awful every day. That's why I said those things at the funeral, because I know what happened, and I am sorry I didn't do something between that Monday and Halloween."

"But you did do something, at that time, didn't you?" pushed DC Jameson.

"You sent Dawn a lot of messages, which she did not reply to, and then you paid her a visit."

Debbie's heart sank as DC Jameson produced two pictures of her car entering and leaving Dawn's road.

"I did, I can explain," she said weakly, as her voice shook.

"Please do, Deborah, because you are in a lot of trouble here. You're at the scene of the crime, within the time-of-death window." DC Jameson raised his voice and leant forward over the table.

"I was driving home from Homestead, there were riots, and I wanted to get my children home. I had to drive a different way. Then I realised we were close to Dawn's house. She hadn't replied to my texts, so I pulled up outside."

"Did you enter the house, Debbie?" asked DS Harris.

"No, I didn't, the lights in the house were off, and I had the kids in the car. So, after a few minutes, I thought better of it and drove off."

"Come on, Debbie, stop messing us around," DC Jameson shouted. "You realised Dawn was on to something about you, so you took the chance to silence her. You've done it before, right?"

"No, no, you cannot think that, please. My children were in the car for God's sake! Ask my son, ask Marco, he'll tell you. I did not get out of the car! You're looking at the wrong person; I was not the only one there that night!"

"Wait, what do you mean, Debbie?" asked DS Harris.

"When I turned my car lights back on, I saw someone, in black clothes and a mask, coming out of Dawn's side gate. That's who you should be looking for, not me. I texted Dawn when I got home, and she replied saying she was OK. That's why I didn't say anything until she didn't come to work. But it was probably the person in the mask, who killed her and stole her phone to text me, right?"

"Deborah," sighed DC Jameson in disbelief. "It's remarkable, and convenient that you remember this figure only once we place you at the crime scene. I think you did leave the car, you killed Dawn and then stole the phone to reply to your own message."

"No, no, I didn't, please."

"Dawn knew your secret?"

"No."

"Janice and Caitlin knew it too?"

"No."

"What is 'Princesses', Deborah?"

"I don't know, but you've got this all wrong!"

Her head was spinning. She needed time to get everything she knew in order. She needed Joe and Marco here with her, to prove she wasn't a murderer.

DC Jameson terminated the interview, and he and DS Harris left her alone in the room.

On the other side of the mirror, Vincent Okafor had watched the entire interview. Despite the mounting evidence against Debbie, he still felt inclined to believe her. Her reactions were the classic ones of innocent people, not the guilty.

"Sir," said Joanne, as she entered the room with DC Jameson.

"Well done in there, both of you," praised Okafor. "Very interesting indeed."

"Do you believe her, sir?" asked DC Jameson.

"I don't think she's lying, as it happens. But there is so much more we need to ask her. We need to check the stories with Joe and her son," replied Okafor, with a sigh

"And in the meantime, we should start on the others who have some explaining to do. Renee, Marie, Jade, Ethan."

As they left the room, a uniformed officer approached them, red-faced and breathless.

"Sirs, Ma'am, we've completed the search of the Gomez house. You're not going to believe it."

Okafor glanced nervously at DS Harris and DC Jameson, and then back to the officer.

"At the bottom of a wardrobe, we found a handbag with a purse and phone in it. It's Caitlin Murphy's, sir."

Okafor felt like someone had punched him in the stomach. His eyes widened, and he had to lean on the wall of the corridor for support. DS Harris' mouth was open with shock.

Could Debbie have another unfortunate 'wrong place, wrong time' explanation for this? Or was she a triple murderer? He now had to admit that the latter was more likely.

"DC Jameson," ordered Okafor. "Change of plan. Forget the other colleagues. Charge her with all three murders. Prepare to question her on this handbag. And DS Harris, get the husband and son in here now."

Okafor and DS Harris returned to the viewing room. They watched DC Jameson charge a sobbing Debbie Gomez with the murders of Janice Locke, Caitlin Murphy and Dawn Smith.

Excerpt: Joseph Gomez interview, Wednesday 12 December 2018, 11.15 am

Officer: What time did your neighbours, the Millers, leave on Friday 3rd August?

Joe: This was four months ago. I said 10 pm last time, I think, I still believe that's correct.

Officer: Why do your neighbours say 9.40 pm then?

Joe: I don't know, I honestly don't, I suppose one of us lost track of time. But it doesn't bloody matter, because whether they left at 9.40, 9.50 or 10, I have told you that my wife was with me after, cleaning up, and then we went to bed together. She didn't leave my sight!

Officer: Sir, calm down, please.

Joe: No, I won't, my wife is innocent, all she has done is try to find out what happened to her friends, and you're holding her like a prisoner with no real evidence.

Excerpt: Marco Gomez interview, Wednesday 12th December 2018, 11.45 am
Present: Joseph Gomez (Parent)

Officer: You're doing very well, Marco. Now, do you remember where you were on Halloween, at about 7.30 pm?

Marco: Yeah, we were at the Halloween party in Homestead, my sister wanted to go.

Officer: And when did you leave?

Marco: I don't know, about 7.45 before the

doors locked. Dad told Mum to take us home because of the riots.

Officer: And did you go straight home?

Marco: We drove to Melwood Junction, but we had to cut through the store because there were people hitting cars. The people who'd been rioting.

Officer: And you stopped somewhere else, do you remember?

Marco: Yeah, on a side road. Mum asked me to check on Twitter to see if our road was safe.

Officer: And what did your Mum do, while you checked?

Marco: Nothing, just sat in the car with us.

Officer: Did she get out, Marco? We need to know if she did.

Marco: No, she didn't. I know she didn't.

Officer: Are you absolutely sure?

Joe: He's answered the question.

Officer: OK, Marco, it's OK, we just need to be sure. Now did anything else happen, before or as you left?

Marco: Mum said she saw someone, with a mask on, by one of the houses.

Officer: Did you see it?

Marco: I saw something, it could have been a person, but it happened quickly, and I'd been looking down at my phone.

Excerpt: Karen Goldman interview, Thursday 13th December 2018, 4 pm

Officer: Thank you, Karen. Now, our search of Debbie's house uncovered a fascinating item. Might you know what that is?

Karen: I don't know, she has a lot of interesting items, you tell me.

Officer: A bag, purse and phone that did not belong to Debbie. Are you with me?

Karen: Yes, yes, I am. I can tell you how that got there, though.

Officer: Please do.

Karen: We were doing a locker search a few months ago, early October, the day you lot came to the store. Debbie was telling me about her chat with Vincent, and then she opened a locker and found it in there. I told her to hand it in, but she wanted to look at it, find out if there was something on the phone before she did. So, she took it home.

Officer: Why didn't she give it to us after she'd looked?

Karen: I don't know, I kept telling her to, but she was intent on finding out who'd killed them before she came to you, she thought she'd be safer that way. There was no telling her, until after Dawn died, when she finally was scared enough to stop digging around.

Officer: Did Debbie tell you about her suspicions regarding Dawn's death?

Karen: She told me that Dawn had believed her theory about the girls at work and that it was linked to Janice and Caitlin's murder. Debbie said Dawn was going to the police. And, after Gill announced that Dawn had died, Debbie told me she'd seen someone at Dawn's house on Halloween.

Officer: Did you believe her, about the girls, the person?

Karen: *sighs* Well, yes maybe, but I wanted to keep out of it. I told her to stay quiet. I mean, look at what happened to Dawn. Look, Debbie is nosy, it's the way she is, and she's too smart for her job, so she gets preoccupied when she sees a mystery to solve. She wants to help people, and it's got her into heaps of trouble. I know how it must look, but she is innocent. That woman is my best friend and she is not a murderer.

22: ATTACK AT THE GARAGES

Friday 21st December 2018 - Jade

Jade clocked out after a gruelling 10-hour shift at the supermarket. The Friday before Christmas was usually one of the busiest days of the year, and today had lived up to expectations. Queues at the checkouts were long, and trolleys crunched against each other in aisles. She'd even seen violence between two customers over the last bag of carrots. Renee intervened, ripped the bag in two and gave them half the loose carrots each. Then, she told them where the carrots would go next if they continued to argue.

She was keen to get home and rest after working her sixth day in a row. She'd finally got the overtime she wanted because they were yet another supervisor down. She could barely move around the store without hearing someone talking about Debbie Gomez, who had been charged with the murders of three of their colleagues.

At first, Jade had thought the arrest was a mistake. Out of everyone, Debbie had been the friendliest and most supportive towards her over the last few months. It was almost like Debbie had known she was in trouble and wanted to help.

But ten days after the arrest, rumours and suspicions about a secret past-life had emerged. Only Karen remained entirely convinced of Debbie's innocence.

Jade wandered out through the store and pulled her black coat tight around her. She wanted to hide her uniform to avoid any further questions from customers. She paused only to say goodbye to Gillian and Renee, who were arguing at the supervisor desk.

"That being said, Renee, we aren't allowed to sell carrots from those bags loose, so… ah, Jade, you're off?"

Gillian's harried, pinched look from a few months ago had returned in full force since Debbie's arrest.

"Yes," replied Jade. "I wanted to say goodbye and happy Christmas, Gillian, I know you're going away to see your family tomorrow."

"That's right, yes, of course, I am," muttered

Gillian. She wrinkled her nose and looked back down towards the schedule.

Renee frowned, then turned towards Jade with a sympathetic smile. Renee looked a little tired too, but she retained a healthy glow that Gillian very much lacked.

"Are you OK, Jade?" she asked in her low voice. "Have you heard from Junior, I mean, your Dad and the others?"

"No, I haven't," Jade sighed, and remembered that Renee used to spend a lot of time with her oldest brother. "And I won't. It's safer that way, isn't it?"

"I'm sorry, Jade. You know, I'm around over Christmas, if you want to pop over, or go for a drink?"

Jade looked up into Renee's eyes gratefully. Gillian stood in the middle, looking back and forth between them, her nose wrinkled.

"You can go now, Renee, Karen's just arrived," said Gillian. "Her and Mard – I mean Marie will have to hold the fort together tonight, there's no other option. Off you go then, both of you."

Jade exchanged a final smile with Renee and dragged her heavy legs out of the store, desperate for an early night. She hoped not to get a call from the man, giving her instructions on where to go that evening. She was thankful that she was no longer forced to work at The Castle. In the last month, a new group of girls who didn't speak much English had replaced her there.

Jade assumed that they could get away with paying these girls less. Or, perhaps the men had started complaining about the cuts on her arms. Either way, she was now made to go out with small groups of others, usually boys, to sell drugs.

The irony hadn't escaped Jade. She'd hated her Dad's businesses, because of the effect drugs had on vulnerable people like her mother. Yet now, she was working for the criminals who'd forced her Dad out of Melwood.

She tried not to dwell on it too much. She'd escaped The Castle, her savings were building up, and she had her secret way of releasing her frustration that she controlled. She stroked her arms before letting herself into her house.

She unlocked her bedroom door and switched on the small, second-hand TV set she'd treated herself to a few weeks ago. She lay on the bed and let her eyes close. A theme tune from a soap played, though she could barely hear it as her body was already drifting into sleep. Then her phone rang, and the familiar voice of the bald man crackled down the line.

"Jade, we need you in South Croydon tonight, we're going to try selling round the garages."

"No, I can't, please.... I'm so tired," she whispered, as she struggled to open her eyes.

"Too tired to stand around and collect money? Come on, Jade. You know how this works. You can go to The Castle instead, for a lie-down, if you're missing it?"

Jade fell silent and rubbed her head; she felt a sharp pain behind her eyes.

"The garages, South Croydon, one hour. The other guys are from New Grange too, you might know them," he chuckled.

She hung up the phone, threw it down on the bed and dug her nails into her forearms. She took off her supermarket uniform and layered herself with T-shirts and a jumper. It wasn't bitterly cold outside, but cold enough to shiver after a few hours of standing around. She turned off the television and bolted her bedroom door closed again.

She paused by the kitchen, grabbed some-one else's bottle of vodka from under the sink and stepped into the night. Her body felt warm under her clothes, but the wind whipped her thin, blond hair away from her face and made her cheeks and nose tingle. She took a few welcome sips of vodka, which burnt her throat.

As soon as she reached the row of old garages, she spotted a huddle of young boys. There were three of them, and by the looks of them, they were indeed from New Grange. She kept her distance and stood on the periphery of their crude and laddish conversation.

"You buying, love?" one of them shouted at her. He looked a bit younger than her and had a gelled man-bun hairstyle, overbite and a spotty face. She ignored him.

"You're a bit early, darling," leered another shorter, heavier boy. "But I've got something for you in the meantime."

She grimaced as he grabbed his crotch through his joggers.

"Enough now," ordered the third boy, the tallest one. "He's here."

The bald man approached the tall boy and passed him a large package.

"Sorry I'm late. I was talking to the boss. She's not happy at the moment, so you had better do well tonight. Right then," he announced, in his East London drawl. "Lay low and wait for the buyers to come to you. Everything is up by £10 a bag and no negotiation, 'cos they can't get it anywhere else. Alright?"

They all nodded.

"Look after blondie," he gestured towards Jade. "She's with you tonight, selling."

The boys turned to Jade with surprised looks on their faces, but they nodded again. After he left, she followed the boys around the back of the garages, which bordered an old housing estate.

Buyers appeared, and often went straight to the tall boy, who somehow knew what they wanted. Most of the buyers blanked Jade, which suited her fine. She perched on the wall, swigging from the vodka bottle when the others were selling.

"Thought it would be busier tonight," said the boy with the man-bun to the tall boy at around 10 pm. "Since we took down the Dimonts."

The fat boy sniggered. Tall-boy stretched his arms out and yawned before responding.

"Yeah, well they were a bunch of amateurs weren't they. They couldn't even control their turf or stop me switching over to 'Princesses'."

"Bit of a weird name for a gang, isn't it?" commented fat-boy.

"We're not supposed to use that name anymore," warned man-bun, as he scuffed his feet against loose paving.

"Yeah, true," agreed tall-boy. "Whatever it's called, I'm glad the boss forced Jack Dimont out. Him and his sons, always walking around New Grange like they owned it. They'll get what they deserve. They snitched, and people know where he's gone."

"Where's that then?" asked Jade, as she staggered towards the conversation.

"Oh, she talks," jeered fat-boy, and the other two laughed. "What do you care, blondie?"

"I know them, the Dimonts. And when they come back, they'll get you first. I'll make sure of it," she slurred. "You traitors."

The three boys laughed back at her; anger bubbled through her veins.

"You're here too, blondie, and as if they'd listen to a dumb thing like you," growled tall-boy, flanked by the other two. Jade took a deep breath, a sip from her vodka bottle, and stepped towards them.

"They wouldn't listen to little bitches like you either, 'cos you'll always be at the bottom of the pile. Selling drugs and going to prison, to make money for rich people who don't give a shit about you."

"Say that again, blondie," dared fat-boy, as he stepped towards her with his fists clenched. Jade looked up and met his eye. At that moment, she didn't care that there were three of them, or that they were bigger than her, or that they might hurt her.

"I said, you're all bitches, and you're all low life New Grange pieces of shit." She revelled at the shocked and confused looks on their faces.

Before Jade knew it, something hard connected with the side of her head. The vodka bottle slipped from her hand and smashed against the ground as another blow hit her legs. She collapsed and felt more kicks all over her body. She heard a cracking sound, accompanied by a searing pain in her chest; at least one of her ribs had broken. When the boys finally paused for breath, she rolled over and vomited over the concrete. She felt a rough hand on her shoulder. Fat-boy ripped her jacket from her and pulled her jumper over her head, revealing her forearms.

"What the hell!" shouted fat-boy as he dropped her back to the ground. She could taste blood in her mouth, metallic and warm, as she struggled to stay conscious.

"Looks like she does have a death wish," muttered tall-boy, as he looked down at her arms. "And someone's coming, time to get out of here boys, grab the gear and run."

She heard their footsteps running away as she tried and failed to sit up from the ground. Her throat was tight, and her whole body ached and burned. She tried to breathe in, but her chest tightened, and everything spun around her. Could she hear more footsteps running towards her, or was it her brain thudding against her skull?

In the distance, she heard someone calling her name. It sounded familiar, like Ethan's voice. Her breathing became shallow, and her eyes dropped.

The sleep that she'd so desperately craved earlier was coming, but this time, against her will. She needed to get herself off the floor, but all the energy had evaporated from her limbs, and her eyes refused to open.

As she slipped out of consciousness, she felt a weight pushing on her shoulder. She heard her name repeated over and over again. With all the strength she had left, she fluttered her eyes and saw a blurred version of Ethan's face in front of her. Then it all went dark.

Excerpt: Debbie Gomez questioning. Friday 21 December 2018 – 2.30 pm

Officer: Tell us again about this figure outside Dawn Smith's house on Halloween.

Debbie: I've told you. They were tall, thin - slender, I suppose. All their clothes were black. Trousers, a hoodie, and they had one of those Guy Fawkes masks on. I've told you all of this.

Officer: Were they male, female?

Debbie: I don't know.

Officer: If you had to guess?

Debbie: Male, I suppose. Something in the way they moved after they saw me. But I'm not sure. Please, my children must have told you that I didn't leave the car. I've explained how I got the phone, please, this wasn't me.

Officer: Then who was it, Debbie?

Debbie: I don't know. It's someone at work. They're putting these girls in danger. Janice, Caitlin and Dawn found out who it was, and then someone murdered them.

Officer: Karen Goldman tells us you suspected Renee Beck and Marie Webster?

Debbie: I did, but I have no proof. Renee's cat is called Princess, and she's been off work a lot recently. I saw her taking an envelope from Gillian's husband which looked like it had money in it. Karen saw Marie spending loads of money in town. They all sound so silly on their own, but yes, I thought maybe they could be behind it.

Renee is from New Grange, too, where the girls are from.

Officer: That's all well and good but unlike you, we have no proof that Renee was at Dawn's around the time of death and we haven't found missing evidence in her wardrobe.

Debbie: Please, this wasn't me! I was just trying to find out who it was; you have to believe me. It's all linked: 'Princesses', the girls at work, Janice, Caitlin, Dawn. And those girls are still suffering because you have got the wrong person here. Talk to the girls. I'll give you their names: Stacy Mackenzie, Louisa Cooper, Jade Dimont. Please talk to them.

23: THE MASTERPLAN

Saturday 22nd December 2018 -
Ethan

Ethan stood outside the supermarket, two hours early for his Saturday evening shift. His eyelids drooped heavily, and he could feel the puffy, dark circles under his eyes. Images of the brutal attack he'd witnessed last night played over in his head, haunting him. Three boys, around his own age, kicking and punching Jade as she lay there, defenceless. He'd run as fast as he could, scared the boys off and called an ambulance. It made all his evenings of watching worthwhile. Though, he wished he'd been closer, rather than on a roof, and that he'd got there sooner.

Jade was unconscious when he reached her.

He thought he saw a flicker in her eyes when he'd arrived, but after that, they wouldn't open again. The ambulance raced through the bright Christmas lights towards the hospital. The paramedics had whispered urgently to each other and exchanged concerned looks. In those moments, they'd confirmed Ethan's worst fears; they weren't sure whether Jade would survive.

He had looked down on her tiny, broken body, her arms covered in self-inflicted cuts, and prayed that she would fight. There was a better future for her, away from the horrible world in which she'd become entangled. He'd run behind the medical entourage at the hospital until they whisked her into intensive care. He'd waited for hours, deep into the night, until a nurse informed him that they'd treated all her injuries. They would keep her sedated, in a critical yet stable condition for the rest of the night. Despite his protests, the nurse had insisted that he go home and return in the morning.

At 9 am, when visiting time started, he'd returned, and sat next to Jade again. Various machines and tubes were sustaining her and, hopefully, helping her to recover. He felt so guilty as he watched over her. He'd let her down by not finding out who was behind her misery and informing the police.

A couple of times, he thought he saw Jade's eyes flutter open and he leapt out of his seat. But, when he stood up to move closer, they'd closed again. He'd have stayed longer if visiting hours hadn't ended at 2 pm. At that point, he'd travelled to the supermarket, to convince another girl to report the crimes of the organisation called 'Princesses'.

He entered the supermarket and battled through the crowds in search of Stacy. He wandered past the Customer Services, then the checkouts. He couldn't see her through all the people finishing their Christmas shopping. He finally spotted her talking to Renee and Marie at the supervisor desk.

As he approached them, Renee and Marie stopped talking and stared at him with hostile, suspicious looks on their faces.

"Err, hi," he said, and he looked directly at Stacy. She looked up at him and gave a weak smile, but then lowered her head back down again, eyes on the floor.

"You're not working until five, Ethan, what do you want?" tutted Renee, who looked hot and bothered under a Christmas fleece.

"I need to speak to Stacy," he replied. Marie raised her eyebrows and Renee folded her arms in front of her chest.

"It's urgent," he muttered. "I need to tell Stace something in private."

"If it's about Jade, she already knows. I told her," replied Renee. She moved her hand to her hip; her left arm now shielded him from Stacy.

"How do you know about that?" asked Ethan.

"She messaged me to say she couldn't come in to work this evening. Gillian has gone on an early holiday and Debbie has got herself locked up, so someone needs to be in charge of this!"

Renee pointed aggressively towards the schedule in Marie's hands.

"Anyway," sighed Renee with a wave of her hand, before Ethan could reply. "I called Jade back, and she told me all about it. She got attacked, then found by you and taken to the hospital."

She's awake, thought Ethan, and a wave of relief swept across him. But why was Renee hostile and accusatory, rather than grateful that he'd been there?

"Yeah, that's right," he retorted. "I called the ambulance and went to the hospital with Jade. I was there last night and this morning. I saved her!"

"So," interjected Marie, with a terse smile. "You just happened to be there late at night, when Jade was walking through the Croydon garages?"

"Yes, good question Marie!" added Renee, and she stared hard into Ethan's eyes. "Bit of a coincidence, isn't it?"

"Yeah, I guess so," he answered, feeling his cheeks flush. "It's a good job I was there, though."

"Well, we don't believe it was a coincidence, so leave us alone," said Marie. Renee nodded and put a protective arm around Stacy.

"Stacy, please," he begged. "Stace, I need to talk to you. It's a-about 'Princesses'."

Renee and Marie glanced at each other as Stacy's eyes widened in shock.

"What are you on about? What do you mean by that?" demanded Renee, but Ethan didn't answer. Stacy stepped away from Renee and tip-toed towards him.

"Oh, Stacy, no," sighed Marie. "I need you to take over from June. She's due a break, and there's no-one else here until 5 pm."

"I'm sorry, Marie, I won't be long," mumbled Stacy.

"Ethan," called Renee as he turned to walk away. "I am watching you. Five minutes max with Stacy, and you had better be here for your shift later. Karen's covering for Jade, but she'll need help."

He nodded and led Stacy away. Behind him, he heard Renee swear loudly, and slam the schedule down onto the supervisor desk.

"Ethan, what the hell?" gasped Stacy as they hurried out of earshot of any other staff members or customers. He turned to her and put his hands on her elbows.

"Stace, you know we spoke a few months back, and a couple of times since then. I keep asking you if you were OK. But I know you're not, I know about 'Princesses'."

"How? How do you know about that? Please don't tell anyone. Promise you won't say anything, Ethan."

Her breathing quickened, and her cheeks flushed despite the chilly air.

"Please, calm down Stace, I've known for ages, and it doesn't matter how," he replied in a harsh whisper.

"There are other girls from the supermarket, forced to work at that old Castle building and sell drugs. I know you don't have a choice, and I know it's making you miserable."

She nodded as tears started welling up in her eyes. Ethan pressed on.

"I've been investigating 'Princesses', looking into it, so I can tell the police and keep you all safe. I've got so much information on them; where they operate, where they store and sell the drugs. I know everything, apart from the main person running it," he explained. "I don't suppose you know who it is?"

"No, I don't," replied Stacy. "But it's a woman. I heard the guy, the one who rings me, on the phone to her a few days ago when he dropped off the drugs. She sounded angry. Then he told us never to say the name 'Princesses' again."

"I know you're scared of her Stace; I bet they've threatened you, but we need to end this. We need to go to the police and tell them your story, and everything I know."

"I can't," Stacy protested. "I've got younger

sisters, and they know where I live. They'll hurt them if I tell anyone or if I don't turn up to work. You don't know what they're capable of, Ethan."

"We'll tell the police that," he pleaded. "And they will protect you and your whole family like they did with Jade's Dad and her brothers. And once the police have used our information to take them down, you'll be free from them."

Stacy started sobbing into her hands and shook her head from side to side.

"You know Jade is caught up in this, too, right?" he pushed on, and Stacy nodded.

"I-I've seen her since we started selling the drugs. Was she at The Castle too?"

"Yes," confirmed Ethan. His eyes stung again, and his lip trembled.

"Yes, she was. And she was selling drugs by the garages in Croydon last night. She got attacked by the guys who were with her, and I saw it happen. They nearly killed her, Stace. I was in the ambulance, and she almost died."

His voice caught in his throat, as he remembered Jade lying on the cold, hard ground; bloody faced and unconscious. How long would she have been there if he hadn't been watching her? What else could have happened to her if he hadn't scared them off?

"We need to stop this," he pleaded. "For Jade, for you all. Please, come with me to the police. I promise you'll be safe. This is part of my plan to end this; it always has been."

Stacy looked up at him, and he saw something steely in her glassy, blue eyes. She slowly nodded her head in agreement and he sighed with relief.

"Oh, Stace, thank you, thank you!"

"I need to start work now, though," she whispered. She wiped her eyes and looked around to check no-one was listening to them.

"Of course," he replied, and he moved his hand to her arm again.

"I'm starting in a couple of hours, too. Let's keep this between us Stace, I mean it. Do not tell anyone what we've spoken about here. We'll go to the police together tomorrow morning, OK?"

She nodded, and they walked back to the store together, towards the supervisor desk. Renee was still there, chewing the end of her pen and staring into space, deep in thought.

"Oh, you're back!" Renee jumped as they reached the desk. "What did he say to you Stace? He hasn't upset you, has he?"

Ethan wondered what he'd done to warrant so much dislike from Renee. She always seemed to think the worst of him.

"Nothing," grinned Stacy convincingly. "He was trying to ask me out again. There's a weird Princess themed bar in London he likes the look of."

Renee looked from Stacy to Ethan and back, and burst out laughing. Ethan winced and blushed; it was a good cover story, but a humiliating one.

"Men!" exclaimed Renee, as she threw her arms up in the air. "All the bloody same. Till 17 please Stace, June needs a break."

Ethan marched away from Renee, who was still laughing and shaking her head. He stepped outside and retrieved his phone from his pocket. There were no messages from Jade, which was strange. He'd left a few messages asking her to call him as soon as she'd woken up. Though, he thought, she may have only had the energy to send one message, and she did need to tell Renee she couldn't come to work.

He dialled the number for Croydon police station. After a brief discussion, they confirmed an appointment with DS Joanne Harris at 10 am the next morning. He told them he had information related to organised crime in Croydon and New Grange. With or without Stacy, he was going to the police station tomorrow, to tell them everything he knew.

24: THE PENNY DROPS

Sunday 23rd December 2018 -
Joanne

"Your 10 am, Sarge, he's downstairs."

"Great. Thanks, Paula," sighed DS Joanne Harris as she came out of a daze. "Ethan Hutchins, right?"

"That's right, and he's brought a young girl with him too. Tiny, blonde thing. Looks terrified."

"Jade?" asked Joanne, in disbelief. Last Joanne had heard, Jade Dimont was at the hospital after a horrendous violent attack. Surely she wasn't in any fit state to leave the hospital and come to the station yet.

"No Sarge," Paula's large fingers flipped through her notebook, trying to find her most recent page. "Her name is Stacy Mackenzie. She lives in New Grange and works at the Melwood supermarket with Mr Hutchins."

Joanne's eyes widened as she grabbed the most recent Debbie Gomez interview transcripts. In black and white, she saw Debbie recorded as saying: 'speak to the girls. I'll give you their names: Stacy Mackenzie...'

"You OK, Sarge?"

"Y-yes, I'm fine, sorry, Paula. Can you settle them in, and I'll be right there."

It looked as though Debbie Gomez would get her wish; Joanne was going to talk to Stacy. She shook her head as she thought of Debbie, who was still sticking to her story and pleading innocence.

Joanne made her way down to the interview room and looked through the glass at the two people sitting within. Paula was right, Stacy did look terrified. Ethan had his hand on her arm and was talking to her in a hushed whisper. Joanne pulled open the door, breaking their conversation.

"Ethan and Stacy, I believe," greeted Joanne, as she held out her hand to both of them. They both returned the handshake without making eye contact.

"I'm DS Harris, and I hear you'd like to speak to me about organised criminal activity in the local area?"

Ethan nodded in response, but Stacy's knees and feet started shaking. Her face reddened around the blemishes on her cheeks.

"Are you OK, Stacy?"

"She's fine," started Ethan, but Joanne immediately cut him off.

"I'm asking Stacy, not you. Stacy, is there something I can get you? Would you rather do this alone, or with someone else here?"

Stacy took some deep breaths and looked up at the ceiling, avoiding eye contact with Joanne.

"I-I'm OK," she stuttered and turned to look at Ethan. "I do want to, I need to tell you, but I don't even know where to start. I'm worried I'm getting myself into more trouble."

"May I?" asked Ethan. Stacy and Joanne both nodded.

"The thing is, Sergeant, Stacy and some other girls from the supermarket have got caught up in a gang, a criminal gang."

He paused as Stacy started crying into her hands.

"It's not their fault. They're not bad people; they're forced into it. They're made to do bad things, like selling drugs and, well, they're made to, you know, be prostitutes, too. That's why they haven't come forward; it's because they're scared.

"But now Stacy wants to tell you what happened to her. And I have loads of information on this gang, what they're up to and who they are.

So, if we tell you all this, you can arrest them, right, and protect the girls?"

Joanne sat back in her chair, struggling to take it all in. Could this be the same gang that forced Jack Dimont out? That was growing in strength and remained elusive to the police?

"OK, thank you, Stacy and Ethan, for coming in today. You've done the right thing bringing this to us. We will take this very seriously, and offer you the protection we need, once we have all the details from you. You're already much safer than you were ten minutes ago.

"What I'll do now is find a colleague who works with young people like you, Stacy, who've been through similar things. We're going to ask you some questions and have a chat on our own. Then I will talk to you, Ethan, about this information you have. Will you both stay right here?"

To Joanne's relief, they both nodded without protest, so she left the room and ran back towards her desk.

"Don't let them leave!" she shouted at Paula on the front desk, as she sped up the stairs. She hurried to Vincent Okafor's office and opened the door without knocking. She recounted Ethan's opening words, and the next steps she was going to take.

"My God, Joanne," grinned Okafor, as he stood up and rubbed his chin. "The poor girl, of course. But it looks like we've got an informant on the rival gang, at last."

"Yes, sir, and a potential corroboration of Debbie Gomez's theory about the girls at work," she commented. "Stacy Mackenzie works at the Melwood store. And in Debbie's latest interview, she suggested that we speak to three girls, including Stacy."

"Jesus, you're right. I'm going to watch your initial interviews with them, Joanne. Set her up in the correct room, please."

Thirty minutes later, Joanne and Denise, a colleague from the safeguarding team, sat with Stacy in the interview room. Denise's calming voice and experience helped ease Stacy into a conversation.

"After I dropped out of college," started Stacy, "I got a part-time job at the supermarket, but only twelve hours a week. It wasn't enough money, but this guy was hanging around the estate one day. He started talking to me, and when I told him I was looking for work, he said he knew somewhere that needed bar staff."

"OK, Stacy," said Denise, in a slow, reassuring voice. "I understand. Did you accept the offer?"

"I gave him my phone number, and someone else called me, a man, and told me where to go. So, I went to this building, an old abandoned one in town, and there was this cash bar inside, selling cheap alcohol. I worked there, and it was OK, they gave me food and lifts home and stuff. Until one night, as I left, the man searched my bag and found loads of money. I didn't put it there, honest, but he said I'd been stealing, that over £2000 had gone missing since I started working there."

Stacy started crying, and Joanne felt a sting in her own eyes, too. It was a classic exploitation technique used against the most vulnerable people. Denise's soothing voice filled the gap again.

"It's OK, Stacy. I'm sure you didn't take the money. What happened next?"

"They said I had to pay it back, but I didn't have it, because I never stole it in the first place. But they said I had to repay my debt, or they'd send bailiffs to my Mum's house. They knew where I lived, from when they drove me home."

"How did they make you repay it, Stacy?"

"They said I had to work at their other business, at The Castle on the old street in Croydon. They said I had to work there for free until I paid off my debt."

Joanne felt an overwhelming sense of pity for the young girl in front of her.

"What were you made to do at The Castle, Stacy?"

"They m-made me," stuttered Stacy, as she wiped huge teardrops from both her eyes. "They made me have sex with whoever came through the door, and I didn't want to, please don't arrest me, I didn't want to do it. They said if I didn't, that they'd make my younger sisters pay."

"Stacy," repeated Denise. "You are not in trouble. We are not going to arrest you, OK? You are so brave, so helpful."

"I've done more, though," cried Stacy.

"It's OK Stacy. Please tell us,"

"Last month, they stopped sending me to the Castle. Now I sell drugs in New Grange for them. I didn't want to, and I hate drugs."

Denise looked at Joanne and gave her a nod.

"OK Stacy," said Joanne, trying to match Denise's tone. "You're doing so well. I need to ask you a few questions about the organisation itself. You mentioned a man who gives you instructions, can you tell me about him?"

"He's old, forty-ish. He's not too tall, bald and he has an accent, like someone off EastEnders. I don't know his name, but it's always him who rings, tells me where to go and now he drops the drugs with us too."

"And is he in charge, is he the leader?"

"No, there's only one leader," whispered Stacy, and suddenly, she looked scared again. "People call her the Boss. I don't know who she is, but I heard her the other day, she was shouting down the phone to the man. I couldn't hear what she was saying, but it was definitely a woman."

"When did you hear her?"

"A few days ago, I think. In the last week, for sure."

"Thank you, Stacy. Now one last thing before Denise has a further chat about witness protection. This organisation that's been exploiting you. Does it have a name?"

"Yes," whispered Stacy, "but we're not allowed to say it."

"Please Stacy, what is it?"

"'Princesses'."

Joanne froze. Her head span as she recalled Janice Locke's last ever message. 'We know something dodgy is going on at work, linked to 'Princesses'. It must all be run by someone at the store...' In the space of a few seconds, the Melwood murders and the organised crime crackdown had collided. Had a 17-year-old girl just given them the key to unlocking both cases?

"DS Harris," prompted Denise. "Have you any other questions for Stacy?"

"Sorry, no, I don't. Thank you, Stacy, you've been ever so helpful."

Joanne watched them leave, raised her eyebrows and looked at the mirror. She wondered if Vincent, who was behind it, also felt like he'd been knocked sideways by a weighty object.

Before Joanne knew it, Ethan Hutchins was sitting in front of her with a folder full of paper notes and pictures. She listened as he talked through the various properties used by 'Princesses'. He knew the shift patterns of the exploited girls, the names and the addresses of the middle-men.

"When did you become suspicious of this,

Ethan? And how did you discover this information?" asked Joanne, when he paused for breath. She already knew the answer - she'd seen it on the CCTV tape from Halloween.

"Back in September, some of Jade's behaviour worried me. So, one night, I followed her and saw her walk into the Castle. She dropped this card, with the 'Princesses' name on. There's a photocopy in the folder, and I've been..."

"You've been following women without their knowledge or consent ever since? Collecting inadmissible evidence without alerting the police to major criminal activity?" asked Joanne, as she leant forward towards him.

"Uh, yeah, but," he spluttered, clearly shocked by her reaction.

"You have spied on these women and their lives. Do you realise that amounts to a crime? If you wanted to protect Jade, you should have spoken to us the moment you saw her walk into the Castle. We could have protected her and gathered this evidence quickly and legally. Instead, you undertook this reckless personal project, Ethan. I urge you to reflect on that."

He sat back in his chair, looking embarrassed and confused.

"Last thing, Ethan. Did you ever discuss 'Princesses' with Janice Locke, Caitlin Murphy or Dawn Smith?"

"No, I haven't told anyone what I've found out, apart from Stacy and you," he grumbled.

"My God," muttered Joanne. Ethan wasn't aware that, according to Janice and Caitlin, one of his colleagues from the store was the elusive 'Boss' that he'd been looking for.

"Thank you, Ethan," she said, as she got up to show him out.

"We will not take the case against you any further for now, but I must insist that you do not discuss this conversation, or any of today's events, with anyone else. Discretion is necessary to protect Stacy, Jade and the other young women mentioned in this folder."

He nodded sulkily and scurried down the corridor towards the exit.

"Brutal, DS Harris, but he needed to hear it," said Okafor. With a grimace, he beckoned her into the viewing room.

"Sir," she said as she entered the room. She tried to find the words to summarise what they'd discovered, but they didn't come. Okafor stepped in.

"So," he started, his hands gripping the back of a chair. "We have a woman running 'Princesses.' She saw off Jack Dimont and has since taken over the South Croydon area, selling drugs, running both brothels and unlicensed bars. She recruits girls from the New Grange estate who work in the supermarket. Janice and Caitlin found out about the girls and the name 'Princesses'. They suspected someone, a colleague, of being behind it all.

"Assuming they were right, then it was that very colleague who murdered them to protect the secret. Dawn was onto it too, according to Debbie Gomez. And now Dawn is dead as well; it could well have been a murder staged to look like a suicide. And this person, this woman who is running 'Princesses', is still at large. The organisation is still thriving, and Stacy Mackenzie heard her on the phone a few days ago. Which means..."

"Which means it's not Debbie," concluded Joanne. "What do we do, sir?" She asked, and she clutched her hands together to stop them shaking.

"What are the next steps?"

"Oh, there is plenty to do Joanne, plenty. I have a working theory that explains all this. It requires some extra CCTV footage and some sensitive personal information, to prove or disprove it. But we should be able to obtain both in good time."

"I don't follow, sir," said Joanne, scratching her head.

"Leave it with me," Okafor replied. "But as an immediate next step for you, I'd like you to organise the release of Debbie Gomez. She didn't leave her house on the 3rd of August. She didn't get out of the car on Halloween. And she really was foolish enough to take home the bag she found in the locker, to try and solve her friends' murders herself. I think she's been telling the truth, and pointing us in the right direction, sort of, all along."

25: THE BIG D

Sunday 23rd December 2018 -
Karen

K aren traipsed, zombie-like, around the supermarket. She couldn't remember how many days she'd worked in a row, but she did know that there were less than two days until Christmas. She wasn't at all ready for it. There was no festive food in her fridge, no presents under the tree, no cards had been posted to relatives.

Christmas preparations weren't the only thing that Karen had neglected recently. For the last six months, she'd kept a secret from her closest friends and family. Her marriage, her relationship with her children, and even her friendship with Debbie had all suffered as a result.

She thought, as she often did, of Debbie, stuck in a cell alone. She wished she'd done more to stop her friend implicating herself in those awful crimes. Her feet carried her around the aisles and back to the busy checkout area. Despite the crowds, though, Renee and Marie seemed to have ample time to chat by the Supervisors' desk. Karen repressed the urge to shout at them both, and instead approached with a smile; she needed to ask a huge favour.

"Busy day, right? I'm exhausted," she sighed. Renee and Marie both looked back at her, their eyebrows raised.

"Girls, look," started Karen, as she ran her fingers through her ponytail. "I need both of you, well at least one of you, to work tomorrow instead of me."

"What?" snapped Marie. To be fair, thought Karen, both she and Renee looked as tired as she did.

"I've worked over ten days in a row," pleaded Karen. "And I've messed up, OK, I've got nothing ready for Christmas, for the kids. I need tomorrow to sort it all out. Ethan is in tomorrow, too; you wouldn't be on your own."

Renee sighed and rolled her eyes.

"No, Karen, we can't do it," replied Marie, her red face clashing horribly with her hair. "I have plans tomorrow, and I can't cancel them, and so does Renee."

"Well..." started Renee, but Marie cut her off.

"No, Renee, you are not working another day," ordered Marie. "You need a break, that's final.

You don't owe Karen any favours."

Renee looked at Marie with a perturbed and moody expression. Marie maintained her very mum-ish look and held Renee's gaze.

Karen caught Renee's eye and whispered, "Please!"

"It's your name on the schedule, Karen," muttered Marie, as Renee sloped off to help a colleague on the checkouts. "And it was your best friend who killed off the other people who would have covered for you, then got herself caught," she added under her breath.

"Debbie is innocent," hissed Karen, for what felt like the hundredth time that week.

"The police have got this all wrong, Marie, none of this is her fault. You must know that?"

Marie shrugged her shoulders and raised her eyebrows, her lips pursed into a smile. Karen resisted the urge to give Marie another slap. At that moment, an announcement rang around the store.

"Karen Goldman to the Customer Service desk immediately please, that's Karen to Customer Services. Thank you."

"Oh, what now!" muttered Karen, as she moved away from Marie and ran around to the Customer Service desk.

"There are three supervisors here, you know, not just me. What do you want?" she grumbled, as she approached the younger girl behind the desk.

The girl pointed at the telephone, which was lying off the hook in front of her. She mouthed 'police' at Karen, then turned away to deal with an approaching customer.

"Hello, this is Karen Goldman," she sighed into the receiver.

"Hello, this is Paula from Croydon police station."

"Right. What do you want?"

"I'm calling to see whether you can come to the station and pick up your friend, Deborah Anne Gomez?"

"I'm sorry," replied Karen, shocked. "You mean she's out? They've dropped the charges?"

"All I know, madam, is that she needs picking up. Can you get her? Her husband is a few hours' drive away and she suggested you would come."

"Um, of course. I'll come right away. Give me half an hour."

Karen glanced towards the crowded checkouts and the swathes of customers. She felt little guilt about leaving Renee and Marie on their own as she returned to the checkouts with a spring in her step. She could pick up Debbie and then prepare for Christmas later in the afternoon.

"Renee, Marie, I have to go," she announced with a smile and her hands in the air.

"Stop it, Karen, it's not funny," muttered Marie, as she looked over the schedule, Tipp-Ex in hand.

"I'm not joking. That was a phone call from the police. They've released Debbie, so I have to go and collect her right now." Renee and Marie froze and looked towards her in disbelief.

"I told you she was innocent," continued Karen with a smile. "Look, don't worry about tomorrow, I'll work it as planned, but I'm not coming back in today."

She jogged up to the staff area, emptied her locker and checked her bag and coat pockets for her phone, but it wasn't there. Strange, she thought, because she remembered putting it in her bag that morning.

"Karen," spoke a voice behind her, and she turned around to see Steve, the store manager, standing there with his hands on his hips. "I thought..."

"Oh, God, sorry, I'm not staying until the end of the day anymore. I have to go and pick Debbie up because they've let her go! And then I have to get Christmas ready, you know, for the kids..."

"Of course, sure, I get it," he paused and looked to the floor. "Say hi to Debbie, tell her I always knew she was innocent."

"That's what everyone will be saying now!" Karen replied with a wink and a forced laugh, as she hurried away from the lockers.

"Where the hell is my phone," she muttered, as she ran down the stairs. There were things on there that mustn't fall into the wrong hands.

Twenty minutes later, Karen reached the police station and spotted Debbie sitting alone, on an uncomfortable plastic chair. She looked tired and pale, like someone who'd lost a lot of weight in a short space of time.

"Deb!" shouted Karen as she ran towards her best friend. Debbie stood up and threw herself into a hug, then burst into tears on Karen's shoulder.

"They've dropped everything Karen, all the charges," she sobbed. "Joe's up at my parents with the kids, but they're coming back now, they'll be here in a few hours."

"That's brilliant, come on, let's get you out of here," hushed Karen, as she supported Debbie outside into the cold wind.

"I'm so sorry about this, Deb, about everything. I should have listened to you, been there to help you. Come on, let's get you home." They got into the car and looked at each other, neither knowing where to start.

"Talk to me," urged Karen. "Are you OK?"

Debbie took a deep breath.

"Yeah, and no. I don't know. I should feel relieved to be out. But I'm scared that they could change their minds at any time and bring me back in. It was awful in there; everything felt so surreal. What does everyone think? Do they think I'm a murderer?"

Karen took a deep breath as she started the car. "No, they don't, everyone thought the police were barking up the wrong tree," replied Karen.

"And now they've released you without charge, everyone will know for sure. I told Renee before I left; word will have gotten around."

Debbie smiled weakly and wiped her eyes as Karen drove through the traffic out of Croydon.

"I had a lot of time to think. I know it wasn't me who killed them, so it has to be someone else, right?"

Karen shifted uncomfortably in her seat.

"And you know..." mused Debbie, "it must be Renee. She's involved somehow. The cat, 'Princesses', it can't be a coincidence, can it? And she's from New Grange remember, where the girls are from."

"Did you say this to the police, Debs? To Vincent?"

"Yes, I said it today when they confirmed they'd dropped the charges. Vincent said he understood why I thought that, but to leave it with him," replied Debbie, with a bitter edge to her voice.

"Well, that's good. You should do as he says. Look where meddling got you last time."

Debbie stared out the window in silence.

"I mean it," warned Karen. "I'm going to keep a closer eye on you now, keep you out of trouble."

"The only way to clear my name is to work out who did do it," Debbie replied. "And I don't trust the police to get there themselves."

Once they reached Debbie's house, Karen poured a large glass of wine for both of them. She tried to steer the subject away from the investigation. But each time, Debbie came back to her theories about Renee, with Marie's name thrown in now and then.

As glad as she was to see her best friend out of a police cell, Karen was also relieved when Joe's car pulled up in the drive. She watched Debbie, Joe and the kids hugging, crying and laughing together. She felt a pang of envy and guilt. Her, Pete and the kids didn't have that same bond; not anymore, anyway.

"I had better go," said Karen, and she poured the remains of her wine into Debbie's glass.

"Thanks, Karen," sighed Joe, pulling himself free of Debbie's hug. "Thanks for picking her up and settling her in. Come around again after Christmas, on Boxing Day, maybe?"

"I'll see Karen tomorrow," grinned Debbie, with her arms wrapped around Marco and Abbie.

"Deb, I told you, I'm working, and I'll need the evening to wrap presents and get everything ready, sorry."

"I'm working too. You said you needed help, and I'm free. I'll come in for the afternoon until closing time. Midday until 5 pm."

"Are you sure, Deb? I'll be fine. Ethan is working too, and you've only just got home."

Karen looked over at Joe and urged him to back her up.

"Karen's right, Deb," he said, reaching over to his wife's shoulder. "There's no rush."

"I want things to go back to normal," argued Debbie, "and I'd like to work a few hours tomorrow. I've got nothing to hide, and I'm coming in."

"OK, OK. Well, I'll see you tomorrow then, unless you change your mind, which would be fine."

Karen said her goodbyes and got back into the car. She checked the floor and glove box for her phone. It wasn't there, and she swore under her breath as she drove home to find it. She pulled up outside her house on the southern edge of Melwood and jumped out of the car.

"Pete? Danny? Becca?" she called out without reply, as she searched the downstairs rooms of her house.

She reached the conservatory and jumped with a start. Her husband, Pete, was sitting alone on the armchair, staring out of the window with a brandy in hand. Her heart skipped a beat; her phone lay on the coffee table in front of him.

"Pete," she whispered as fear began to creep up her chest towards her neck.

Her husband turned to face her with a sigh. The cheeks on his round face were a blotchy pink from the brandy. His small eyes stared at her with a look of pure hatred.

"Your secret is out," he slurred, tapping the screen of her phone in front of him with a stubby finger. "Now I know what you've really been up to these past few months."

"Pete, I...,"

"No, Karen." Pete held up his hand and looked down at the phone. "I don't want to hear it. It's unforgivable, and I'm divorcing you. You're not getting half my money. You're not staying in this house. And you're not getting the kids."

Karen felt a surge of anger. There was no point trying to protest the divorce itself; she knew the marriage was over and had been for some time. But he couldn't dictate terms.

"You can't decide that Pete, it all has to go through lawyers. This house is half mine, and so are the kids. I'm their Mum! What you're saying, it's not going to happen."

"Yes, it is, Karen," he replied and took a large swig of brandy. "Because if you don't do what I say, I'll tell the police the truth. I'll tell them that I lied about your whereabouts. Twice."

26: THE DAY BEFORE CHRISTMAS

Monday 24th December 2018, 12:00 - Debbie

D ebbie took a deep breath of chilly air before entering the supermarket. Despite Joe's further attempts to dissuade her, she felt compelled to come to work with her head held high. After all, she had nothing to hide, and this was the best way to prove it to her friends and colleagues. No matter what Karen said, Debbie was sure some people had doubted her over the last twelve days.

Twelve days didn't sound like a long time, but it had felt like an eternity. Interviews were the only thing which broke the silence, but they weren't enjoyable. In them, the police tried to make her confess to murders which she hadn't committed. It was her innocence, she supposed, which had kept her sane throughout the quiet hours. It gave her time to reflect on her friends' murders and to try and push the police towards the person behind 'Princesses.'

Did I succeed? Debbie wondered as she wandered through the supermarket. Had the police released her because they lacked evidence against her? Or because they had mounting evidence against someone else? As she walked through the store, colleagues looked away, pretending they hadn't seen her. Others gasped and stared at her with their mouths open in shock. Only a few of her close friends gave her a nervous smile and mumbled 'hello.'

She reached the staff area and exhaled; the bright lights had already caused a pain behind her eyes. She stared at the locker she'd opened, which had once contained Caitlin's purse and phone. She pushed her coat and bag into it and saw Edith strolling towards her with a grin. The knot in her stomach loosened slightly.

"Police let you out then?" she croaked, with a smile and a pat on Debbie's arm.

"Sure did. They finally figured out that I'm innocent," replied Debbie. She sounded braver than she felt, and was able to return Edith's smile.

"I always knew you were. You're not the type. But you've got guts coming in today. Well done."

"Thanks, Edith," sighed Debbie, as some of the tension in her shoulders eased.

"I don't suppose you saw Karen in the canteen? I didn't see her on my way in."

The corners of Edith's mouth twitched, and she raised her eyebrows.

"Why don't you ask Steve?" Edith grinned and gestured back towards the Manager's office.

"What do you mean by that? Is Karen in trouble, I mean, has she messed something up?"

"Oh, you could say that!" cackled Edith with a chesty laugh, as she hobbled towards the stairs to the shop floor.

Debbie rolled her eyes, put her locker key in her pocket and followed Edith's path towards the checkouts. She wondered what Karen could have done to warrant a ticking off from the Store Manager. Had she taken another swipe at Marie in the last twelve days, and not told her about it? Or perhaps Karen was in trouble for leaving work yesterday to collect her.

She arrived at the Supervisors' desk to more shocked stares from colleagues. But more pressing was the complete chaos in the department. The queues of customers ran four-deep, and Ethan was caught in a heated discussion at the self-checkouts, unable to help. She smiled to herself; this was the type of gritty normality and distraction she needed.

Within twenty minutes, the queues had eased, all the tills were open, and she'd extricated a shocked-looking Ethan from his argument. He then dealt with the various customer requests while she planned out the lunch breaks.

A few times, a colleague looked around for help but then pretended they hadn't seen her. In those instances, she went over and helped regardless. After all, it was an opportunity to mention that the police had dropped all charges against her. Every time it happened, she hoped she had convinced another person of her innocence.

She was almost enjoying herself until Karen finally appeared. She stomped towards Debbie with a face of thunder.

"Where have you been? Oh God, Karen, you look awful!"

It wasn't an understatement. Karen's hair, usually straightened and tied up in a neat ponytail, was loose and frizzy. She wasn't wearing her usual perfect make-up. Instead, she had a pale, more wrinkled and blotchier complexion. The deep frown was doing little to improve matters.

"Oh, thanks, Deb," snapped Karen, with a roll of her puffy, bloodshot eyes.

"What's happened then, what have I missed? Did you slap someone again?" asked Debbie, with a sympathetic smile and tap on Karen's shoulder.

"What? No, it's not that," Karen replied with a whimper. "Can we go somewhere after work, Deb? I need to talk to you and tell you something I should have told you a while ago. It's quite serious."

"Oh, yes, of course," agreed Debbie, her face now full of concern and worry for her friend. "Are you sure you're OK to keep working? You really do look terrible."

The Supervisor call button rang incessantly, but Debbie held back from answering it. Karen's arms had started to tremble against the desk.

"I can't talk about it here. But after work, I'll tell you everything, I promise."

Debbie battled through the rest of the busy shift. Christmas Eve was always challenging, given the crowds, the stress and the low stock. But also, neither Karen nor Ethan seemed capable of concentrating or helping anyone. By 4.30, even the colleagues who had given Debbie the most fearful looks were opting to call her to assist them.

One by one, the last customers and checkout staff members left the building. The ones that didn't run away from Debbie wearily wished her a Merry Christmas. While Ethan and Karen began collecting banknotes from the tills, Debbie reviewed the schedule. She noticed that someone had scribbled out both Jade and Stacy's names.

"Hey," she called to Karen and Ethan as she

approached them. "Why couldn't Jade and Stacy work today?"

"You didn't tell Debbie about Jade?" snapped Ethan, and he looked at Karen with narrowed eyebrows.

"It didn't come up, we had other stuff to talk about," sulked Karen, still frowning.

"Uh, tell me now then," demanded Debbie. "What about Jade?"

"She got attacked, beaten up, a few nights ago in town. She's in the hospital," mumbled Ethan, as his face flushed red.

"Oh God, that's awful," replied Debbie. "What happened Ethan? Was it a random attack, or was she caught up in something else? Is she OK?"

Ethan sighed, and his cheeks and ears went pink.

"I guess you can ask her when she comes out. It was serious, but she's out of the danger zone now. She texted Renee to tell her," he added bitterly.

"I'll go and see her. And Stacy?"

Ethan looked down at the floor. Debbie glanced at Karen, who tutted and raised her hands in the air.

"He knows, but he won't tell me," explained Karen, with a glare at Ethan. "So, don't ask me."

"Tell me now, Ethan," ordered Debbie, in her most stern and mother-like voice. "I need to know what's happened."

"Leave it, Debbie, she's asked him not to say,"

warned Karen.

"Ethan, trust me, if something has happened to that girl, I need to know. Has someone attacked her, too?"

"If I tell you, Debbie, you can't say anything," he whispered. Karen rolled her eyes and groaned as Debbie nodded eagerly.

"I took Stacy to the police station yesterday morning. She told me she'd got caught up in something, a gang who are forcing her to do things she doesn't want to do. She's gone to the police to tell them everything. She's going to need protection, so she can't come and work here. She can't even stay in this area."

"Is this gang called 'Princesses'?" whispered Debbie to Ethan.

He gasped and stepped back from her, his cheeks now a brighter red.

"How do you know that name?"

"Ethan, I'm not part of it, I promise. I've been trying to work out who's behind it for months. Janice and Caitlin figured it out, and so did Dawn, but they were all killed by someone before they went to the police."

"Debbie," hissed Karen, but Ethan cut across her.

"What has this got to do with the murders? How did Janice, Caitlin and Dawn know about 'Princesses'?"

"Don't you see Ethan?" prompted Debbie. "The person running it works here. It's someone in the store."

"That's why so many girls from here are part of it," he said to himself, with a rub of his forehead. Debbie could see the dawning realisation on his face.

"Who is it then?"

"Well, they thought it was me," replied Debbie. "But when you brought in Stacy yesterday, it must have proven it to the police. That this is all linked, and that I'm not the person they're looking for. I know it's Renee, and Marie, too."

"Debbie!" shouted Karen. "Shut up will you, you can't go accusing people like that. It's not them!"

"Renee and Marie," interrupted Ethan, with a gasp. "They hate me. They're always watching me, trying to stop me from speaking to Jade and Stacy..."

"And Renee is from New Grange, like the girls, and her cat's name is Princess," added Debbie, ignoring Karen's protests.

Ethan froze.

"You're kidding!" he whispered. He scratched his head and ran towards the staff area.

"Stay right there!" he shouted back towards them.

"You see, I was right all along!" cried Debbie.

"Yes, I can see that this is all linked," replied Karen. She was no longer frowning, but she did look furious. "But it's a police matter. It sounds like they've got a statement from Stacy now, so stay out of it."

Debbie raised her voice.

"How can I stay out of it? I'm part of this, and I have to clear my name!"

"Look where meddling got you last time," hissed Karen in return. "Look where it got Dawn, Janice and Caitlin. Now you're putting yourself in danger again, mouthing off about your suspicions to Ethan! We barely know him!"

Debbie paused for a moment. Did Karen have a valid point? Had she been too quick to trust Ethan? Before she had a chance to consider it, she heard the sound of his footsteps running towards her. Ethan approached her at pace and held out a small, crumpled business card.

"What is that?" asked Karen, as Debbie took the card.

Debbie couldn't believe her eyes. She saw the words 'Princesses' and 'escort services' and a picture of a white, fluffy cat, winking up at her.

"Oh my God," she whispered. "It's the final piece of the puzzle, Karen, look! The cat!"

"Where did you get it? I mean, did you not give this to the police?" Karen asked as she stared at the card in disbelief.

"Jade dropped it, and I picked it up. I gave the police a photocopy, but it's in a big folder with hundreds of other documents. I didn't realise how important it was."

"Oh, I bet they won't even spot it," muttered Debbie. "Let's take it to them now, and wave it in front of them, spell it out."

Ethan nodded as Karen sighed again and looked up to the ceiling.

"Deb, I thought we were going for, you know, a chat. Just the two of us?"

"We can, we will," promised Debbie, her eyes fixed on the card. "We'll drop this off with the police first, and then we'll take Ethan home, then go for a chat. It's quarter to five now. Let's finish closing up, and then we'll go."

27: THANK YOU, JADE

*Monday 24th December 2018,
16:45 - Jade*

J ade's hospital taxi pulled up outside a row of semi-detached houses in South Croydon. She winced in pain as she sat up straight and attempted to haul herself out of the car. Despite her broken ribs, the doctors insisted she was ready to go home. She trusted their opinion, but also saw first-hand how short of beds they were at the hospital. That, too, may have had something to do with her early release.

The taxi driver had asked for her address or the address of someone who could look after her. Various options ran through her mind. She thought of her Dad's, but then she remembered that he and his real family had moved away to an unknown location. Then, she thought about her mother's flat, but she hadn't told her about the attack. Telling her about it could tip her over the edge again.

She also couldn't bring herself to give the driver her address. The thought of going back to her small, cold room in Melwood was unbearable. She could deal with loneliness and discomfort, but not the fact that people from Princesses knew she lived there.

She considered giving him Ethan's address, but she knew he wouldn't give her any proper space. He'd demand answers to questions she wasn't ready to answer. Why was she hanging around the garages with those boys that night? And why did she have so many cuts on her arms?

There was only one person she could think of who might want to help. Who wouldn't question her, and who'd offered to meet up over Christmas, even before the attack. So, she gave the driver Renee Beck's address and hoped that she'd find her at home alone. She thought about messaging Renee to check, but it felt too awkward, so she decided to turn up and hope for the best.

As she struggled out of the car, she looked down the street at the many festive lights. They'd started to sparkle and twinkle in the dusk. Fake frosted snow and 'Santa Stop Here' signs covered the surrounding gardens. There were no decorations on Renee's house, but the living room light was on behind the blinds, and her car was on the drive.

Jade thanked the driver as he passed her a small bag and a pair of crutches. She approached Renee's front door gingerly and winced again with each step. She rang the doorbell twice and hoped she wasn't interrupting anything important.

After a few seconds, Renee opened the door wide enough to expose her head and bare shoulder. Jade felt the warmth from within the house rush out towards her. She looked up at Renee and mumbled "Hi.'"

Renee looked back down at her, shocked and flustered.

"Jade!" she exclaimed after a short pause. "Oh my God, I didn't even realise you were out."

Jade wondered why Renee stood with the door ajar, shielding herself and her hallway from Jade's view. She guessed it was a sign that she didn't want Jade there, bothering her.

"Yes, they let me out. I thought, well you live close to the hospital, and it was easy to get here. You did say I should pop round. But, sorry, I'm sure you're busy. I'll go."

"Oh. No, no don't go," replied Renee. "You should come in, of course, we can talk. Go through to the living room, and give me a minute, I'll go and get changed."

Renee spun around and pulled the door open

behind her. She ran, in shorts and a vest top, up the stairs without looking back. Jade was sure she heard Renee swear under her breath.

Jade entered the warm and cosy house, removed her coat and hobbled into the living room. The fire was on and magazines, books and an open laptop were spread out across the floor by the armchair. She didn't want to pry, so she walked past them, sat on the sofa, and stared at the swirling flames in the fireplace.

A minute later, Renee reappeared in leggings and a woolly jumper and gasped at the mess on the floor. She scooped up the books and magazines and threw them all behind the armchair.

"Drink?" she asked. Her face was reddening in the heat.

"Oh, thanks, I can't have anything strong, you know, because of the painkillers."

"Herbal tea, biscuits, on the way," grinned Renee. She closed the lid of her laptop firmly as she left the room. As she left, a large fluffy white cat padded in. Princess jumped up onto the sofa next to Jade and stared back at her curiously.

"What's up with your mum then?" whispered Jade, as she started petting the purring cat.

It was a bizarre coincidence that this Princess resembled the cat on those horrible old business cards, thought Jade. Princess yawned and rubbed her head against her shoulder. As the kettle started to boil, she climbed onto her lap and settled down.

Jade absent-mindedly removed her phone from her pocket and checked her messages. There was one from Ethan earlier, telling her he'd visit her at the hospital after work. She rolled her eyes; she'd have to reply to him now, to let him know she wasn't there. She shifted Princess gently to make herself more comfortable and typed a response:

Hi, don't go to the hospital after work, they've let me out early. I'm at Renee's, but she seems busy, a bit frantic about something, so I'm not sure how long I'll be here, will let you know when I leave.

She started to balance her preference to avoid his fussing and questions with her desire not to be alone in her room. At least at Ethan's house there would be a warm bed and food; his parents had always been kind to her.

Renee returned with a tray of tea and chocolate cookie-style biscuits. Princess leapt off Jade's lap and trotted over to join her on the armchair.

"I can't stop eating these," laughed Renee. She dunked a cookie into her mug of steaming tea and stroked Princess with her free hand. "But what about you, are you OK? What on earth happened?"

"I got attacked and beaten up. Didn't see who

they were. Random, I suppose. But the doctors say I'll be fine if I can rest somewhere warm and comfy for a bit."

"Was Ethan with you when it happened?" asked Renee through a mouthful of biscuit.

"Um, no, he wasn't. He found me on the ground and called an ambulance."

"Bit of a coincidence, that he just happens to be walking by the Croydon garages late at night, at the same time as you. How can you be sure it wasn't him who did it?" probed Renee, as she leant forward to grab another biscuit.

"Oh, no, it wasn't Ethan who attacked me," answered Jade. However, she paused to consider Renee's question; what *was* he doing there at that time?

"Thought you didn't see who attacked you," mused Renee. She stared at Jade with an eyebrow raised, her amber eyes reflecting the firelight.

Jade looked into her lap. She didn't like lying to Renee, but at the same time, she didn't have the energy to tell anyone the whole story. Where would she even start?

"That's the problem with secrets, Jade, they catch up on you," sighed Renee. "Take it from the expert."

"Is everything OK, Renee? I'm sorry I disturbed you, you seem…"

"Oh, no, don't be sorry," replied Renee with a wave of her hand. "But you should know, nothing good comes from having secrets. Especially ones that you can't keep hidden forever. Don't make the same mistakes that I have, Jade."

"I don't know what you mean. Has something happened?"

"I've got a secret Jade. Well, many secrets. And everyone is going to find out sooner or later," hushed Renee. "I think someone already suspects something. If so, I'll have to deal with her. And, of course, there is someone else I have to tell first."

Renee's eyes flitted around the room. Jade was lost for words, but Renee filled the silence again.

"How can I sit here and tell you not to keep secrets? When what I should be doing is coming clean about mine. I have to. The walls are closing in, so to speak."

"What's going on, Renee? I don't understand..."

"Ah, it's a long story, Jade, such a long story. You will find out, everyone will, and when you do, please try not to think the worst of me. Think of it from my perspective-and what you would have done." Tears welled up in Renee's eyes as her voice shook.

"Tell me what it is," urged Jade.

She suddenly yearned to get lost in someone else's secret. Already, it made her feel less alone. Renee put her biscuit down, removed Princess from her lap and put her head in her hands. She took deep breaths as if she were trying to stop herself from crying.

Jade hadn't expected this at all. Renee was always so sure of herself, and Jade had no idea what to do to comfort her.

"It's such a mess," cried Renee from behind her hands. Before Jade could attempt to move from the sofa, Renee's mobile rang.

"My cousin," she muttered. "She'll try and stop me, just you wait."

Renee got up from the armchair and left the room. Jade remained on the sofa, feeling both shocked and curious. She could hear Renee on the phone in the kitchen, raising her voice at her cousin.

"No, I need to do it now, Claire," shouted Renee. "I should have done it months ago. Gillian is going to find out if she doesn't know already. So, I need to go and explain myself to Kevin. He deserves to hear it from me…"

There was a pause - presumably, Claire was trying to talk Renee out of her plan. What could Gillian have found out about Renee? And why on earth would Renee have to explain herself to Gillian's husband?

"I've made up my mind, Claire. I need to deal with this. I'm going to Fair Lawns now."

A minute later, Renee marched back into the living room and threw her phone into her handbag. "I'm sorry Jade, I have to go out, something urgent has come up," she announced without making eye contact.

"Stay here if you like, make yourself comfortable, or leave if you have somewhere else to be. I'll be a while. And thank you, Jade, for listening and making me see what I need to do."

Renee grabbed her car keys and left the house before Jade could respond.

Princess meowed at the door and then at Jade, who shrugged her shoulders in return. She checked her phone and saw that another message from Ethan had popped up.

Jade, you have to trust me. Get out of Renee's house now, make an excuse and leave. If you can't, don't worry, we're on our way there now.

She re-read the message in disbelief. What on earth was going on with everyone this evening? Why was Ethan telling her to get out of Renee's house, and what did he mean, 'we're on our way'? Who was 'we'? Whatever was going on, she wanted no part of it; she'd had enough drama already.

She hauled herself up with her crutches and shuffled towards the living room door. She leaned over and peered behind the sofa at the books and magazines Renee had thrown there.

"Ah," muttered Jade as the penny dropped; "that certainly explains a lot."

With a final, apologetic glance at Princess, Jade put on her coat and left Renee's house. She limped away down the street, with no firm idea of where she was going.

28: FIGHT AND FLIGHT

Monday 24th December 2018,
17:25 - Marie

Marie drove through the busy Melwood Junction, casting an eye towards the supermarket. As expected, the front doors were already locked, and the lights dimmed. She smirked and wondered how Karen and Ethan had coped with the crowds. She didn't feel guilty about leaving them to it, after working back-to-back days over the last two weeks. She'd needed the day off to wrap and deliver presents before she returned to her mum's home in Sussex.

Renee, who was more of a people-pleaser than her, had almost agreed to cover for Karen. But Marie had put a stop to that; Renee had enough to worry about without adding a Christmas Eve shift into the mix. She drove towards Croydon town centre, then veered into a quiet, well-decorated road. In the distance, she saw a young girl on crutches, struggling to walk along the pavement.

Given her tight schedule, Marie considered driving past. But at the last minute, she slammed on the brakes. She had recognised the blonde hair and pale face of Jade Dimont. She swerved into a parking space ahead of Jade and lowered her window as she approached the car.

"Jade! Jade!" she called, and the young girl turned towards her with a scowl on her face.

"Are you OK?" asked Marie.

She took a closer look at the crutches and the yellowing bruises on Jade's face. She looked awful, and Marie couldn't believe she was wandering the streets alone in that state.

"Oh, yeah, I'm just great," replied Jade through gritted teeth. She was breathing heavily and sweating despite the cold outside.

"Do you need a lift somewhere local? I can squeeze you in if you want."

"No, thanks, I don't even know where I'm going," mumbled Jade. "You get on with whatever it is you're doing."

"Well, I'm going to drop Renee's present off."

"Yeah, good luck with that," snapped Jade before she hobbled off.

Marie sat for a moment, perplexed. She was

only trying to be helpful, so why had Jade reacted in that way? No answer came to mind immediately, so she shrugged it off. She drove another hundred metres down the road and reached the front of Renee's house.

She grabbed a massive gift bag from the boot, containing presents for both Renee and Princess the cat. She walked down the front garden path and rang the doorbell twice, without response. She turned to the living room window instead and peered through the blinds. The lights and fire were on, and she could see Princess on the coffee table, licking a plate of biscuits.

Marie turned to the driveway, and to her disappointment, she realised there was no sign of Renee's car. She sighed, took her phone from her pocket and dialled Renee's number. There was no answer, so she sent her a message instead.

Ren, I'm at yours with presents. I thought we said 5.30? Can't wait long, got to go to Rachel's before leaving for Mum's. Hope you're OK xxxx

She sighed and slouched back towards her car. "Typical Renee," she muttered.

She'd have to come back after Boxing Day with the gifts unless she received a reply in the next five minutes. Before she reached the top of the path, a familiar car screeched to a halt in front of her.

"It can't be!" Marie gasped. But then she saw Debbie Gomez climbing out of the driver's seat with a clenched jaw. Even more bizarrely, Ethan jumped urgently out of the back seat. Karen then got out of the front passenger's seat, with a more reluctant look on her face.

Debbie rushed towards Marie and blocked her exit from Renee's front gate. She looked fevered.

"What are you doing here?" she demanded.

"I could ask you the same question. Last I heard, you were in a cell," replied Marie, as she attempted to shove past Debbie and get to her car. She had no desire to hang around, answering to her three least favourite colleagues. Debbie, however, continued to block her way.

"Oh, for God's sake," protested Marie, holding up the gift bag. "I came to drop off Renee's Christmas presents, but obviously, she's not here, so I'll try again later. What's it to you, anyway? Why are you here?"

"Where's Jade?" asked Ethan, from somewhere behind Debbie. "Is she inside there?"

"No," replied Marie as she craned her head to look at him. "If you're here for her, I saw her heading down the road five minutes ago. It won't take long to catch her up. She wasn't going very fast." Ethan nodded, turned on his heel and ran in the direction Marie had indicated.

"Right, can I get through now please," Marie demanded, as she tried to shuffle forward.

She avoided eye contact with Debbie, who

was still glaring at her. Though Marie was trying her best to hide it, she felt quite scared. She was alone in the dark, with her exit blocked by a woman who'd spent two weeks under caution for three murders. What if the police had made the wrong call, and shouldn't have let her go? What if Karen had given her an alibi, but was some kind of accomplice? Marie swallowed and tried to keep her composure.

"No, you can't," replied Debbie, her arms outstretched.

Marie looked past Debbie and saw Karen leaning against the hood of Debbie's car, picking her nails. If she could get past Debbie, she'd be able to run to her car and leave.

"Tell us where Renee is," Debbie continued.

"I don't know. I came here because I thought she was here, but she's not," rushed Marie. She tried to push past, but Debbie reached out and grabbed her arm to hold her in place.

"No, Debbie, get off me!" Marie twisted and turned but couldn't shake her off.

"Debbie!" gasped Karen, paying attention at last.

"What are you doing? She doesn't know where Renee is, so let's go. We have other things to discuss, remember?"

For once, Marie agreed with Karen. She tried again to wrench her arm away from Debbie, who tightened her grip in return.

"She's lying Karen," hissed Debbie. "She knows

where Renee is, and she knows what horrible things Renee has been up to, what she's capable of."

Marie bristled. "It's none of your business what Renee does in her own time. Who are you to judge?"

"None of my business?" roared Debbie, frenzied. "How can you say that? I know everything Marie, I know about 'Princesses', I know about the murders, and I know you're involved in it all."

With her spare hand, Debbie thrust a crumpled business card in front of Marie's face. It had a cartoon cat on it, and the word 'Princesses' written in pink italic letters.

Marie stared at it, confused.

"I don't know what you mean. I don't know what this is, I've never seen..."

"How could you, Marie?" interrupted Debbie with disgust. "How could you sit by and let Renee get away with this? She's killed innocent people to protect her secret, she's killed my friends, and they arrested me for it! Can you even begin to imagine what that was like? And you say it's not my business! Can you hear this, Karen?"

"You've got this all wrong," trembled Marie. "I know she's not perfect, but Renee has nothing to do with any of that, I promise. She's not a killer; she couldn't even..." Marie paused, unsure whether to break Renee's confidence.

"Couldn't what?" snarled Debbie.

"Perhaps you should look a little closer to home for Janice and Caitlin's killer," cried Marie. "Haven't you noticed your best friend over there has been acting strangely lately?"

"Oh, don't start that again, Mardie," laughed Karen. "I had nothing to do with it, and Debbie knows it. Deb, this is ridiculous. Let's go."

For a fraction of a second, Debbie's grip loosened, but then Marie's phone beeped in her other hand. Renee often didn't bother messaging her back, and for once, Marie wished she hadn't. She glanced down at the screen and tried not to react.

Gone to Fair Lawns – sorry. I think she knows. I need to sort it out.

"Is that from Renee?" asked Debbie, her grip tight again.

"No."

"You're lying again, give me your phone."

Marie lurched forward and tried to free herself, as Debbie reached across her to snatch the phone. Their heads clashed, and Marie turned on her ankle. A searing pain shot up Marie's leg as she fell to the ground with a thud. Her head bounced off the side of the path. The bag of presents and her car keys flew out of her hands, out of reach.

"Argh, help me!" she cried, as she tried and failed to sit up.

"Oh God, Debbie, what have you done?" tutted Karen.

Debbie was staring at Marie's phone, wide-eyed.

"Oh, Karen, look at this message," urged Debbie. "What does this mean? She's gone to kill Gillian?"

"I don't know," whispered Karen. "I thought Gill was away?"

"What if Gill didn't go?" asked Debbie. "Renee seems to think she's there. We need to go to Gill's house; we have to stop her."

From the floor, delirious from the pain still shooting up her leg and the bump on her head, Marie looked up and laughed. Debbie and Karen both looked back down at her with a mixture of shock and disgust.

"You idiots," said Marie, as she winced in pain. "That's not why she's there. It's Renee's business, not yours. Stay out of it."

"I knew it," shouted Debbie as she shook with rage. "I knew you were in it together."

She stepped forward, Marie's phone still in her hand, and grabbed the car keys from the floor.

"We'll take these; we don't want you warning her, deleting evidence or running away, do we?"

"Not much chance of that," groaned Marie, as she looked down at her leg with another delirious smile. She'd started to feel lightheaded, and she wasn't in control of what she was saying.

"But wait, no, don't take the phone. I need to call someone. Rachel. Call Rachel, please. You can't leave me; it's cold here. Christmas Eve. I'll tell you the truth, everything, about Renee and Kevin, I'll explain. Check the presents, you'll see. Need an ambulance, though, I-I don't feel good."

"I am taking these Marie," confirmed Debbie. "You've had your chance to explain. I knew Kevin was involved anyway, and you're just trying to delay us."

"Deb, are you sure?" asked Karen, as she looked down at Marie on the ground with a mixture of concern and contempt. Debbie had already returned to the car and started the engine.

"Karen, please!" pleaded Marie, her voice trembling. Her head had started to throb, and her ankle was swelling.

Karen sighed and looked between Marie and the car. Debbie was already shouting Karen's name and encouraging her to get in. With a shrug of her shoulders, Karen turned away from Marie and got into the car.

"Help!" yelled Marie, as Debbie and Karen sped off into the distance.

29:
CONFESSIONS

Monday 24th December 2018,
17:40 – Kevin

The grandfather clock ticked in the reading room at The Manor. In the corner, a record player deck turned without sound. Kevin sat in the largest armchair, a glass of freshly poured scotch in one hand and an open book in front of him. He had been sitting there for the best part of an hour, yet he hadn't read a single word.

He stared into the ornate mirror between the bookcases on the opposite side of the room. He rubbed his short, spiky beard, and then his temples, where grey flecked his dark brown hair.

His mind drifted, as it so often did, back to Renee. When they were together, he felt so alive, happy, even. But he hadn't seen her in almost two months. He looked around him and sighed. He had a big house, money, a marriage of over twenty years. Yet, he felt so empty and alone without Renee.

He'd fallen for her, every side of her. There was the Renee that everybody saw. Confident, bubbly, brash. She sometimes went too far, but always charmed her way out of trouble. And then, the Renee underneath who was kind, caring, vulnerable and desperate to prove her worth to people.

There were moments when he thought she'd fallen for him too. But then something changed. Her messages became less frequent, and she didn't even respond to his requests to meet up. She was pulling away from him, and he couldn't blame her. After all, he'd had a year to leave Gillian, and he hadn't done it.

He took his first sip of scotch, which warmed and soothed his dry throat. He picked up his phone, and his thumb followed a familiar path to one of Renee's social media profiles.

He flicked through the old photos and smiled to himself. He looked deep into the mischievous eyes that stared out at him from every picture. In all of them, Renee was having fun, surrounded by friends. In some of the images, there was a man alongside her. Each of them looked a bit shell-shocked but very pleased with themselves.

A notification popped up on his phone, and he looked at it in disbelief. Had Renee felt the intensity of his thoughts? He took a sharp intake of breath and opened the message.

I'm outside. Are you home? Need to talk.

He sat up straight in the armchair. Of course, he wanted to see Renee, but not here. She shouldn't have come to The Manor; what was she thinking?

He tiptoed down the hallway and looked through the front window. Sure enough, Renee was striding towards the front door. He gently opened the door, held it ajar and tried to play it cool.

"Renee, what a surprise. Let me get my coat, and we'll go out somewhere?" he suggested as he cast a furtive look around the street.

"No, I need to talk to you right now. Gill's away, right?"

"It'll be nice in the pub down the road, Christmas Eve..."

"It needs to be now Kevin, and in private, we won't get a better chance," said Renee.

She looked at him with sadness in her eyes, which caught him off-guard. As he lowered his defences, she pushed the door open and strolled towards the reading room, her heels clicking against the wooden floor.

"Shit!" he muttered under his breath as he followed her hastily down the hallway.

His heart thumped against his chest as he closed the door to the reading room. He turned to face her, to attempt to get her out of the house again. But she'd already sat down on the velvet sofa and started crying into her hands.

"Oh God, Renee, what's happened?" he whispered as he sat down next to her and put his hand on her shoulder.

As he touched her, he felt a spark, like a static shock. A tingle ran up his arm towards his chest, doing little to ease his heart rate. He pulled her close, inhaled the smell of her and her perfume, and kissed her on the head.

"Talk to me, please Ren."

She rested her elbows on her knees and balanced her head on top of her hands. How was it possible for someone to be so beautiful, when tears fell from their eyes, and their lips trembled?

"Kevin," she whispered. "I need to tell you something,"

"Come on then," he urged. He dared to be hopeful.

"Before I tell you, I need you to know how I feel about you."

Finally, she looked up, and her fierce amber eyes met his.

"I know I've not been myself these last few months and I'll explain why. But first, I need you to know that I care about you, more than I've ever cared about anyone else before. I want to be with you, Kevin, and I have missed you so, so much."

His heart leapt; he couldn't believe what he was hearing.

"I thought... I thought you'd found someone else," he mumbled. "Or that you didn't want to see me, after, you know, the abortion."

She looked back at him, and the tears came again.

"Shh," he hushed as he pulled her back towards him.

"I'm sorry, I'm sorry. It's my fault. You shouldn't have had to go through that alone. I should have left Gillian and told you that you're everything to me. I love you; I have done for a long time. These last two months without you have been hell. Our relationship was never over for me."

"So," she sighed as she pressed her head into his chest. "Whatever I tell you now, whatever happens, you'll want to be with me? You'll leave her?"

He took a deep breath and closed his eyes. Of course, he wanted to be with Renee; he wanted it more than anything. But it wouldn't be easy, and he needed to be honest.

"Me and Gillian, it's not a real relationship anymore, you know that. But it's so complicated, beyond what you could imagine."

"What do you mean?"

"I will leave her, Ren. Whatever you say to me, I want to be with you. But it won't be as simple as me packing my bags and moving down the road. We'll need to leave, go abroad even, without telling anyone until we got there. Could you do that?"

"Yes," she agreed instantly. "I don't have anything here to stay for. I've got an apartment in Spain, near Torrevieja. I bought it years ago, when I sold my businesses. No-one knows about it; we could start there."

He lifted her head gently with his finger and wiped the tears from her cheek with his thumb. She leaned into him, and he kissed her. It was soft, at first, and for a few seconds, he felt as though they were the only two people in the world. But then, the upstairs floorboards creaked, and he came back down to earth, reminded that they weren't alone.

"Let's go to yours, we can plan it all out," he suggested, and he stood up, holding her hands.

"I haven't told you what I came to tell you yet. I have a confession, Kevin."

"Come on then," he urged. "Nothing you say could change my mind."

Renee took a deep breath, closed her eyes, and squeezed his hands.

"I'm pregnant. We're having a baby."

"No, we can't be!" he said, his mind racing. "You had an abortion. I haven't seen you properly since then."

"I didn't go through with it," she whispered, her eyes were still closed.

"I'm sorry, I should have told you, but I kept putting it off. I didn't know how you'd react, whether you'd want any part of it. That's why I've been avoiding you."

If he were anywhere other than The Manor, this could have been the happiest moment of his life. He felt the shock of the news, but it didn't upset him in the least. It was the most beautiful bombshell anyone had ever dropped on him.

"It's OK," he assured her, as he pulled her up to her feet and into an embrace. "It changes nothing, and it gives us another reason to escape together, doesn't it?"

He moved his hands from her back, towards her waist, and ran one of them tenderly over her stomach. "I wondered why you were wearing this old jumper," he smiled.

"I'm four months gone, it shows through most of my clothes, except this," she chuckled.

"Any other secrets, Renee?"

"Only that I've spent the money I asked you for, for the abortion. Sorry. If I'd given it back, you would have known."

He laughed and pulled her closer. "I can't wait to spend the rest of my life with you, Renee Beck. Just you, and me, and this one," he whispered, his hand still on her stomach. Despite the circumstances, he couldn't stop smiling.

"Now I want you to go back to yours. I'll move some money around, grab a few bits, find my passport, and then I'll come over. We'll work it all out from there."

"You want to leave tonight?" Her face was suddenly alive and excited at the prospect of adventure.

"Why wait?" he beamed. "Now come on, let's get you out of here." He re-opened the door to the reading room and looked down the hallway. All was clear. He led Renee down the hallway, avoiding the creakiest floorboards.

As he walked, he felt lighter. In a few hours, he thought, he could run away, and start a new life with the woman he truly loved, and their child. They had almost made it to the door when three loud, urgent knocks broke the silence. The hairs on the back of Kevin's neck stood up, and the smile faded from his face.

"Are you expecting someone?" asked Renee, as she put her coat on.

"No. I suppose it could be carol singers. Wait there."

Renee stepped into the lounge, hidden from view, as Kevin opened the door. When he did so, he came face to face with Debbie Gomez, who looked angry and scared in equal measure. Behind her was Karen Goldman, who looked more embarrassed and apologetic.

"Debbie, Karen, what are you...?"

"Where's Renee?" demanded Debbie.

"Not here," he shrugged.

"Her car is literally right outside." Debbie gestured to the vehicle parked diagonally across the driveway. He looked at his feet, bit his lip and didn't respond.

"Where's Gillian, is she safe?" continued Debbie.

"Of course, she is, didn't she tell you, she's gone away," he replied, through a strained voice. "Now, sorry you've wasted your trip, but I'm a bit busy."

Karen rolled her eyes and tried to drag Debbie away, but she remained resolute.

"Renee!" she shouted, and Kevin winced.

"Shh! Please go away," he begged. It was in everyone's best interests, including his own, to get away as soon as possible.

"What?" Renee's voice came from behind him.

"What on earth are you two doing here?" she asked, a look of bewilderment on her face.

"We're here to see Gillian," answered Debbie and without warning, she pushed past Kevin into the hallway.

"No," he hissed. "You can't be here. You all need to leave now!"

But Debbie was already halfway down the hallway, looking into the rooms. Karen trailed behind Debbie, trying to persuade her friend to leave.

Renee turned to Kevin with a confused expression and a shrug. He delicately closed the front door and hurried towards Debbie and Karen. They had reached the entrance to the reading room.

30: APOLOGIES

Monday 24th December 2018,
17:50 – Ethan

E than redialled Jade's mobile number, but it went straight to voicemail again. He'd followed the direction Marie indicated, but then he had to choose which route to take at the end of the road. He'd opted for Croydon but was now backtracking to Melwood.

He finally caught sight of Jade on Melwood High Street. By the time he reached her, she'd hobbled beyond the junction and was opposite the pub they had lunch in a few months ago. A misty rain had started to descend from the darkness above. He needed to get both himself and Jade inside and safe.

"Jade," he called through deep breaths, as he ran in front of her. "Jade, are you OK?"

She stopped in her tracks, her thin face illuminated by the garish Christmas lights above. Her hair and forehead were damp from a mixture of rain and sweat.

She rolled her eyes, clenched her jaw and muttered, "for God's sake,' under her breath.

"What are you doing out here, it's starting to rain."

"What does it look like I'm doing?" she snapped, and stared at him, deadpan. "Walking along minding my own business, unlike everyone else."

"Where are you going, though? To your house?"

She sighed again and shrugged her shoulders. Ethan took a deep breath and tried to put himself in her situation. Of course, she wouldn't want to return there, but she needed to rest and didn't have anywhere else to go. That might be why she'd ended up Renee's.

"Jade, why don't you come to my house for a few nights? I won't pester you, I promise, and I'll tell my parents not to bother you either. But at least you'll be comfortable, and there will be plenty of food. You know how much my Mum cooks. And it's Christmas!"

He watched her pull a familiar facial expression. It meant that she was thinking something through, and weighing up the pros and cons. His promise not to bother her seemed to have made an impact.

"OK, fine," she accepted, and her face finally

flushed with some colour. Despite her hesitation, his chest flooded with relief.

"Great, let's get a quick drink in the pub and get out of the rain. Then I'll get us a cab home?"

"Sure," she sighed again. "But all this - it's on one condition."

"What's that?" He asked, frowning as he took her bag and put it over his shoulder.

"I don't want you to ask me any questions. But I have a few for you. And I want the whole truth."

"All right then," he responded, reluctantly, and they crossed the road together to enter the busy pub.

Thanks to Jade's crutches and bruises, the barman served them first. A large group even offered them a couple of chairs.

"The first question," began Jade, over the blaring Christmas music and chatter around them, "is what were you doing that night I got attacked? Why were you at the garages?"

He took a deep breath and looked down at the table. "I don't know where to start," he mumbled.

"Well, I've realised you weren't there by coincidence, so tell me why you were." She picked up her drink and stared at him with bruised, bloodshot eyes.

"I suppose it started the night of Gillian's meeting, you know, the one at her house when I walked you home. You said you were going out, back into town, and that worried me. So, I waited until you left your house, then I followed you. It was me by the bins; you shouted at me. And I saw where you went."

Jade put her drink back down and stared at him, her mouth open. "Jesus Christ, Ethan!"

"So, some evenings since then, I'd hang around, make sure you were OK. But also, I was trying to figure out more about... you know," Ethan looked around and lowered his voice, "Princesses, and who's behind it, so that I could tell the police."

Jade looked away from him, shaking her head. "So, you know about everything I suppose."

"Yes, I do. I know about 'Princesses', the drugs, and that you're not the only girl from the supermarket working there. I know how they operate and where their buildings are. Are you angry with me Jade, for what I've done? I know it was wrong, but..." he paused; there wasn't an acceptable excuse, and he knew it.

"Angry? Of course, I'm bloody angry, Ethan!" she clenched her jaw, and her eyes looked glassy.

"You've been following me without me knowing. But you saved my life, so what can I say? Thank you for stalking me?"

She raised her hands in the air and gave an entirely humourless laugh.

"I'm sorry, Jade, I am so sorry. I got it wrong. I should have gone to the police straight away.

I know that now. I thought if I could figure it all out, then I could tell them who to arrest and keep you out of it completely. If it had worked, you wouldn't have had to give any evidence or move away."

"Right. How selfless of you," Jade replied in the same deadpan tone.

He knew he deserved it and thought better of trying to defend himself further.

"What do you plan on doing now then, with everything you know?" she asked.

"I've already been to the police, with Stacy," he mumbled, knowing that it might enrage her further.

She stared at him wide-eyed again, her eyebrows raised.

"After you got attacked, I realised I couldn't wait any longer. I had to go to the police and tell them everything so that they could take 'Princesses' down. I spoke to Stacy, and I told her what had happened to you. She agreed to come to the station with me, to prove that what I was saying was true. She was so brave, Jade, she told them everything. But her family have had to move somewhere else, under protection."

"Jesus, poor Stace!"

"I'm sorry, I know I've messed up. But Stacy is safe now, and so are you, once the police figure it all out and arrest whoever is behind it all."

He sat opposite her for a few minutes, watching her take it all in.

She shook her head a few times and took several deep breaths.

"Next question," she broke the silence as she turned to face him. "What was your message about earlier, telling me to leave Renee's?"

"Oh, it doesn't matter," he replied. Debbie and Karen would have dropped the card off at the police station by now, and DS Harris will take it from there. He was nervous about upsetting Jade further by telling her that Renee might be the elusive 'Boss,' who had exploited her for months.

"No more secrets Ethan! Tell me," she pressed, as her bright blue eyes bored into his.

"Fine. But you won't like it. Debbie said something to me at work today," he started.

"Debbie?" replied Jade, over the noise. "I thought she was in prison for murdering Jan and Cait?"

"No, the police were holding her, but they dropped the charges, so she was back today. Debbie said that the same person who killed Janice, Caitlin and Dawn was also the boss of 'Princesses'. And that they worked at the supermarket with us."

"No way, no it can't be... how does Debbie even know about 'Princesses'? This is mad!"

"Is it mad? Think about it. Isn't it a coincidence that at least three girls from the supermarket got caught up in it? What if Janice and Caitlin, and then Dawn figured out that a colleague was behind it? And what if they got killed because of it?"

Jade looked shell-shocked, and he couldn't blame her. It was a lot to take in at once, particularly on top of his confession and apology.

"But who would do that?"

"Well, Debbie thinks it's Renee. You see, that's why I sent the message, and why we drove to Renee's to find you, after you told me you were there."

Jade burst out laughing.

"No, no, you've all got that wrong! Renee? No way, she's not a murderer!"

"Well, what about her cat, Princess," he protested. "Just like the cat on those horrible business cards, isn't she?"

"It's a coincidence," Jade replied with a dismissive wave of her hand.

"She wouldn't have put such an obvious link to herself on them, would she? More likely it's someone trying to frame her."

"But think about how she's been, missing days at work, moody. You said yourself; she was frantic earlier."

"Yeah," replied Jade with a smile. "She's in trouble alright, but it has nothing to do with 'Princesses'."

"What is it then?"

"It's her secret Ethan, so I'm not going to tell you. But you'll find out soon enough. Trust me, it's nothing to do with 'Princesses'," answered

Jade.

She rubbed the condensation from her glass with a wry smile.

"You know, Ethan, people are so quick to think the worst of Renee, because she's from New Grange. But more often than not, the richest people are the worst, not the poorest. We're just exploited and judged more."

Ethan sat back in his chair. He'd been quick to believe Debbie when she voiced her suspicions about Renee. But that was more about the evidence in front of him, than Renee being from New Grange, wasn't it? He shifted uncomfortably in his chair.

"Well if it's not Renee, then who is it? Seeing as you seem to be in the know."

Across the table, Jade's contemplative expression returned. Her eyes darted back and forth; her eyebrows narrowed. After a minute, her breathing quickened, and she grabbed the edge of the table.

"What?" he leaned towards her.

"If Debbie's right, and it is all linked, then I think I know who it is. Oh, God. It could be. That's why she..."

"Who?" he asked as she strained to get her phone from her pocket.

"Oh no, my battery has gone. Do you have Renee's number on your phone?" she asked.

"Renee? No, I don't. I thought you said she wasn't involved?"

"She isn't, but I need to speak to her. Have you got money for a taxi?"

"Yeah, of course, I can order one now. Back to mine?"

"No, not to yours. If we can't ring Renee, we need to go to her. She's at Fair Lawns. I heard her say it earlier."

"Fair Lawns?" he repeated. "Why would she be there?"

"Do it, Ethan, please order the cab, and I'll explain on the way."

He followed Jade out of the pub. Her realisation, which she hadn't shared with him yet, seemed to have energised her. They saw their cab in the distance and waved at it eagerly. The driver flashed his lights through the rain in return. As the car waited to clear the traffic lights, Ethan turned to Jade and took a deep breath. She looked up at him, her jaw clenched.

"Thanks, for getting us the cab," she muttered.

"Does this mean we're still friends, then?"

"Possibly," she replied with a sigh. "But that is all we will ever be."

"I know," he mumbled and, for the first time, he accepted it.

31: REVELATIONS

Monday 24th December 2018,
18:00 – Renee

R enee followed Debbie, Karen and Kevin back into the reading room. Her two colleagues' sudden presence at The Manor left her perplexed. What on earth could they need to tell Gillian on Christmas Eve? And didn't they know she was away?

A few minutes ago, Renee had felt so relieved, happy, and most of all, excited about the future. Kevin had reacted the way she'd hoped he would. Soon enough, they'd be setting up a new life far away. And this, she realised, was what she'd wanted all along.

It amazed her that no-one, apart from Marie, had figured her secret out before now. Her sudden abstinence from alcohol and cigarettes and her baggy clothes, her time off of work and last-minute sick days, were all dead giveaways.

The thought of bringing up the baby alone didn't trouble her too much. But she'd lived in fear of Gillian, or anyone, putting two and two together about the father. It didn't matter anymore though; by the time everyone at the supermarket found out, she'd have left Melwood for good. She would already be on her way if it wasn't for Debbie and Karen's sudden arrival. It seemed that she and Kevin had one last hurdle to overcome before they escaped into the night.

"What are you doing here?" snarled Debbie, pointing her finger at Renee.

"Well, I see the inside of a police cell has done little to improve your manners. What does it matter to you?" asked Renee, as she turned to Karen with a baffled look. Karen shook her head and looked away immediately, refusing to meet her eye.

"Don't look at her, answer me," growled Debbie, her shaking hand still pointing towards Renee.

"Look, it's really none of your business," sighed Renee. She turned to look at Kevin for support but didn't get any.

"You're interrupting a very private conversation, and I don't know why."

"I'm here to see Gillian, to warn her," replied

Debbie.

Renee wondered if the police had made the wrong decision, letting Debbie go. She felt a prickle on the back of her neck.

"She's not here, Debbie. Please leave, you'll see Gill after Christmas," interjected Kevin, with an attempt at a laugh. A redness was starting to creep up his neck.

"So," mused Debbie, as she pulled her phone out of her pocket. "If I call Gill now, she'll answer and tell me she's away as planned, and that she's well?"

"No!" Renee and Kevin shouted at the same time, but it was too late. Debbie raised her eyebrows and pressed the call button.

"Debbie, hang up now, don't tell her Renee is here," hissed Kevin.

Beads of sweat had started to form on his forehead. Debbie held the phone to her ear for some time. Please don't pick up, willed Renee. She breathed a sigh of relief when Debbie muttered 'answerphone'. But instead of hanging up, Debbie walked to the far corner of the room to leave her message.

"Gill, it's Debbie, I'm at your house, but you're not here. I need you to let me know you're OK. I have to speak to you, urgently."

Kevin reached Debbie as she finished her message. He grabbed her by the arm and began to drag her towards the reading room door.

"You need to leave," he ordered, as Debbie dug her heels into the carpet and struggled to free herself.

"Let go of her!" cried Karen, and Kevin loosened his grip. "Kevin let go. I'll take her home, I promise, Debbie, come on," she continued, grabbing her friend's other arm.

"What, leave the house without Gillian, with her still here?" replied Debbie, as she threw them both off and pointed again at Renee.

"What exactly do you think I'm going to do?" asked Renee in exasperation. She stepped back from the altercation, perched on the sofa closest to the door and folded her arms over her stomach.

"Oh, I don't know! Maybe kill Gillian to protect your secret, as you did with Janice, Caitlin and Dawn?"

Renee opened her mouth to respond, but, for once, she didn't know what to say. She looked at Kevin for support, but he was staring at Debbie wide-eyed, rubbing his jaw. A vein on the side of his temple had started to twitch.

"What? What the…?" stuttered Renee, as she struggled to process Debbie's accusation.

"I had nothing to do with that. Is that what you think of me? That I'm capable of murder?"

"That, and the rest!" accused Debbie, as she glared down on her from the middle of the room.

"Your time is up, Renee. We've figured it all out. 'Princesses', the cat, the girls, the drugs, the murders, and you."

"I don't know what you're on about. Do you need help? Karen, she needs sectioning! Kevin, does this mean anything to you?"

Renee laughed and looked at Kevin, but he stood by the armchair, staring out of the window. Why wasn't he telling Debbie that her accusations were baseless?

"I'm calling the police, to tell them to come and arrest you," muttered Debbie. She removed her phone from her pocket again.

"Oh, go ahead, but it would be a waste of time! I can prove I didn't kill anyone straight away," replied Renee with a dismissive wave of her hand.

"How's that then?" asked Debbie, as her thumb hovered once again over the dial button. "I'd love to hear this!"

"I was with him," Renee pointed at Kevin. "The night Janice and Caitlin died. And yeah, we were up to no good, but not the murder kind of no good. We were right here, in a room upstairs. Do you understand what I'm saying?"

"Renee!" Kevin groaned, finally turning away from the window. He raised his hands and pushed his hair away from his face. "What are you doing?"

"Oh, for God's sake Kevin! They were about to find out anyway, given what we've decided tonight. What does it matter?" She turned back to

Debbie.

"We've been seeing each other for over a year. I know, awful us, poor Gillian! But it's become a serious thing, and I'm here because I'm pregnant and he's going to leave Gill. I was sick on the night Dawn died, after my scan. So, there it is, my big secret is out. Now can you do one and leave us to it, please?"

Kevin groaned again at Renee, his face now a very dark red. Karen turned towards her, too, looking both shocked and amused. Debbie shook her head in disbelief.

"No! You're lying..." Debbie whispered. "You're in it together, the two of you. You're making up this affair to cover yourselves!"

Renee rolled her eyes, stood up, lifted her jumper to her waist and shrugged her shoulders.

"Oh my God," laughed Karen. "Well, this explains a lot. Come on Deb; we've embarrassed ourselves enough. Let's go."

Debbie's shoulders dropped, and she slumped towards Karen. "Just because she's pregnant doesn't mean she wasn't involved in the other stuff," she grumbled.

"Kevin, was I with you on that night Jan and Cait were killed?"

Renee paused as Debbie and Karen turned to Kevin, who gave a stiff nod, then resumed looking out of the window.

"So, Debbie, why don't you head off to think about who doesn't have an alibi?"

"Marie, I bet she'd do it if you asked her to…" replied Debbie, the accusatory tone returning to her voice.

"Well, I can tell you now she didn't. She was at home on the night Janice and Caitlin died, messaging me, and she was with Rachel on Halloween night. Rachel, her girlfriend. I've met her, and she told me all about their cosy night in together watching horrible scary films."

"Girlfriend?"

"Yes, she has a girlfriend," laughed Renee. "I told her to come out with it, but she was nervous. Especially as someone called her a fat dyke in front of all her colleagues recently."

"Well, I didn't know she actually was," muttered Karen.

"And what about you, Karen?" continued Renee. "Marie thought it might have been you. God knows why you would do it, but Marie seemed certain that you had something to hide. Why don't you go and reflect on that, Deb, and leave us alone?"

Renee had expected both Debbie and Karen to leave at that point, tails between their legs. Instead, Karen turned a shade of red which rivalled Kevin's, and Debbie turned to her best friend.

"Well, Karen? Tell her! You were with Pete."

"Yes, I do have something to hide," spluttered Karen, as Debbie's eyes widened. "But it's nothing to do with this, I promise. Deb, I wanted to talk to you about it this evening, but you've dragged me here instead."

Debbie waved a hand, encouraging her best friend to speak.

"Fine. OK, fine," rushed Karen. "I've been having an affair with Steve. I was with him on both nights."

"Oh, you could have come up with something a little more original Karen," laughed Renee.

"It's true," snapped Karen as she took her phone from her pocket and passed it to Debbie.

"Check the messages. He's saved in my phone as 'Steph.' Pete found out yesterday, he saw the messages, and he's divorcing me. Says he's keeping the kids."

Debbie comforted Karen as she suddenly burst into tears.

Jesus, thought Renee, will they ever leave? She looked at Kevin and gestured for him to take control of the situation and remove the two women.

"Right," said Kevin, "now we've cleared all this up, you need to leave, both of you."

Karen nodded and reached down to grab her bag. Debbie remained rooted to the spot; her eyes stared into space.

"Wait," she muttered. She looked down at the phone in her hand, and her face turned pale.

"If you're telling the truth, Renee and Kevin, then there's someone else who isn't."

"That's enough. Get out, Debbie. Now!" Kevin ordered as he reached out to grab her again.

"Oh Renee," groaned Debbie, as she grabbed Kevin's wrist to hold him off. "How could you not have realised this, all this time?"

For the second time that evening, Renee's neck prickled with fear. Not only did Debbie look terrified, but Kevin's face had drained of colour too. The vein on his head was twitching non-stop. Even Karen dropped her bag, her eyes open wide in fear. But what did Debbie mean? What should she have realised?

Behind her, just beyond the door to the reading room, the hallway floorboards creaked. A chill ran down Renee's spine as she realised that there was someone other than herself, Kevin, Debbie and Karen at The Manor.

32:
WHODUNNIT

Monday 24th December 2018,
18:00 – Vincent

Two emails arrived in Vincent Okafor's inbox in quick succession, breaking his chain of thought. He looked at the subject lines, took a deep breath and sprang to life with a grin. Despite the importance of his requests, he hadn't expected a response this side of Christmas. He opened the attachments and rushed through the text. At a glance, it seemed to confirm the hypothesis he'd worked on for the last 24 hours, since the release of Debbie Gomez.

"DS Harris," he called out over the Christmas playlist. He pressed the print button on all the documents. "Office, now!"

Joanne dropped her mince pie and shared a significant look with the rest of the team around her. She grabbed her notebook from the desk and joined Okafor at the printer.

"I'm not clocking off anytime soon, am I?" she asked with a smile on her face.

"Not if you want to crack the Melwood case with me, Joanne, no," he whispered, and her eyes widened in interest. They entered the investigation room, where Okafor laid out the various printed documents. Joanne looked over his shoulder, eagerly.

He sent a short message to his Superintendent, asking him to set the wheels in motion as planned. Adrenaline coursed through his veins. Finally, it all made sense to him - and he had enough evidence to prove it.

"These documents and pictures are all about Renee Beck, sir," said Joanne, with a note of surprise. "Was Debbie Gomez right, then?"

"Renee is integral to this case, Joanne. Not because she's guilty, but because she isn't. And by exonerating her through the evidence, we reach the truth."

He saw the perplexed look on DS Harris' face as she tried to keep up with his thinking. In years to come, thought Okafor, the College of Policing would make a case study of this. But this was a live case, and he needed to bring Joanne up to speed quickly before they made the arrests.

"Here, we have Renee Beck's mobile phone

records from the last year. Though we can't see or hear the content of the messages and calls, we see this number over and over again. It belongs to Gillian's husband, Kevin."

"Ah," acknowledged Joanne. "I expect the most obvious explanation is the correct one, sir?"

"Yes, it is, and sometimes these romantic affairs have unexpected consequences. The devil is in the detail here, and it was you who first spotted something, Joanne."

"I did?"

"After the store party, you asked, 'does Renee Beck strike you as the designated driver type?' It was a pertinent question, because, of course, she doesn't. What would make Renee take that role? What would keep her at home alone, instead of working or raising a glass for her birthday?"

"She's pregnant," whispered Joanne, with a look of dawning realisation on her face.

"Quite," he replied, as he tapped on the second document; Renee's medical records.

"These records that she had a 12-week scan on Halloween. It was the morning she booked off from work, knowing she had an appointment. Can you hazard a guess at the estimated date of conception?"

"Surely, not Friday the 3rd of August?" replied Joanne, shaking her head in disbelief as Okafor nodded. "Now, we know from our investigation that Renee lied to us in her initial statement. She did leave her house on the night Janice and Caitlin died. She drove off-grid and returned later in the evening. Given what we now know about the pregnancy, we can guess what she drove off to do."

"Or who," replied Joanne, and Okafor chuckled, despite the seriousness of the situation.

"Now, previously Joanne we asked for images of cars leaving the Fair Lawns estate. This time, I asked for images of people. Renee wouldn't make a habit of parking outside Kevin's house, so I assumed she parked outside and entered on foot." He paused and tapped two pictures of Renee Beck entering and exiting Fair Lawns via a footpath on the evening of Friday 3rd August.

"So, Renee is in the clear for Janice and Caitlin..." surmised Joanne. "She's busy with Kevin. Though, if she was with Kevin, then..."

"Where was Gillian?" Okafor finished her sentence gravely.

"I believe, Joanne, that Gillian slipped out of Fair Lawns earlier in the evening. There is a path from the estate to the neighbouring woods, which she could have taken to avoid cameras. She gets into the vehicle, commits the crime, and then drives back off-grid. We found the torched car on the edge of a large field, which borders those very woods.

"Back at home, the neighbours see Kevin drawing the curtains, and he later gives Gillian her alibi. Gillian's car never leaves the estate, and no-one sees her leave on foot. It's a near-flawless plan, right? Except, once Gillian leaves, Kevin couldn't resist an opportunity to invite Renee over."

Joanne exhaled and scratched her head.

"But Gillian, sir, she has never seemed nervous with us, she's complied fully with the investigation. She always seemed very composed, very together."

"Think of the details again, and the type of person capable of committing such a crime," urged Okafor.

"Janice and Caitlin's murders were cold, callous assassinations. 'Princesses' is an organisation which exploits the most vulnerable. These are crimes which the emotional and irrational types of Renee, Debbie, Karen and Marie couldn't have committed. But Gillian," he continued, "has she ever shown you or me empathy or emotion? Anything other than rational, reasoned answers and performances? Remember how convincingly she contradicted Edith Coaker's account of the staff party? She wanted the investigation to go away, so she lied."

Joanne nodded her head.

"As well as that," Okafor pushed on, "until May this year, she was a local Councillor for the Homestead ward in Croydon. She would have known about unoccupied but unregulated local buildings, like The Castle. She would have known how to avoid cameras."

"She sure would," sighed Joanne. "But how does Gillian, a Councillor and checkout manager, start exploiting people like this? And why?"

"Only she can tell us that, Joanne, and she will. I guess that she's been at this for years in Surrey. But I think it's no coincidence that 'Princesses' ramps up in Croydon when she loses in the council elections. Rejection doesn't play well with cold, nasty people who are capable of extreme violence and exploitation. And, maybe she also knew her husband was playing away with a woman from New Grange. That might have been enough to trigger her worst instincts and capabilities. She could easily identify vulnerable girls from New Grange through the supermarket, to expand her enterprise into Croydon. But after a few months, Janice Locke and Caitlin Murphy started joining the dots..."

"I'm with you," confirmed Joanne. "But what about Dawn Smith? Dozens of people gave Gillian an alibi that evening."

"Indeed," sighed Okafor. "Gillian made sure she surrounded herself on Halloween. Imagine how thrilled she was when she got to lock herself in the hall. There are two possibilities here, Joanne. First, that the coroner had it right; Dawn Smith, weighed down with the stress of the secret, decided to end it all."

Joanne raised her eyebrows in disbelief.

"Or, we go back to Renee's records. On Halloween, she receives an unanswered call from a burner phone in the vicinity of Dawn's house. Well, I traced the sale of this phone and SIM card back to a shop in Croydon and look who we have here." Okafor pointed to a picture of Kevin handing over cash at the till.

"Kevin's letting the side down, sir, he's not as savvy as his wife."

"He had a Renee-shaped weak spot, yes. Now, this suggests that Kevin went to see off Dawn. He was the person Debbie Gomez saw outside the house: tall, slender, and male at a guess. Why he called Renee, and what he was going to tell her, we don't know, because she didn't pick up. And did he go to kill Dawn because he's complicit in all this? Or was he coerced by his wife? Again, we don't know."

"So, we need to bring them both in, sir?"

"Yes Joanne, the Super is liaising with Surrey police now. We'll send a joint convoy down to Fair Lawns as soon as it's all squared. For Gillian and Kevin, the party is very much over."

One of Joanne's phones buzzed from her police belt.

"It's the private phone line for the Melwood investigation, sir. Should I answer it?"

"How curious," mused Okafor. "Yes, please do."

"Hello, DS Harris speaking," answered Joanne,

and she switched the call to the loudspeaker.

"Hello," shouted a familiar, abrupt voice. "It's Marie Webster here. I'd like to report a serious assault on myself and theft, by Deborah Gomez."

Okafor rolled his eyes, and Joanne bit her lip.

"She pushed me outside Renee's house, stole my phone and my car keys, and left me for dead on the ground. Karen Goldman was there too, and she did absolutely nothing to help."

"Ok, Marie," said DS Harris. "Where are you now? Are you receiving medical attention?"

"I managed to get up and hop around the corner to my, uh, friend Rachel's house. We called 999, but they don't have an ambulance available unless I'm actually dying, apparently."

"Right, if you're safe there Marie, if Debbie and Karen have gone, I suggest you await medical attention. We'll take a statement from you about the assault once they give you the all-clear."

"Oh, they've gone all right, sped off to Fair Lawns," grumped Marie.

Okafor and Joanne looked up at each other in shock.

"Why? Why have they gone there?" asked Joanne, her voice strained.

"They think Renee is there. Well, they know she's there because they stole my phone and saw a message from her. Debbie and Karen think Renee is some sort of criminal mastermind, but I can assure you that she isn't. She's gone to tell Kevin something."

"OK Marie," interrupted Joanne. "I'm afraid I need to go. Urgent call on the other line. Please get back in touch once you've received medical attention."

She hung up the phone and looked at Okafor.

"I don't think we can wait for Surrey, sir," she whispered. "Renee, Debbie, Karen - they've all walked into the lion's den."

Together, Okafor and Joanne ran into the main room and grabbed their equipment. Okafor ordered the quick assembly of the convoy. He alerted his Super that, due to an immediate threat to life, Croydon police would be going to Fair Lawns, with or without their Surrey colleagues.

Ten minutes later, Okafor sat next to Joanne in the leading car of the convoy. They were moments away from departing the station.

"Renee Beck," he muttered, shaking his head. "Wandering over to her boyfriend's house on Christmas Eve, unaware of what his wife, and indeed he, may be capable of doing. What if she tells Gillian she's four months pregnant with her husband's child? I wonder, who would Kevin choose if it came down to it?"

"I guess that depends on how strong Gillian's control over him is. And how strong his feelings for Renee are, of course," replied Joanne.

"We don't know if she's a bit of fun for him, or if he's madly in love with her. We don't know much about Kevin at all."

"True. And bloody Debbie Gomez," Okafor cursed. "Couldn't resist getting involved, putting herself and Karen in danger yet again."

"Sir, Marie said Renee had gone to see Kevin, right? Gillian may not be there. Best case scenario, they'll all confront each other while Kevin looks on. They'll exonerate themselves and leave unharmed?"

"I don't know Joanne," said Okafor grimly. "It's a big house, and I don't have a good feeling about this. Something tells me Gillian is there, whether the others know it or not."

At 18:20 on the dot, their driver pulled away, the rest of the convoy in tow. Joanne looked pale yet resolute.

"Are you sure, sir? Absolutely sure we've got this right?"

"Oh, I'm sure, Joanne. You see, there's something else I haven't mentioned to you yet, that was pointing us towards Gillian all along."

"Sir?"

"We spent so long dwelling on Renee's cat, that we missed the other 'coincidence' that was staring us in the face. Sociopathy and narcissism always leave a trace."

He paused and turned towards a confused-looking DS Harris.

"Gillian's surname, Joanne. And don't worry. Everyone else missed it, too."

33: BANG

Monday 24th December 2018,
18:20 – Gillian

G illian Prince held her breath, out of sight of those inside the reading room. Silence had fallen. She assumed that the creaking hallway floorboards had finally given away her presence. Not that it mattered now, she supposed. Debbie had finally worked out the link between Gillian, 'Princesses' and the murders. So, Gillian had no choice but to intervene and to silence her. It was a shame that it would have to end this way. But needs must.

She'd been quite content for most of the day. Upstairs in her study, she'd played her favourite classical music slightly louder than usual, keen to avoid distractions. She'd organised piles of banknotes, checked in with her various fixers. She'd completed all sorts of admin that came with running off-the-books businesses. Over the last few weeks, she'd fallen behind with it all. She'd fabricated a Christmas vacation to justify a few days off, to get on top of more important matters. And she'd made exceptional progress. She would have had everything shipshape if it wasn't for this unwelcome interruption.

She wasn't sure how long the uninvited guests had been at The Manor, or the order in which they'd arrived. She only realised they were there when she listened to the unexpected voicemail from Debbie Gomez.

She was curious about why Debbie had dropped by, and what she needed to discuss so urgently. So, she'd crept downstairs and followed the noise to the reading room. As she approached, she realised that Karen and Renee were there too, so she had hovered outside. She had stayed there as Debbie accused Renee of the things that Gillian was in fact responsible for. Her jaw had twitched as she listened to Renee's defence.

She had discovered her husband's affair with Renee almost a year ago, in January. He was terrible at lying, and he'd hardly covered his tracks. The thing that annoyed her most was the timing. Shortly before she'd found out, Gillian had used her savings to bail out Kevin's collapsed business. An affair with a loudmouth woman from New Grange was a poor way to repay her.

But the pregnancy was news to her, as was the

fact he'd invited Renee over on the 3rd of August. That hit her like a gut punch. Both errors were utterly unforgivable, and he would pay for it.

She'd planned to dip into the kitchen opposite and wait for Debbie, Karen and Renee to go. Then, she'd deal with Kevin. But Debbie, once again, couldn't keep her mouth shut and her nose out.

"Did you hear that?" asked Renee, inside the room. "Who's there?"

Gillian took a deep breath, stepped towards the door and nudged it with her foot. It creaked open, and four terrified faces stared back at her.

"Well isn't this cosy!" she remarked.

She took a step forward onto the reading room carpet with her hands behind her back. She wrinkled her nose and smiled sweetly, taking in the scene. Renee was in front of her, to her left. Karen and Debbie were next to each other towards the opposite corner of the room. Kevin shook nervously on her right.

"You're not on holiday!" gasped Karen.

"It certainly looks that way, doesn't it?" replied Gillian, still smiling. "So, to what do we owe this visit?"

"Gill, this is all a misunderstanding." Kevin stepped forward, trying and failing to appear nonchalant.

"The girls were all worried about you, for some reason. Spooked by everything that's gone on recently. I didn't want to disturb you, because you were busy, but now they can see that you're OK, I expect they'll be off."

Debbie and Karen nodded, but Renee hadn't quite got the memo; she was staring daggers at Kevin.

'Ah', thought Gillian, 'he didn't tell her I was here'.

"Came to check on me, did you, Renee?" she asked.

Renee clenched her jaw, turned towards Gillian and gave a stiff nod of her head.

"So very kind of you. And there was me thinking you were a no-good New Grange slut, who came here to steal my husband."

The colour drained from Renee's face as Gillian turned to Kevin. He raised his hands in front of him.

"You could do better, dear," Gillian commented with contempt. "I mean, she's pretty enough, but the child probably isn't yours. And you two," she turned to Debbie and Karen before Kevin could respond. "You're here to catch a killer, to clear your names. Well, I suppose you found one. Well done!"

"I actually followed Debbie," mumbled Karen. "I didn't want any part of this."

"Look, Gill," pleaded Debbie. "We don't know anything. Nothing at all. We can go on like normal, can't we, Karen? Let us get out of your hair."

"I don't think so, Debbie. Do not play dumb

with me, and do not treat me like an idiot!" warned Gillian, as the smile slipped from her face.

"You can't keep us here," whispered Debbie. "You can't hurt us all."

"I never planned for anyone to get hurt, Deborah!" Gillian raised her voice, causing the others in the room to jump. "I never planned to kill anyone. I didn't want to kill anyone. I wanted people to stay out of my business, and to not poke their noses in. Janice and Caitlin gave me no choice, just like you've given me no choice now!"

"You did have a choice Gill," protested Debbie. She appeared to be the only one with an ounce of bravery. "You do have a choice. You could've shut down 'Princesses' and you could have handed yourself in. Those poor girls. Jade, Louisa, Stacy, how many more? You can still do the right thing, though."

"How on earth is sending myself to prison for life the right thing? How would that benefit me? And those 'poor girls' are happy to be earning money," argued Gillian. "At least it gives them something productive to do with their time. Better than being on the dole."

"Why are you doing this?' asked Debbie, shaking her head in disgust. "You have a job, and you have money, you don't need any more!"

"I had money; I had a reputation. I was quite happy, running a smaller, off-the-books operation away from Melwood for the last ten years! Then this fucking idiot," Gillian glared and gestured at Kevin, "tanked his business. He almost bankrupted us. I bailed him out, with a considerable chunk of my savings. And then I lost my place on the Council and the money that comes with it. Do you think a small enterprise in Surrey and my supermarket salary would match the payments on this house? On his debt? No. I had to take a risk and expand 'Princesses'. And now, it bankrolls everything you see here, our entire life, and I have every right to protect that."

"No," Debbie shook her head. "This isn't only about money, is it. That's a convenient excuse, but that's not why you did all this."

"Debbie!" whinged Karen, grabbing her friend's arm.

"You like it!" Debbie continued. "You think you're better than us, and you like being in control. You've killed and exploited innocent people. You think some women are worthless because of where they're from. The fact your husband has fallen for one of them can't have helped. Probably made you want to punish them more."

Gillian flushed and made a noise through her nose as she locked eyes with Debbie. Who was Debbie to judge her? She ground her teeth and took a deep breath.

"What about Dawn?" Debbie demanded. "She didn't deserve to die, and I know you had something to do with it."

"Don't you dare talk to me about Dawn!" shrieked Gillian.

She'd reached the end of her patience with Debbie's accusations and opinions. Kevin gestured at Debbie, imploring her to calm down, but Debbie kept her eyes fixed on Gillian.

"I didn't even know she was onto me," muttered Gillian. "Until I heard you talking to her by the lockers on the day of the inspection. I was around the corner when she told you she was going to the police. I had no choice."

"Who did you send to do it while you were at the Halloween Party?" asked Debbie.

"Good question. Dawn's killer is standing in this room," answered Gillian, as the three other women turned to Kevin in shock.

"I didn't!" he protested, but Gillian cut across him.

"You may wish to cover your ears, Renee. Yes, Kevin went and took care of that for us. A very nice touch to make it look like suicide, I must admit."

"I didn't do it," repeated Kevin. "Renee, look at me, I didn't. I got there, and she'd already killed herself, I promise. I would never have done it! I was going to tell her to disappear, then I was going to run away myself. I tried to call you, I was going to tell you everything, to ask you to leave with me that night, but you didn't pick up. Then I could barely get you to talk to me."

"Enough!" Gillian insisted icily. "As I said, it's sometimes necessary for me to do things to protect myself. And you three are a threat to me. One of you is trying to steal my husband from under my nose. One of you has figured out enough to get me sent to prison for life. And the other is a witness to it all. You've left me no choice."

"Gillian, I won't let you do this," declared Kevin, as he stepped forward and rolled up his sleeves. "Step away from the door, all four of us are going to leave now, and you can't stop us."

Gillian smiled and wrinkled her nose.

"It's a bit late to play the hero, Kevin." She smiled as she finally removed her hands from behind her back, revealing two loaded guns.

There was a collective gasp as Gillian lifted her left hand and pointed the gun directly at Renee.

"Nobody move!" she ordered, and they all froze. "Got anything to say, Renee? No humorous observations? No quick-witted little one-liner for us?"

Renee shook her head and started crying as she folded her arms over her stomach. Debbie and Karen looked on in fear; Kevin looked on the verge of a breakdown.

"Well, it's not like you to be lost for words," sneered Gillian, with a shrug.

"Now, Kevin, I have a proposal for you. When I say so, I want you to come and take this other gun from me. Then, I want you to shoot Debbie and Karen dead, leave the weapon and run away."

"No, Gill, I can't do that!" he whimpered. "Please put the gun down; we can work this out another way."

"Do it, Kevin, and you can leave with Renee. The two of you can vanish off into the distance, which is what you wanted, right? I'll give you a head start and then I'll call the police. I'll tell them that the two of you were behind 'Princesses' and the murders. I'll say that I knew nothing about it until tonight when the girls came here to confront Renee, and you killed them. I get to keep my life outside of prison. You get to keep Renee. Good deal, right? Everyone's a winner! Well, apart from you two," Gillian glanced menacingly at Debbie and Karen.

"Though I will have to shut 'Princesses' down, so I suppose you won't have died in vain."

Kevin looked from Gillian to Renee, then to Debbie and Karen.

"No, Kevin, no, don't do this," begged Debbie and Karen together.

"Shut up!" shouted Gillian, her gun still pointing at Renee. "One more word from anyone and I will shoot her, where it'll hurt most." She lowered the weapon towards Renee's stomach.

"Kevin, come and take the gun now, come on!" urged Gillian, as silence fell.

He stepped towards her, his eyes staring at the floor. He took the gun from her and shuffled back. He was shaking, mentally preparing himself to kill two women in cold blood, as Gillian had done back in August. It was about time he pulled his weight, she thought.

"Right, Kevin, come on now, you know what to do. Debbie first," encouraged Gillian.

She couldn't wait to watch Kevin commit the crime. She would then pull the trigger anyway and watch him suffer as his girlfriend's life evaporated. It would serve him right for humiliating her by choosing someone like Renee.

Behind her, she heard a thumping noise on the front door. Unless she was mistaken, a boy and a girl were shouting Renee's name.

"Ignore that, Kevin." Gillian raised her voice again. "I'll count you down. Three,"

Could she also hear sirens in the distance? Had someone alerted the police? Either way, the need to resolve the situation had become critical. Kevin's hand wavered; had he heard them too?

"If you don't do it, Kevin, I'll kill Renee, I mean it. She is less than nothing to me," spat Gillian. "Two."

Kevin raised the gun and pointed it at Debbie. He gulped in air and shuddered. Debbie grabbed Karen's arm and whispered something that sounded like, "I'm sorry."

"One," shouted Gillian, and she turned her head from Kevin to Debbie, to watch the impact of the bullet.

Screams pierced the night as a loud bang re-verberated around every corner of The Manor.

34: THE SURVIVORS

Monday 24th December 2018,
18:40 – Debbie

Debbie had closed her eyes after Gillian said 'two.' Her whole body tensed, and she squeezed Karen's hand tighter than anything she'd ever grasped before.

Thoughts raced through her mind: her and Joe on their wedding day and Marco and Abbie on their first days at school. The coming days the three of them would have together, without her. I'm sorry, I love you, she thought, over and over again. Her heart pounded against her chest, savouring its last beats.

And then it came; the sick crack and bang of the gunshot. Debbie imagined, in slow motion, the bullet moving through the air towards her.

How long before it made an impact, and where?

Seconds later, her ears were ringing, her eyes were screwed shut, yet she didn't feel any physical pain. Is this death? If it was, then why was she still standing up, and not crumpled on the floor? And if she was dying, then why were her senses heightening? Why could she feel a pair of hands, gripping her shoulders and shaking her back and forth? Why could she smell something pungent and metallic? And why, through the ringing in her ears, could she hear someone shouting her name?

She realised that she hadn't breathed in a while. Alongside the other sensations, she felt a tightening pain around her chest. At once, she opened her eyes and inhaled as much air as she could in one gulp. All she could see was Karen standing in front of her; it was Karen's hands on her shoulders, Karen's voice calling her name. She looked panicked, but not hurt, and she was also still standing up. Debbie didn't understand; they were both supposed to be dead.

"Deb, Deb, oh thank God, she's opened her eyes," gasped Karen with relief. "It's OK, Deb."

Debbie took deep breaths, still compensating for all the time she'd held her breath. Her eyes focused and moved towards the place where Renee had stood moments ago. She wasn't standing up anymore.

"Oh, please no," she whispered. Her eyes moved downwards, and she hoped desperately not to see Renee, slumped or lying still. But Renee was sitting upright on the sofa, her arms wrapped around a cushion on her lap. She was taking short breaths and rocking back and forth as she stared at something behind Karen.

"What happened?" whispered Debbie to Karen. She couldn't see past her taller friend.

"Don't... don't look, Deb, you don't have to."

But she did have to. Debbie stood on tiptoes and tilted her head over Karen's shoulder. Kevin perched on the small chintz sofa; the same one she and Karen had sat on a few months ago. His head was in his hands, his elbows shaking in his lap. In front of him, Gillian's body lay on the floor, motionless. Her eyes were staring blankly at the ceiling. Underneath, blood pooled and seeped into the cream carpet fibres.

"He shot her," whispered Debbie. "Kevin shot her, and he saved us?" Karen nodded.

"I saw it. I saw him do it. Gillian turned her head at the last second, away from him and towards you. So, he turned the gun on her. What do we do now? I think people are banging at the door, I thought I heard sirens, but my ears are ringing. Tell us what to do Debbie, please!"

Debbie took another deep breath and stepped sideways past Karen. She placed a hand on Renee's shoulder and squeezed it as she walked past her. She couldn't quite bring herself to look towards Kevin again. She stumbled into the hallway and looked towards the front door. Her ears were still ringing, but she could see two distressed faces at the window. A young girl and boy were waving at her. She heard police sirens again.

She shook her head at Ethan and Jade through the window.

"Renee?" Jade shouted through the window, as tears ran down her face.

"She's OK. Renee is OK," shouted Debbie. "But you can't come in."

She turned her back on them and willed herself to walk back towards the reading room.

"Ethan and Jade are at the door, the police are on their way," she called from the hallway. She tried to step back into the room, but she struggled. She felt weak, as though her legs were about to give way underneath her.

"Police. K-Kevin," stuttered Renee from the sofa. Debbie watched her put her cushion to one side and approach him. Gently, she placed her hands on his and prized them away from his face. Tears streamed from his eyes, which looked up at the ceiling; he too couldn't bear to look down at the corpse in front of him.

"Kevin," she repeated, "you have to tell them the truth. Tell them everything. You had no choice because she was going to kill us. Tell them she tried to force you to kill Dawn, but you were never going to go through with it. Tell them you knew nothing about this 'Princesses' thing."

Kevin turned his head towards Renee, and moved his hand towards her cheek, wiping away the tears.

"Are you OK, Ren?" he asked tenderly, and she nodded in return. "I couldn't let any harm come to you. Even if I'd done what Gill said, she would have killed you, to punish me," he stuttered. "But we both know I need to run. I can't defend myself from a police cell."

"No, Kevin, no!" begged Renee. But he ignored her. He ran out of the reading room and up the stairs. Renee hauled herself up from the sofa and followed him.

Debbie looked at Karen, who stood, shaking, with her back to the corpse.

"Karen..."

"I can't turn around," she whimpered. "I saw it happen, but I can't look at it. Oh God, Deb, I thought we were about to die."

"I'm so sorry, Karen, let's get out of this room. We can wait for the police in the hallway. Close your eyes and take my hand."

She led Karen out of the room, as two pairs of footsteps crashed down the stairs. Kevin reached the bottom first, stuffing bundles of money into a holdall.

"I'm coming with you then," yelled Renee, who was close behind him. "We said we were leaving together tonight, didn't we? So, let's do it."

"No," shouted Kevin, as he reached the door to the kitchen, opposite Debbie and Karen. "Being on the run from the police is different from leaving Gillian. I'm not putting you through that. I'm not putting our child through that."

"Our daughter, Kevin, she's a girl. I was going to tell you later. Please don't leave us, we only just got you. Please!" she begged.

He pulled her close, his hand on the back of her head, and sighed. Debbie and Karen looked at each other, away from the intimate moment. It was surreal and felt somewhat inappropriate, given the circumstances.

"I love you, Renee," whispered Kevin. "Look after our daughter; look after yourself. I will see you again, I promise."

Police lights flashed through the front window. Kevin threw the holdall over his shoulder, sprinted into the kitchen, through the patio doors, and into the garden.

"Kevin!" screamed Renee, as she ran after him.

Suddenly, the front door burst open and several armed police officers rushed in. Debbie and Karen threw their arms up in the air and stood to one side, as the officers ran past them. In turn, they swept the many rooms of The Manor.

At the front door, DS Harris had stopped Jade and Ethan from entering the house. Debbie's eyes met Vincent Okafor's, and he urgently beckoned her and Karen towards him.

"Renee. Is she alive?" he asked as they reached the front doorway, concern etched across his face.

"Yes, she's not hurt. She ran into the garden, after Kevin. He's leaving."

"And where is Gillian?"

"She-she's dead. It wasn't me!" gasped Debbie, with her hands in the air. "She was going to kill me, but Kevin shot her. We can explain it all. She was behind everything."

Okafor held up his hand, nodded and held his radio to his mouth.

"All armed officers to the garden. Debbie last saw Kevin Prince entering it to flee, accompanied by Renee Beck. Bring them both in. Force is not authorised until Renee is safe."

"IC1 female corpse in the third room on the right, sir," announced an officer, who had appeared behind Debbie and Karen.

"Officers have Renee Beck in the garden; they're bringing her indoors now. No sign of Kevin Prince, sir."

Okafor nodded and picked up his radio again.

"Pursue Kevin beyond the garden. There is a path out of Fair Lawns into the woods. Proportionate use of force authorised."

Debbie shuddered as she imagined Kevin sprinting through the woods. She could hear the shouts of the armed officers and the barks of the police dogs in pursuit.

Down the hallway, two officers appeared,

with Renee crying between them. They left her with Okafor at the front door, then turned back to join the rest of their team. Okafor looked at Debbie, Karen and Renee and shook his head.

"You three are lucky to be alive," he muttered. "But I'm glad that you are. DS Harris is going to take you straight to the station. You can make phone calls, they'll look after you, and you'll get the support you need. But you will also give statements, and you are all going to tell the absolute truth, do you understand?"

Debbie nodded and to her left and right, Renee and Karen did the same. He turned away to greet the arriving forensic team, while DS Harris settled Jade and Ethan into one of the cars.

"Renee. I'm...I'm so sorry," stuttered Debbie. "We should tell them to take you to the hospital to check the baby."

"She's fine, I'm fine," hiccoughed Renee, one arm still around her stomach.

"It's not your fault Debbie," she continued after a moment of silence. "This is all on Gillian. I didn't know what she was capable of."

"No-one did. None of us would have come here if we knew. But you and Kevin, you were about to escape... If I hadn't come here..."

"Gillian was in the house the whole time," whispered Renee. "She would never have let us leave. Even if we snuck out, she would have found us; that's why Kevin said we'd have to go abroad. Now I understand why he couldn't just leave. We would have been in so much danger."

"Do you think he knew about 'Princesses' and killed Dawn?" asked Karen.

Debbie shrugged, and Renee shook her head.

"He couldn't have known the whole story," Renee replied. "But he couldn't have known nothing at all, either. I don't know what to think. He didn't kill Dawn though; I can promise you that. He doesn't have it in him to kill people."

She hiccoughed again as Debbie and Karen exchanged a glance. After all, Kevin had just shot his wife in front of them.

"Ladies," called DS Harris, from a car at the front of the convoy. "This way, please."

Debbie held out her hands to Renee and Karen. They took one each and, together, they walked away from The Manor towards the flashing lights.

Excerpts: Interviews with Renee Beck, Karen Goldman, Debbie Gomez
Monday 24 December 2018 – 9 pm

Officer: Why did you go to The Manor this evening?

Renee: To tell Kevin I was pregnant. I couldn't hide it any longer, physically it was obvious. I missed him, and I hoped that he'd finally agree to leave Gillian. And I got what I wanted; he said he'd leave her to be with me. But he was also trying to get me to leave the house, and I should have listened to him sooner, but when I finally agreed to go, Debbie and Karen arrived. I thought Gillian was away. I had no idea that she had this other life; I didn't know about 'Princesses' or the murders. I would never have gone if I did. I wouldn't have put my baby in danger like that.

Debbie: I thought Renee was behind the murders and 'Princesses.' I wanted to warn Gillian. You can imagine how stupid and awful I feel about that now.

Karen: I went with Debbie. She – I mean we – thought Gillian was in danger. When we got there, we realised what was going on, between Renee and Kevin. You know, the affair and the pregnancy. And we were about to leave them to it. But then Gillian appeared and blocked the door to the room we were in.

Officer: What happened directly before the shooting?

Karen: Gillian was saying we were all a threat to her, that she didn't want to kill us, but we'd left her no choice. Debbie was so brave. She said to Gillian, 'you can do the right thing, you could stop 'Princesses', turn yourself in.' But she didn't want to do that.

Renee: Kevin said he wouldn't let her harm us, that we were all leaving together, but then Gillian pulled out the guns. Then he stopped because we were all unarmed and she had two guns. She pointed one at me, and I can't remember much until, well, until Kevin pulled the trigger.

Debbie: Gillian gave Kevin an ultimatum. She said, if he killed Karen and me, she'd let him leave with Renee. Gillian said she'd blame 'Princesses' and all the murders on them. She didn't know that you'd already figured it out.

Officer: Who shot Gillian?

Debbie: I can't be sure, because I closed my eyes, I didn't see it happen, but surely, there's only one thing that could have happened? Kevin shot her.

Renee: You have to understand; she was forcing him to kill Debbie and Karen. He had no choice but to turn the gun on her. And you know, even if he'd done it, killed Debbie and Karen, Gillian would have killed me anyway. He saved our lives, all three of us, and our baby's, so if you find him, please remember that.

Karen: It all happened so fast. Kevin pointed his gun at Debbie, and Gillian was counting down, pointing hers at Renee, and looking at him. She said, 'do it now, Kevin, or I'll kill Renee.' Then she turned her head to look at Debbie and me like she wanted to watch us die. But that meant she couldn't see Kevin, and at the last second, he turned away from us and shot Gillian instead.

Officer: Why do you think Kevin ran?

Renee: Because he's scared. Look at what happened to Debbie! Locked up for two weeks even though she wasn't involved. He ran because he knows he'll get the blame for it all, but he doesn't deserve it. He had no choice but to kill Gillian, and he didn't kill Dawn, he looked me in the eye and said it.

Debbie: Look, he saved my life, and I am so

grateful. And he genuinely loves Renee. They love each other, that's obvious. But that doesn't make him innocent. I saw him, the night Dawn died, and I still don't believe she killed herself. And even if Gillian was running it, how could he not have known about 'Princesses'? He must have known where the money was coming from. He must have known why Gill sent him to kill someone, even if he didn't do it in the end. He ran because he has stuff to hide.

Karen: I don't know Kevin. And I can't tell you whether he helped Gillian with the murders or with 'Princesses'. But think about what he went through this evening. He found out the woman he loves is pregnant, so he agrees to this new life with her, to run away. Then we storm in and start accusing her. His wife appears with guns and makes him choose between Renee and us, and then he has to kill Gillian to save three innocent people and his child. The fact he ran doesn't make him guilty or not guilty. I think he ran because he was in shock and wanted to buy himself some time.

EPILOGUE: ROSIE

Monday 27th May 2019 – Renee

Renee stood in the middle of her garden on a warm Bank Holiday Monday. She frowned as she absent-mindedly prodded the food sizzling on her barbeque. She'd turned the burgers a few times, but she hadn't paid attention to the instructions on the packet.

"Rachel!" she shouted, and Marie's partner ran down the stairs from the patio to join her.

"Are these done, do you think?" asked Renee, as she prodded the food again. "I don't want to lose another colleague by accident..."

"Oh, Renee! Why don't you leave me in charge of this, so you can go and greet the guests? They're arriving now, and Marie is trying to welcome them, but, well, you know..."

"Oh God, say no more!" chuckled Renee.

She passed the tongs into Rachel's more capable hands and made her way towards the house. Through the patio doors, she could see a group of her aunts and cousins in a huddle. Jade was in the middle of them, holding a tiny bundle in her arms.

Renee's cousin, Claire, looked up from the crowd with a smile.

"Finally, Ren, someone's getting more attention than you!"

Jade passed the baby to an aunt and turned towards Renee and Claire with a sigh of relief.

"You're a natural, Jade," commented Claire, and Jade smiled and blushed.

"She's a Godsend," sighed Renee, as she put her arm around Jade and kissed her on the head.

"She's staying with me for a little while, aren't you? She's working full time and helping me out with Baby."

"That's amazing," replied Claire. "Then what, are you off to Uni or something?"

"Oh, no," replied Jade. "My friend Ethan, he's going to study law in September, but I'm staying here. My new boss has got me onto a management training scheme at the supermarket."

"Speak of the devil," announced Renee, as she peered out the window. "Here she is, mine and Jade's new boss."

Claire followed Renee's gaze towards the woman and her family walking through the front gate.

"And do we like her, this new boss?" whispered Claire.

"Well, she can't be worse than the last one," muttered Jade, with a glint in her eye.

Renee burst out laughing as she swung the door open.

"Renee," greeted Debbie, with her arms outstretched. "You look amazing, and it's only been two weeks since you gave birth, it's not fair!"

"Oh, stop it. Not everything is back in shape yet, let me tell you..."

"You've met my husband Joe, and these are our children, Marco and Abbie," interrupted Debbie, as Renee ushered them in.

Debbie's son gave Renee the slightest of glances as he hurried in, and turned a dark shade of red.

"Well, where is she then?" asked Debbie, as she looked into the crowded living room.

"Here," answered Renee as she reached over and retrieved Baby from the group of family members. "Here's Baby, her real name to be confirmed soon."

"Oh, look at her!" gasped Debbie, as Baby wiggled her arms and opened her eyes for a few seconds at a time. "She's adorable, Renee, just perfect."

"Apple didn't fall far from the tree," commented Joe. "She's gorgeous."

Debbie raised her eyebrows and gave Joe a

sharp look. He continued to stare and smile at Baby, oblivious to his faux pas.

"Don't worry, Debbie," whispered Claire. "I think Renee's learnt her lessons about messing around with her boss' husbands."

"Jesus, Claire!" laughed Renee.

Debbie's eyebrows lifted even further, and Joe turned his head in shock.

The doorbell rang again; Claire opened it for Karen, who stood at the door hand in hand with both Steve and her daughter.

"Ahhh!" she beamed as she stepped inside and looked at Baby. "Renee, she looks just like you! Look at her hair, Steve."

"Claire, this is Karen and Steve,"

"Oh, the ones who…"

"Yes, I told you, they had an affair," stated Renee, as Karen's daughter frowned. "Terrible behaviour, obviously, but now they're together, which is lovely. Come in, come in."

"Thank you, Renee, for the introduction," grimaced Steve, as he wiped his shoes on the doormat.

After an hour or so, Renee had lost track of time again. Everyone seemed to be well fed and watered, thanks to Marie and Rachel. Princess the cat kept a watchful eye as the guests passed Baby around. She hissed and pawed at Renee's leg whenever Baby seemed unhappy.

When some of her older family members had

left, Renee noticed Karen, Debbie and Jade talking on the patio. She grabbed Marie and a fresh glass of fizz and joined them.

"I think we should have a little toast, don't you? To the Supermarket Supervisor Survivors Group!" she announced, and they all raised their glasses.

"That's not a thing, Renee!" said Debbie, with a roll of her eyes.

"It is! Look at us all, still standing after Gillian Prince's reign of terror. Just you wait until they start with the TV documentaries, the dramas. We could play ourselves!"

"Renee," implored Marie. "Four people died..."

"You're not drinking, Marie," interjected Karen, gesturing to the glass of orange juice in Marie's hand. "Are you pregnant too?"

Renee and Debbie exchanged a glance as Marie scowled at Karen with narrowed eyes.

"So," said Debbie, breaking the silence. "When are we going to hear the name, Renee? You must have one by now."

"Oh, not quite yet," smiled Renee. "Though I suppose we can rule out any variation of 'Gillian.'"

"Renee!" Debbie and Marie objected, as both Karen and Jade stifled a giggle.

"Oh, come on," laughed Renee. "The therapist said we should try and joke about it if we need to, you know, lighten the mood. It's good to talk about what happened to us!"

"Have you heard from Kevin then?" asked Karen, eagerly.

"Nope, nothing," sighed Renee as she shook her head. "I thought, maybe after Baby was born, I would hear something. The police thought so, too. They've been here twice in the last two weeks asking me if he's been in touch. But he hasn't, and they can't find him. He must have made it abroad somehow, I suppose."

She sighed and looked down at her glass.

"He had a lot to answer for, Renee," said Debbie, as she reached out to touch Renee's arm. "You and Baby are going to be fine without him. Look at everyone you have here to support you."

Renee took a deep breath and nodded. Since Kevin fled on Christmas Eve, she had tried to push him from her mind, but she hadn't succeeded. He always hovered on the periphery of her thoughts.

Often, she slipped into a daydream of a different life, that featured only herself, Kevin, and Baby happy and safe together. Despite everything that had happened, she would embrace it all in an instant.

Half an hour or so later, she saw the last guests out. Her eyelids felt heavy, and she craved a lie-down. In the garden, Marie and Rachel laughed and joked as they packed up all the food. In the kitchen, Jade was part-way through a massive stack of washing up.

"Leave some of that for me, Jade," yawned

Renee from the sofa, where she'd sprawled her-self.

"Don't be silly," replied Jade with a smile. "Why don't you take Baby upstairs and have a nap with her. She's almost asleep too, look."

Renee peered into the little Moses basket and saw her daughter rubbing her eyes for the first time. Her heart jumped, and she felt another wave of love course through her. With a weary smile, she carried Baby up the stairs.

She placed her gently in the middle of her bed. She could see why everyone thought Baby was the spitting image of her. The thick dark hair and the chocolate brown eyes flecked with gold were a giveaway. And whenever Baby yawned or made a noise, two little dimples appeared on her cheeks, exactly like Renee's.

But as she stroked her daughter's head, she looked for a resemblance to her father as well. And although she was only seventeen days old, Renee found shades of Kevin in the shape of her eyes and the arch of her eyebrows. She lay down next to her and pulled a light blanket over them both. She placed one of her fingers in her daughter's hand, and she gripped it tightly in return and yawned again. It was the most heart-warming, adorable thing Renee had ever seen.

"Goodnight, Rosie Kay Beck," whispered Renee, as they both fell asleep.

Her name was Rosie. It had been Rosie ever since the doctors told Renee she was expecting a healthy little girl. And for a short while longer, her name would stay Renee and Rosie's secret.

THE END

ACKNOWLEDGE-MENT

A massive thank you to the readers who have made it this far! This is my debut novel - the first of many more to come. I very much hope you've enjoyed it. If you did, I'd be so hugely grateful if you'd leave a review and recommend it to others. It is difficult for self-published authors to compete with the giants - but with your help and a solid word-of-mouth campaign, I'm giving it a go.

Thank you to my sister Cath, and my wonderful friend Becca, who both read various drafts and gave me the encouragement I needed to publish. I acknowledge that my other sister, Lucy, has agreed to give feedback following the release of an audiobook version!

Thank you to Martin, for the much needed and thoroughly executed proofread of the final draft.

And to Drew (for making me go through a final proofing phase, and) for so brilliantly designing one of the two front covers.

ABOUT THE AUTHOR

Jennifer R Hollis

Jennifer R Hollis is a crime and mystery author from Croydon, South London. She studied law at both undergraduate and postgraduate level, before beginning her career in campaigning organisations, solving complex social problems.

She now works in Political Communications. By night, she pursues her ambition to write books full time. Killer Princesses is her debut novel; she hopes the first of many in the crime and mystery categories.

Follow her on:
Twitter: @JenniferHollis
Instagram: JenniferRHollis
Facebook: JenniferHollisBooks
Website: www.JenniferHollis.uk

Printed in Great Britain
by Amazon